UNDER THE GOWN

PAYTON FRISCHHERTZ

WOLFFISH PRESS

WOLFFISH PRESS LLC
NEW ORLEANS

For Mom,
You brought me into this world, and you've kept me in it.

Cover designer: Kamil Rekosz

Paperback ISBN: 979-8-9906975-1-5

Hardback ISBN: 979-8-9906975-2-2

Ebook ISBN: 979-8-9906975-0-8

CHAPTER 1

THE CRESCENT CLUB PRESENTATION

Tonight, the ballroom bleeds red and white.

Between the white silk gowns, red sashes strapped across starched tuxedo shirts, and crimson bouquets of roses each girl holds, we look way more presentable than we had at the haphazard practice a few days ago. Thankfully, I can say the same for my family.

"You look gorgeous. I couldn't be prouder," my dad trumpets for nearly the thousandth time. "I'm sure I'll be saying that a lot with so many upcoming debutante events. Certainly worse things to hear more than once, right, Ainsley?" He bumps my shoulder, laughing, since it's become an inside joke between us after I'd reminded him one too many times not to be late for this presentation.

"Sure, Dad. I can always endure more flattery, so thanks. And for being here. I know you've been slammed, but with me at college, there's been no time to talk football. You're my one sports salvation in this family. Especially since Mom cheers for the wrong team. And Luke—well, he's just . . . *Luke*."

"Your mother has always picked her team by the uniform she likes best." He rakes a hand through his hair, one of the few physical traits we have in common. "By the way, I saw Leslie earlier. Which makes that twice in a very short span of time, considering she also appeared on our Ring camera holding a bottle of wine and ringing the doorbell twenty times while we were out of town."

Straightening my pearl necklace, I nearly choke as I try to come up with the right response regarding my ex-girlfriend and our recent wine-induced hook up. How did I forget about that doorbell app? I should've made her climb the tree again, like she did after senior prom. "We're old friends, Dad," I finally say. "She wanted to celebrate me being back in town."

"While it's none of my business who you choose to spend time with, I certainly hope she didn't drink all of that wine *and* drive herself home." His expression changes as he morphs into doctor mode.

"The bottle is in the wine fridge, and she drove home safely— the next day." I reassure him. Leslie is infamous for having the worst taste in wine, so when she came over wielding her five-dollar gas station bottle of wine, I stashed it with zero intention of drinking it, instead substituting a better bottle from my dad's collection.

He cups my chin. "Did you not want to escort her? Or have her escort you? I don't know how all this debutante stuff works, but if you didn't need separate escorts, your mother and I are more than fine—"

"Dad, stop. I realize you're trying to be accepting, but I didn't want her to escort me, or the other way around. We're not dating. We really are just friends these days. Besides, you don't get to pick your escort for the presentation. It has to be a club member."

"Okay, honey. I'm fine if you're fine." He plants a kiss on top of my head.

Ever since I came out in high school, my parents have gone above and beyond to show how comfortable they are with my sexuality. The first year, they set up a rainbow balloon arch during Pride month—which my brother Luke made sure to photograph for our digital family album—that took a solid hour to take down.

"Besides, I don't want to be *that* girl, you know."

"What girl?" he asks.

"The gay one," I whisper, acutely aware of how close everyone is standing to us.

"What about Leslie? Surely, there are others." His brows furrow.

"And all their dates are *men*, Dad. Have you ever seen a female escort at a deb ball? I'm not ashamed of my identity. Quite the opposite. But I have no need to trailblaze at one of these orthodox social events. I'm confident with who I am and have nothing to prove. Plus, I have a ton of guy friends. So . . . no big change."

While my relationship (or lack thereof) with Leslie seems to be, at present, tenuous, I'm proud of who I am and have never hidden it. But I'd prefer to assume the reason people are staring is because of my amazing dress and *not* because of the arm linked to mine for the span of 180 seconds during our post-presentation dance.

"Go take photos with Mom and Luke while he still looks presentable." I push my dad toward our table in the area reserved for the debs, their dates, and family members. "We'll chat after I make my debut."

As I walk off, my phone buzzes. Peeling off one opera-length leather glove, I click on the text. It's from Violet—the girl I'm dying to see. The girl I never expected to meet, but haven't been able to get out of my mind since we talked two weeks ago at Leslie's debutante luncheon, and again at rehearsal for tonight's event.

VIOLET

You look nice.

Scanning the room, I spy her black pinned-up hair and green

eyes drilling into me. Her dress is strapless, like mine, with a white corset and barely there lace that reaches her waist before it pools out, and she's wearing an emerald choker around her neck.

A

Is it platonic for me to say you look far better than nice?

She shakes her head from across the room, and I shoot a wicked grin.

A

Save a dance for me?

VIOLET

As long as your curtsy tip works, sure.

In my book, that's a yes. I'd been using that trick since I was a princess in my first Carnival ball. When my mom forgot my flats, I dug out a pair of Converses and never looked back. I even changed into my blue high-tops when I was queen, immediately following the bal masque.

I tap on my cell phone's camera to make sure my braid hasn't fallen apart.

This wait is driving me crazy.

Wish I had a drink.

Eli—one of my closest friends and current plus-one—looms over my shoulder, giving an exaggerated wink as I snap his photo and tag it *#UndertheGown*. Might as well stay on top of the ship and not get sunk by the questionable Instagram account that's reared its ugly horns since the start of deb season. "Thanks for asking me to be your *date*." He laughs. "You know I don't love these events, but I'm honored." He bows. "Want to trade?"

Nodding, I swap my bouquet for his glass of champagne, forever mindful of the sloshing liquid and potential for disaster should I move too quickly. Pre-presentation, we're only allowed water and brut champagne. No dark liquids or food that could possibly stain our white dresses. Not that any girl would dare risk it.

"You were bound to come, even if I hadn't invited you," I say. "No doubt Cooper would have scored you a ticket, right?" I scan the ballroom to see if I can spot Eli's older brother, who is not just *here* but a member of the Crescent Club, one of the seven official debutante nominating clubs in the city. Of course, Crescent is not the only club he's part of, though no one knows that but me. Not even Eli, as far as I can tell. For now, it needs to stay that way. "Where is he, anyhow?"

"I'm not a member, so no, I only came for *you*, and I'd bet money Coop's hiding backstage. During lunch, he kept complaining about how bored he was of this scene, though he says that every year." He gives me a side eye. "Why? What do you want with Cooper? Did you secretly ask him to escort you first, and he turned you down? What about Peyton? Did you ask my cousin too? I hate being sloppy thirds."

"Shut up." I elbow him. "I did *not* try to poach your brother or cousin, who, might I remind you, is still in high school. That's weird on so many levels."

"You're nineteen, not ninety. Besides, your friend *Laney* doesn't care about those things. Hunter is a senior in high school. Not abnormal, just saying. But you promised me all the amicable love in the world, so I expect to be number one. I only accept second place to Piper because she'd kill me if I tried to usurp her. Just please don't cheat on me with my brother or relatives."

"No worry. You're officially the most tolerable *man* I know." I smile sweetly, and he pretends to swoon. "Speaking of Laney, she wasn't at Leslie's party or at practice a few days ago. Do you have any scoop on why she's been off the radar? I really need to talk to her."

"Actually, I do. I ran into Hunter at their store, and he

mentioned she was dropping out of Crescent to focus on one presentation."

My mouth falls open. "Laney Wilson doesn't want to be presented more than once? Are you kidding? She's been nuts for this stuff since we were infants. All she talked about in high school was our presentations, what kind of party she'd throw, and if she'd get picked as queen for any Carnival courts. Hell, her Pinterest board of deb dresses makes mine look like a fifth-grade school project."

He shrugs. "I don't know . . . maybe she outgrew it? You saw her posts from the Clemson game. Seems pretty busy with her Tulane gig." He holds his palm up. "Before you go on a rant, I know their team isn't SEC, but it looks like she's having fun."

Of course I'd seen every one of Laney's posts about her shadowing their football training staff. Who hadn't? And while I'd do practically anything to land an opportunity like hers to jazz up my resume—and plan to do just that during deb season—it's a stretch to believe she's too busy for more than one presentation or ball. Guess it's possible Division I football went to her head. Stranger things have happened.

"Maybe," I say. "But hopefully, in some utopian future, we'll both land jobs with an NFL physio staff. Until then, I need you to take more photos with me. Then, of just me. And later, me and Piper. Wait—gotta go. See you after the presentation."

I plant a kiss on his cheek and sprint for the procession of white-gowned, long-gloved girls exiting the ballroom.

Showtime!

"Fuck, I'm nervous," a girl blurts, and I nod in sympathy. Stuffed into a narrow staff tunnel, I listen to the Crescent Club president's introduction speech until my best friend sprints from her spot farther back in line.

"Ainsley, final check. How do I look? I hate that our names are so far apart. I had to haul ass in these heels"—she sticks out her Louboutins from beneath her dress—"to get up here in time."

Spinning her, I scan Piper's dress for spots or awkward creases, then readjust her pearls. "Perfect, Richards. Just don't bow as low as you did in practice. A long-necked swan, you are not."

"Eff off, Clarke. It's so damn hot, I'm about to have a panic attack in these miles of silk. Soon, you may be chasing a *runaway* swan."

"As long as it's after they call my name. Otherwise, you'll have to wait."

She glares, and we both jump when a trumpet blasts.

Piper's escort waves frantically, but she shakes her flowers at him, then presses her hands onto my shoulders, trying to get a look at who's being presented first. "Ladies and gentlemen," the master of ceremonies says, "I'd like to present Miss Violet Easton Anderson."

"Holy shit!" Piper shouts and a chorus of shushes ensues. "Forget anything bad I said about your new crush. Dude, do you know who she is?"

"Miss Violet Easton *Anderson*," I mock, confused why Piper looks so shell-shocked.

"No, Ainsley . . . *Anderson*. Like Anderson Oil. As in *the* Andersons of Texas. They're ungodly wealthy. A few are in politics, but most are huge corporate titans."

"You know this how?" I grab her arm, so she won't flee to her increasingly flabbergasted escort.

"Remember when I applied for my summer internship?" she asks, and I nod. "It was with them. If you get a shoe in at Anderson, and they like you, you're basically guaranteed a job as a petroleum engineer anywhere they own land." She pauses. "Haven't you seen their commercials? I think they own a basketball arena somewhere," she explains.

"What did you say?" I stare at Piper.

"Yes, a basketball arena, Ainsley. But don't bring up anything political, or like, business related. There have been a bunch of boycotts at their Texas jobsites lately. Said they're stealing jobs from locals. A colossal cluster—ooh, got to go before my weird escort starts sobbing."

After receiving several more glares, Piper leaves, and I mull over her news. Most people in these clubs are wealthy. No surprise there. And if they're not flush with cash, they wield some sort of power. Academic. Political. Anything which holds a ton of sway, but if Piper's right, Violet's in a whole different league.

Her family is corporate elite, yet there I'd been, flirting with her at practice last week, looking like a mismatched sports urchin.

One more girl, and it's my turn.

"Miss Catherine Cho." The girl ahead of me disappears through the parted drapes.

"Miss Ainsley Prescott Clarke!"

My escort, Chuck, nudges me to start walking, so I plaster on my million-dollar smile as the spotlight hits my face. The dance floor is lined with eager parents, craning their necks to get the best photos of their daughters. Luckily, I spot mine right away. On cue, I curtsy, then wheel around to finish the procession. Climbing the steps, I take my place on stage with the other girls, peering now and then over my shoulder at Violet. At one point, she tilts her head to the smallest degree to let me know she sees me.

"Miss Isabella Diaz."

"Miss Leslie Rory Hart."

I grin at Leslie. When she passes me on stage, she gives me a fist bump.

"Miss Claire Levenson."

"Miss Piper Eleanor Richards."

Clapping for my best friend, my pride surges. We did it! We are official New Orleans royalty. Tomorrow, our names and faces will be splashed across the internet. While it may sound lame to others, and maybe to me if I hadn't grown up here, I'm as proud of this moment as any lifetime achievement.

Name by name, girls promenade into the shimmering ballroom under the glow of crystal chandeliers, and the applause elevates the energy in the room while the space on stage grows tight.

Piper makes the sign of the cross, exclaiming, "Thank you, St. Anthony!" and climbs the riser without tripping. Piper is Catholic, and these days, he's her favorite saint after she'd promised twenty bucks in his name and her grandmother's passed-down-to-her pearls that went missing ten years ago were miraculously found.

Tonight, they're securely fastened around her neck.

Widening my elbows to keep girls from penning me in, I chew my lip, hoping not many names are left.

"Miss Alexandra Joan Williams."

I raise my hands to clap, but the velvet drapes don't part, and no one comes out. Since I'm closest to the entrance, I hear whisperings. A man's voice rises above the rest. "Just do it! One step at a time. Come on!"

Clutching her escort's arm, the girl emerges and wobbles to her first cue.

Piper and I exchange shrugs, and a stilted round of applause fills the room. The girl hits her second cue, then turns toward the stage. Her eyes are glassy. Blinking slowly. And her escort—holy shit, it's Cooper—whispers something, steadying her elbow as she walks.

"She's going to faint," I say to the girl next to me, then I wave at a club member, hoping to catch his attention, but he doesn't notice.

I try the same with the blonde den mother standing nearby.

Again, no response.

The girl, Alexandra, hesitates, then her bouquet plummets, red and white petals scattering on the wooden parquet dance floor. As she follows the path of her bouquet, she paws the air, like she's trying to catch herself, but her body wilts on top of her mushroomed-out, white puddle of silk.

The crowd gasps. People stand. Shout.

A group of Crescent Club members encircle her.

I rise on my toes, trying to see what's going on, but since Cooper towers above the rest, I fasten my eyes on him.

He pushes the others aside and kneels, apparently trying to prop her up.

A girl elbows me. "Should've bent her knees. My friend passed out last year from standing too long." Nodding, I keep my gaze riveted on Alexandra. When she finally stands, Cooper and another member flank her sides to steady her. Once they start walking, they practically drag her through the cues, proceeding across the room, past center stage.

I'm on the end, stage right. When Alexandra is nearly a foot away, the spotlight illuminates her face. Not only is she pale, her front teeth are coated red.

Blood?

She must have hit her head. Hard.

They disappear behind the drapery, and after an awkward break —during which time, I spot my dad rushing backstage—Patrick taps the microphone. "Um, sorry, folks. Seems Ms. Williams had an unfortunate case of nerves, but we're happy to report she's feeling better. She'll be rejoining us shortly."

The crowd erupts into whoops and applause.

"Please continue to enjoy the procession, and in a few moments, the dance floor will be yours," the club president says, charisma oozing, as we wait for the final girl to be presented.

"Miss Laney Wilson."

Say what? Eli just said she'd dropped out—

"Miss Laney Wilson." Her name is called a second time, a bit more emphatically. Whispers ripple throughout the audience and across the stage. A guy dashes to the podium to speak with Patrick and his face reddens. "I'm sorry for another interruption, but there seems to be a mistake. Miss Laney Wilson will *not* be joining us tonight. I apologize for the mix-up."

Like at practice, Patrick's neck grows mottled, and I can't help wondering how such a colossal error has been made. Surely, Laney notified the club that she would no longer be participating.

Definitely not Crescent's shiniest moment.

Moments later, the music fades and we're dismissed. When I reach my table, I plunge my hands into the frigid ice bucket to retrieve a bottle of champagne, then pour myself a glass. It's the only way I'll be able to shake off the image of Alexandra Williams's bloody smile or forget about the mess-ups that have occurred.

When my dad returns from backstage, I barrage him.

"No. I didn't see her, honey. She's being assessed by her family doctor, who, by sheer luck, happened to be in attendance."

Relieved to know this girl is being looked after, I pour another glass and down it.

My dad leans closer. "I know this is your moment, but you may want to pace yourself, hmm?" He taps my champagne flute. "Don't you think there have been more than enough mishaps tonight?"

Nodding, I swallow the last drop. "Sorry. Just needed a little liquid memory remover," I say, without realizing it might stir a parental inquisition, which it does.

My dad crosses his arms and stares, seemingly waiting for a detailed explanation. "Dad, I'm fine. A bit thirsty, but this isn't my first rodeo. Girls have been known to faint at these things, and life goes on. But hey, if you happen to spot that orthopedic surgeon friend of yours who treats the NOLA Gold team, can you please introduce us?"

Shaking his head, he shoots me a look.

If there's one thing he doesn't believe in, it's fishing for favors, so I make a pout face and loop my arm around Eli. "Ready to complete your first duty as my date?"

He extends an elbow, and we head to the center of the ballroom to join the other debs and their partners for our first official dance.

When it ends, I drag him to find Piper.

Just like that, we're back in party mode.

"Screw these shoes." Piper balances on one foot, trying to remove her studded heel. "Next presentation, I'm copying you—Converses for the win. While I may have appeared all grace and poise, my life actually flashed before me because of this bougie-ass dress." She puffs out her voluminous skirt. "It caught on my heel going up the steps. I was certain I'd face-plant." Leaning on Jamie's chest, she slips off her other shoe and into a pair of tennis shoes. "Maybe if I'd had these strong arms guiding me—"

"These scrawny things?" Jamie flexes, then locks his muscled arms around her shoulders. "Gotta say, you looked pretty hot up there, Ms. Richards. No one would've guessed you almost tripped."

Tonight, Eli's college roomie, Jamie, looks polished in his tux and is beaming at Piper, who seems equally pleased with his undivided attention and agreement to be her last-minute date.

I couldn't be happier.

"Can't say the same for Ms. Grace." Eli pats the top of my head. "Ainsley stomped on my shoe when we were dancing, but being the chivalrous gentleman I am, I didn't say a word." He winks and slams a vodka shot.

"I think you just did, so scratch the *chivalrous* part. And if you didn't have such oversized hands trying to lead me around, I wouldn't have stepped on your feet. But being the polite, mild-mannered woman *I* am, I kept quiet and followed my un-gentleman's lead."

Leslie, who happens to be passing our table, whirls around. "Did you just call yourself mild-mannered?" She laughs. "I know a lot of things about you, *Ms.* Clarke, but mild-mannered is not part of that definition."

Happy to see Leslie's back to her normal, sarcastic self, I give her a hug. "Hey, enough with the talking. C'mon. Let's dance!"

She grabs my hand, Eli wraps an arm around my waist, and we head to the dance floor with Piper and Jamie trailing behind. Minutes later, we're dancing and singing in sync with the band.

"You make me wanna shout!" Jamie yells, while Piper shakes him back and forth.

I twirl Leslie twice, then switch to Eli and he expertly dips me. When I'm whisked upright, I catch a glint of green—

Violet.

Spinning myself out, I yell, "I'll be right back" and streak toward Violet, liquid courage propelling me onward. When I reach her, I hold out both hands. She hesitates long enough for my ego to plummet, then grabs hold.

"That was cruel," I say, but she ignores my comment, her toned body moving in rhythm with the music. The band breaks into a slower part of the song, so I pull her to me, hands on her waist. "Did I mention you look much better than *nice*?" Leaning closer, the warmth of her laughter tickles my neck.

"Maybe you did, but it's more effective hearing it in person and . . . up close." She squeezes my hand. "Pretty brave of you to charge over for a dance, all graceless like that."

"Me? Graceless? Gee, thanks. As always, you're full of compliments." I fake a frown because not only does she seem happy to see me, she's actually flirting. "Besides, why wouldn't I ask you to dance? It's a supper *dance*."

Violet stops. "You know my last name now, right?"

"Yes."

"And—"

"And what?" I ask. "It's just a name, *Anderson*."

Her face tightens.

"Okay. I admit, when I found out who you are, I may have been the tiniest bit intimidated." Her face freezes, and she tries to untangle our hands, but I tighten my grip, not letting go. "You're upset? Well, I may not have been wearing *basketball* clothes the other day at rehearsal, but I'm the one who should be offended."

Her eyes widen. "Oh. Why is that?"

"Because you never asked me to any games, Ms. Anderson.

Rumor has it your family owns a basketball arena, and this avid sports fan is crushed." Though I'm teasing, she doesn't laugh. "C'mon, Violet. It's a joke."

"Seriously? That's it? No questions?" she yells over the song, while I continue to dance erratically.

I shake my head. "Other than the arena part, I didn't learn anything that wasn't general knowledge from my best friend, who, by the way, *is* gunning for an internship. Apparently from your family's company." I spin her out, then pull her back. "If you care to share more, I'll be happy to listen another time. Right now, all I want to do is dance with you."

"Like I've said before, you're certainly odd," she says, cheeks reddening.

"*Let's get low. A little bit lower now . . .*"

Everyone drops down and we whisper-sing to each other. Several feet away, Eli appears to be unsuccessfully lowering himself, but even with his deepest knee bend, he towers over the hunched-over crowd.

I motion to Violet and guide us across the crowded dance floor to reach Eli.

With his back to us, I snatch a drink from his outstretched hand. Mainly, so he doesn't fall on his ass and ruin some girl's dress with a spilled drink, but also because—*I desperately need a drink.*

"Ainsley!" He whips around, but before he can object further, I give him a thumbs-up, sipping his drink while he's pulled lower by a random girl.

"You better finish that before the next part," Violet warns, so I down his screwdriver, placing it on a waiter's tray as the music kicks up.

"*Let's get high, now!*"

"Hey, hey. Hey, hey!" we shout in unison, and Violet clings to my neck as we move across the dance floor, laughing and grabbing anyone close enough to join in on the fun.

"Ainsley, wait!" Piper pushes her way through the crowd. When she reaches me, I grab her hand to dance, but she swats it away. "Stop! And listen. It's important. Alexandra—"

"Yass. Where is that girl?" I tug on Violet's hand. "Let's go find her to dance."

Piper steps in front of me, stretching her arms to block my way. "Stop! I mean it!"

"What is your problem, Pipe—"

"She's dead, Ainsley! Cooper just told Eli. She started throwing up and she got really, really sick. They rushed her to the hospital, but she's dead. Like never coming back. *Dead-dead!*"

Violet drops my hand, and before I can say a word, she's gone.

CHAPTER 2

TWO WEEKS EARLIER

For a trip I've made dozens of times, heading back to New Orleans last night felt like driving into a war zone. Of course, it's one I'd happily accepted an invitation to and purchased the proper uniforms for—white formal gowns and opera-length leather gloves —but a war, nonetheless, where bullets often rain down in the shape of rumors.

The first bullet: Leslie and I are dating again. Which is *not* true, but it didn't stop her from bombarding me with messages the minute I updated my Snapchat to a driving-home post. Nor did it prevent her from asking to come over, me caving, and well, to Leslie in my bed this morning.

Crossing the room in baggy sweats and a tee, I pluck a garment bag labeled LESLIE HART/ANTOINE'S LUNCHEON from the rolling rack that, after shopping for months, has become a perma-nent fixture in my bedroom. Sliding a mustard bodycon dress over my head, I pose. "Oscar de le Renta once said 'the modern debu-tante is more concerned with the perfect dress rather than the perfect suitor.' Sound familiar?" I complete a twirl. "Zip me, will ya?"

"You can always go with me, Ainsley. Not like I won't be there." Leslie's fingers trace down my back, but when I flinch, she rushes them back to the zipper. "Careful," she says. "If you hurt my feelings, I just may uninvite you from my party."

"You wouldn't dare. Your family loves me too much," I joke, pressing a kiss to her forehead. While Leslie and I dated exclusively junior and senior year of high school—essentially coming out together—after we broke up, we made a pledge that since we'd been friends longer than girlfriends, we'd do our best to keep it that way.

And we had . . . for the most part.

"I've grown a lot in the maturity department since our breakup," she says, flipping her long copper hair. "You'd realize that if you came home more often. But texting on holiday breaks for blue-moon visits? I don't know, sometimes, it makes me think I'm being used."

"You broke up with me, Hart." I lob my stuffed tiger mascot at her, which she deftly deflects. "Besides, you've drunk-texted me enough after your dates. Pretty sure we're even."

"Yeah, whatever." She picks at her fingernail.

Leslie's go-to has always been hyperbole, but she's acting strange. Almost sad. I can't imagine what's wrong, considering her deb luncheon is tomorrow, and last night, she was more than in a celebratory mood. We drank too much and kissed—venturing a bit past the friend zone—but all in all, no big deal.

At least, it shouldn't be a big deal. It's happened once or twice before, and we've always returned to a platonic status the next day. According to Leslie, the occasional hook-up after a breakup is a normal part of the separation process.

Attempting to shift the attention back to my dress, I step back. "But do you think it's appropriate for your luncheon?" I'd labeled this dress, along with coordinating accessories and shoes for her event, just as I'd done for the rest of the season. Which at present includes four, maybe five presentations, six brunches, five luncheons, three teas, and seven headliner parties all crammed over our Thanksgiving and mid-semester breaks. "Some girls put their OOTD in the group chat. Are you sure this gives off the same daytime vibe?"

"It's fine," she says, but *fine* is not what I'm going for, so I linger in front of the mirror, tugging the hem higher, then lower, smoothing its fabric. Deb season begins the moment you receive an invitation the summer before freshman year of college from one or more of the bachelor clubs to its exhaustive, decadent finish Mardi Gras day, but the perks can last a lifetime. Or hopefully, in my case, long enough to lay the groundwork for my future career.

I glance at Leslie. "You didn't add to your guest list since the last time I saw it, did you?"

She shakes her head. "Why?"

"No reason," I say, when in reality, I'd checked every deb's list I could get my hands on to see if anyone from our local sports world had been invited to their party. These are the people I'll need to meet *and* impress if I want to land an internship this summer that carries clout. Not only will it amp up my resume, I won't have to cram the two hundred or so observation hours required to apply to physical therapy grad school over my sophomore and junior year. Which means I'll be ahead of the game.

At least that's my backup plan—if my dream internship doesn't work out.

"Stop staring at the mirror. Your dress is *killer.*" Leslie jars me back to the sight of her, once again snuggled in my down-filled comforter like she's ready to stay awhile. "By the way, when will your parents be home? I don't need a repeat of senior homecoming. Your tree up front? Not as strong as I thought."

I think of the remnants of silver duct tape still on our scarred oak, where Leslie attempted to perch after our all-nighter. Instead, the branch snapped, and she fell on her ass at five in the morning, and stupid, drunk me thought I could tape it back together. "No need to remind me, Les. My parents make sure to do so whenever they need leverage. *It's a registered, historic oak, they say. No amount of money can undo a hundred years of growth.*"

"On that note, this ecoterrorist better get her ass out while it's safe." She sits up, ready to bolt.

"Relax. They're with Luke at some wrestling match, and I haven't heard a peep. Which means he's winning, and they'll be gone another day. Guess I'll need to take you up on that ride after all." I bat my eyelashes playfully. "Especially since someone picked a restaurant with zero parking. You know I hate to Uber by myself."

"What about Piper? She's coming, right?"

I shake my head. Piper's grades had slipped a little, and our GPA-obsessed, czar of a sorority president, Shelbi, had assigned her mandatory exam prep, but Piper wouldn't want me to share those gritty details. "She's not feeling well. She doesn't want to infect anyone."

"Ooh, that sucks, but yes, I can bring you. As long as you promise to be on time. Can't be late for my own party."

Nodding, I slide next to her while she peruses Instagram. "Wait. Stop. Who's that?" Scrutinizing the photo of five girls perched at the Carousel Bar, I notice a bartender in the background flashing a cheesy smile. Either their fake IDs were hella good, or he ignored them to let in a flock of pretty girls. But I know that flock. I also know their actual age. All, that is, but a dark-haired girl, face half-turned from the camera. On her wrist, a gold bracelet with a huge green gem shimmers. "Whoa. Look at that bracelet."

"The bracelet or the *girl?*" Leslie snorts. "If you're trolling for a new conquest, you're out of luck. She's not tagged." She shakes her head. "Are you *not* following this account? It's only deb central. Covers the presentations, the parties, and—"

Grabbing her phone, I read the screen. "Under the Gown? Never heard of it."

I copy the username into the app on my phone, sighing when a locked symbol appears. "It's private? Like why? They literally announce us in the newspaper."

"They announce *most* clubs," she says, no doubt referring to the official, yet off-the-books, secret club that if you ask around—*it doesn't exist.* It's the most coveted invite a deb can score, though no one knows who does, unless you're chosen. And the one I've been secretly gunning for, but have yet to receive.

"Maybe they don't want just anyone gawking at our events. Send a DM. Tell them you're a deb. That's what I did after the Madisons told me about it."

"The Madisons?" I raise an eyebrow.

She laughs. "Yes. I had the misfortune of running into them while I was picking up my gloves from Town and Country. That account was all they could talk about." She twirls a lock of my hair around her finger. "Sometimes, small talk pays off. Guess there's a lesson there, even when you dread it, right Ainsley?"

I have no clue what she's talking about, or why she's still being so touchy-feely, but my head is starting to pound from the wine, and I'm certainly not up to deciphering one of her psychological riddles.

Ignoring the comment, I follow her instructions.

Minutes later, a chat bubble appears. I had typed in my name with no proof I was a deb, and presto. Guess they could've perused my social media for confirmation. It's how sororities gain intel for rush, so why not?

UTG

We know who you are. You have open access. Feel free to send any posts or pictures for our page. A fiver's content is worth gold here. Don't be shy now, Clarke. You never were.

I tilt my phone her way. "What the hell does that mean?"

"Fiver means you've been invited by at least five clubs."

"I know what fiver means, ass." I wave her off. "I meant the message. Creepy, right? Especially that last line."

She gives me a side-eye. "*You* watch far too many true-crime shows. Probably just trolling for content for their page. Which is why you should pick a different pair of shoes." She points at my feet. "Unless you'd prefer to look like a mustard bottle sporting retro Minnie Mouse clogs."

"Exactly why I don't text *you* more often," I snip, and she flips me off.

"Aw, Clarke, don't get pouty. Tomorrow is my party. You'll look fab, and we'll both drink far too much for a brunch and get to do it again and again. This is our year. We deserve to have fun."

They don't deserve it.

These girls with their connections and knotted-up family roots that leave everyone without power choking on them. They're scurrying home, back to their high school breeding grounds, which laid the foundation for terrible personalities and beautiful lives. Currying favors to place a crown on their head or a bouquet in their hands.

I want to stomp their tails.

Watch them scamper away in heels with their wasted preppy escorts, too witless to offer help and too selfish to care.

They're all a joke. Because really, how special can you be?

Just a girl in a white dress or a dude in a tux. Yet, each year, there's another season of fresh, eager faces to fill their clubs. You'd think it would no longer pull so much weight, but it does. Wasted on reputations that are never put to good use. They could be the keepers of this city with the power of one invite. Not to mention all that money spent on nothing, for one night of nothing, yet their faces will be splashed across social media the next morning, just to let us know . . . we're nothing.

Nope. Not this year. This year, every member will be presented for who they truly are.

It's been hard coming to grips with that. Even harder to stay quiet, to be invisible, but it will come in handy when I need it. They made us ghosts. Now, I'll haunt each and every one of them.

Welcome to debutante season, ladies!

CHAPTER 3

LESLIE HART'S BOUTIQUE LUNCHEON
NOVEMBER 9

Sitting on one of the twenty uncomfortable chairs surrounding the mahogany dining table, I tap *speaker* on my phone, trying to comfort my best friend. "It's one party, Pipes. You're not missing much." Rubbing my eyes, I curse as my fingertips come back glittered with makeup I most certainly just botched. "Plus, it's Antoine's. We have four more parties here."

"No way are you at Antoine's. Why is it so quiet, hmm? If the food wasn't so amazing, I'm not sure I'd eat at that echo chamber again."

"It's quiet because no one's arrived yet. And sure, you wouldn't," I tease, knowing it's her all-time favorite restaurant.

"Yeah, maybe. I *do* love their Baked Alaska presentations, especially when they light the meringue on fire. Wait . . . where are you exactly?"

"I'm hiding in the Rex Room, so Leslie won't make me check

the placement cards in the dining room for a *fifth* time. And it's doubtful anyone could forget your spectacular act of heroism."

During our high school graduation luncheon, Piper had been the only one brave enough to smother out the flames when a waiter accidentally lit the tablecloth on fire with a piece of ignited dessert, and the moment went viral. "Don't worry, Pipes. I'll be sure to send you an SOS if the party goes up in flames."

"Please do, and hold that thought. I have to text my mom back."

While I wait, I survey the emerald wallpaper, the display cases stocked full of jewel-encrusted scepters, and the crowns from past Carnival royalty. To most, this room is sacred. An honor to host a luncheon or dinner in, but honestly, though I appreciate the allure, it kind of creeps me out. Just a bunch of dead people's stuff forever protected behind glass, while their bodies rot away at some lofty, above-ground grave. Depressing isn't an adequate word. Especially since I'm stuck as the first guest at a party with nothing to do until the rest arrive.

Note to self: *Never accept a ride with the host of the party.*

"I'm back." Piper's voice resurrects me from the entombed royalty. "Okay, have a blast while I live vicariously through the snaps on Under the Gown. They accepted my request this morning."

"It took a whole day for their response? Did they send a personal message or something?"

"No, why? Were they supposed to?"

Before I can explain the eerie message they had sent me, Leslie pokes her head in, motioning for me to join. "Never mind. Gotta run. Study your ass off and get home as soon as possible. It appears the pastel parade is incoming."

Sure enough, aquatic-blue, coral, and seafoam-green dresses drift in, creating oceanic displays of girls clumped into their former cliques, both figuratively and literally. Doesn't seem to matter that we've graduated. Apparently, high school rules still apply.

"Ohmygosh. Ainsley!" A trio of girls swamp me. Known to most as the Madisons, these same-named girls—Madison N, Madison J, and Madison K—are a three-headed beast, rarely spotted alone, who've not only been best friends since middle school, they used to run the rumor mill at our former high school. And they probably have every intention to do the same here, considering nearly one-fourth of this season's girls hail from St. Claire's lofty halls.

Including me.

Giving hugs, I scan their dresses. It figures none are the ones posted in the group chat, which is obviously a part of their strategic plan. If they showed their actual outfits, they'd be afraid someone might outdo them. "Should be a cool party," I say, trying to be cordial, since it will be a long season, and I have no way of escaping them.

"I guess." Madison N grimaces. "If nothing else, they don't card. Being at a school in a dry county gets boring fast." She pauses, like she's waiting for her other two heads to nod along.

"Fortunately, I cannot relate," I say, happy to be enrolled at a more lax, liquid college. "I saw your posts during rush. Where did you pledge again?"

"Sigma Sigma Delta," all three chime, and I press my lips together, trying not to laugh. Of course they pledged the same sorority. Why should I assume differently?

"Rushing was *so* stressful"—Madison J talks with her hands— "but when the girl interviewing us said, 'Hope to see y'all soon,' I knew we were a shoo-in."

"You mean the sorority that creates a maze to walk through while random strangers shout your name to see how nervous they can make you? That Sigma Sigma Delta?" I ask, and the three glare like I'd just swiped their Netflix password. "I'm sorry. Maybe your maze is much smaller," I joke, and they force smiles back onto their perfectly made-up faces.

Someone behind us laughs, but when I try to glance over my shoulder, Madison J waves her hands in my face. "You're so funny, Ainsley. Yes, it's *smaller*, but we're transferring to Alabama next year. We figured private college was the best idea after being in classes of max fourteen our entire life, but that's a lesson learned the hard way."

Leave it to the Madisons to play the long con. Getting into a top-tier sorority at a smaller school so they didn't have to take the risk of being rejected at a more selective, larger Greek school. In all honesty, I'd been paranoid about rush too, but not enough to move halfway across the country just to pledge a more prestigious sorority.

"How tragic," I say. "Now, we'll be official enemies. Football-wise, that is," I say, but they don't seem to get my joke. Not like I care about their new college choice since you couldn't pay me to cheer for Bama. I'd turned down a scholarship from the university entirely due to sports loyalty. One has to draw a line somewhere, and I'd always been a Tiger, through and through.

Madison K bristles. "I see someone's still obsessed with sports." She says it like it's a curse, and I imagine to her—*it is*. "Practically the only thing you post about, but aren't you majoring in sports medicine or something like that?"

"Physical therapy with a sports specialization. Close enough," I say, yearning for a drink to make this high school reunion of sorts more manageable. "Speaking of that, has anyone seen Laney? I'm dying to find out how she scored the Tulane gig. Lucky girl. I've texted a few times, but she hasn't answered. She *is* being presented by Crescent Club, right?"

Laney was closer to the Madisons than most of us in high school, so if anyone knows where she is, or when she might show, it's them, and I'm hoping it will be today. The only way I can submit an application for my dream internship—a summer shadowing stint with the Saints' PT staff—is to include a character reference. If anything can help me rise above the pack for that spot, it's a reference from one of Tulane's physical therapists. Though Laney and I had both volunteered at their sports camp senior year, she now has an inside track. Since I haven't gotten a response to my emails, I'm hoping Laney can help.

"She's around somewhere," Madison N says.

"She's not done with classes," Madison J says.

The two heads turn on each other, while the one silent Madison glares at the offending girls.

Someone's lying. I just don't know who or why. "Alrighty then. Regardless of where you find her, can you ask her to text me?"

It's not worth getting sucked into whatever spiderweb of drama these three are weaving with Laney, though I certainly hope my little chat will pay off. Searching for an out, I spy a waiter balancing a tray of champagne glasses with the mystery girl from the photo steps behind.

"Um, Madisons. Do you know her?" I nod in the girl's direction, and the three glance her way, shaking their heads dismissively. Even more of a reason *not* to linger a second longer.

I make my way across the room and catch up with the waiter, sneaking a look at the girl. Her hair is dark and worn loose. Not like the perfectly styled updos or flat-ironed hair of other debs, including my own. Her skin is a shade of golden brown that makes her green eyes pop.

Accepting a flute from the waiter, she takes a sip, and her bracelet shimmers—the one from the photo at the Carousel Bar. But even up close, can't say I recognize her. While I don't claim to know everyone, a completely new face around here is rare.

Catching my gaze, she raises an eyebrow, and my cheeks flame. "Sorry. I was just, um, trying to place you. I hoped I might remember your name before embarrassing myself. You know,

Southern manners and all that." It's a lie, but what am I supposed to say? That I suddenly find it hard to speak because I think she's *cute?*

I point at her outfit. "Love your dress, by the way."

Her eyes lock onto mine, and I don't know whether to look away or engage in her stare-down. "Thanks. The dress is old, and no, we've most definitely never met. This is my first event. I didn't go to the summer mixers. I stay pretty busy at school."

"Well, I'm Ainsley. Ainsley Clarke," I say. "Nice to meet you." We shake with a bit too much enthusiasm on my part. "What college has you too busy to miss out on all the fun?"

"Fun?" she scoffs. "I go to Rhodes. Geographically not far, but it's hardly worth getting behind in my classes to attend these parties. I'm Violet, by the way."

"Violet?" I pause, waiting for her last name to follow, but it doesn't. "Okay. Just Violet. From Rhodes. Got it," I say, trying to fill the awkward void. "Rumor has it your campus looks like one of the Ivies with its gothic architecture. Unfortunately, I never made it there during college tours. Did you um, rush?"

It's a safe conversation starter, and my go-to at events like this.

Her face brightens. "And experience the maze of witches chanting my name? I'm afraid I passed on that enlightening experience. Sounds like I dodged a bullet though."

She grins and my eyes widen. "You were the one eavesdropping?" I laugh, my curiosity further piqued. "Glad I made an impression on someone," I say, "but yes, their sorority can be a bit hyper-aggressive during rush, in my opinion. Most aren't nearly as stressful. The one I pledged is more, um, academic-based, but fun. At least, I hope it will be. Still a newbie."

She raises an eyebrow. "I wouldn't know about that, but I definitely think you made an impression. After you left, those three made a beeline for her." She points with her chin. "They've been whispering ever since."

Following her gaze, I spot the Madisons locked in conversation with Leslie.

Leslie shoots me a look and shakes her phone. Mine buzzes.

"Pretty sure they're spreading rumors about me to the host," I say, figuring that's why Leslie looks so annoyed. Everything seemed fine when she picked me up this morning, but now, I'm no longer sure. "Guess it's collateral damage for engaging with my former high school's gossip queens."

"So when the local rumor mill didn't recognize me, this was your plan B?"

"Wow. You really were eavesdropping," I say. "Don't know if I should be offended or flattered."

"I could say the same, since you don't know who I am, which *is* surprising . . . but still." Raising her flute, she takes another sip.

Am I supposed to know who she is? And if so, what does that say about my vetting skills for identifying clout-worthy guests? "More a plan C for champagne," I say. "Full disclosure, I did see a photo of you on Insta yesterday. So technically . . . not lying."

"Under the Gown, right?" She drums her pale pink fingernails on the side of her glass. "I didn't post that. My friends did. They're obsessed with that moronic account."

I shake my head, grateful someone shares my skepticism about the site. "'Your daily dose of debutante drama behind the gowns and gloves,'" I recite their tagline. "A tad theatrical, but what better season to lose your mind and become a baby gossip girl?"

"Sounds like a whole mess of avoidable problems to me." She swirls the remaining liquid in her glass. "Though I'll toast to the fact that after Mardi Gras, I'll never have to hear about another *season* again."

I stare at the green-eyed girl. "You really don't want to be here, do you?"

"Why would I? This whole scene is"—she rolls her eyes—"self-aggrandizing."

"So is *your* plan to show up at parties with a designer rain cloud as an accessory and make everyone miserable?" I pass my comment off as a joke, but if you're going to be a deb, you need to own it. Kind of hard to feel pity for this girl in her thousand-dollar outfit and jewels, attending a score of glamorous parties she doesn't care to be at. I can think of a hundred places worse to be and a million girls who would trade places with her or me in an instant.

Not to mention, it's Leslie's party, and I know the amount of booze, therapy sessions, and tears that went into her planning efforts. "If you don't want to be here, surely you can find a better way to amuse yourself than listening in on conversations of people talking about the thing you're presently hating on."

"If the party isn't too dull, sometimes my cloud can contain a bit of lightning." She grins. "Not like I have a choice about being here, if you must know. A friend dragged me along, and it's way easier to actually attend these events than explain to my family the twenty reasons why I didn't show."

While her attitude is annoying, deb season isn't everyone's thing, and besides, certainly none of my business. Even so, I'd rather spend time talking to Miss Dark Cloud than return to the present mix of girls milling about. "What clubs are you being presented by? Maybe I can make that twenty-one reasons?"

"Crescent, Le Orleanians, and M—" She snaps her mouth shut. "That's all."

"Perfect. I'm in both. Since we have rehearsal for Crescent soon, you'll get to see my extremely inspiring face again."

"Not sure that's something to look forward to."

I can't tell if this is another bad attempt at humor, or she's actually insulting me, but my phone buzzes for the trillionth time, so I swipe through the multiple notifications. "Apparently someone thinks we look good." I flash the photo posted to Under the Gown, and scan the crowd, hoping to spot who uploaded it, but everyone seems absorbed with their own group of friends. "Because according to this, I'm 'on the prowl,' and you're 'the prettiest prey by the liquored-up watering hole.' Get it?"

"I don't know which is more offensive. The fact that you're prowling, like some crocodile, or someone is suggesting I could ever be *your* victim." She shakes her head.

"The hashtag says *#deblooks*. Pretty sure it's a compliment. At least we've passed someone's standard of fashion."

"Are you that concerned with someone else's opinion? Please, you look better than most of the girls here."

Before I can digest her out-of-left-field compliment or dizzying change of moods, she shrugs. "Guess it's my turn to pull a plan E, as in *evacuate,* before you start explaining the meaningful tradition of why my parents were asked for their permission to have me escorted by a pack of men who voted me in. Have fun gossiping."

CHAPTER 4

CRESCENT CLUB REHEARSAL
NOVEMBER 18

It's finally Thanksgiving break, and Piper and I catch every red light on our drive down Canal Street. "Ooh, look." Piper points at the neutral ground. "The Roman Candy cart. Can we get taffy?"

"Are you like five? And no, we don't have time, Pipes. We'll be late."

"I don't know why we have to practice. It's just *walking*," she laments.

"Probably more for the guys than us," I say. "They need to meet who they're escorting and learn where their family will be sitting. Remember what Eli said about Cooper last year? He didn't know who he was escorting until he showed at the event. Not to mention, he was fifteen minutes late. And drunk."

"It's *Cooper*. What do you expect?"

I start to reply, but really, what can I say? That I *don't* know what to expect from Cooper, but I'm hoping he'll procure an invitation for me to the most coveted debutante ball of the season? The

32

one I suspected he was a member of, then bugged him nonstop to put me up for consideration? And if he does come through, it won't include an invite for her because each member can only nominate one prospective debutante?

Is that what I should say? Because I can't.

Not just because I feel rotten keeping this from her and Eli—because I do—but for so many other reasons I'm not ready to share or have had the time to process myself.

Forcing the thought from my brain, I swerve into the Hilton's circular drive. Fifth in line for the valet, Piper gathers our totes stuffed with bottled waters, snacks, and heels so we can break them in for the event while I grab a baseball hat from my glove compartment. The air is more humid than normal—87 degrees in November—and my hair is already screwed. Might as well commit. Besides, it's practice. Not like I need to impress anyone.

Or do I?

"Exactly why are we walking this fast?" Piper huffs as we book it through the main lobby and down the hallway to the Grand Ballroom. I've been to so many Carnival balls here, I could practically sleepwalk to the location, but today, I refuse to be late.

"Ooh, I know. You're hyped to see that bitchy girl who rejected you at Leslie's luncheon, right?" she snipes as we sweep past the gift store. "Sorry, Ainsley. This is how it feels when you meet someone who may not find you as charming as you find them."

"Encouraging. Wow, thanks." Piper is not known for having a filter, but today, I figure her comment has more to do with her anxiety over Jamie rather than my situation, so I let it slide.

Opening the door to an empty ballroom, I raise an eyebrow. "Which room did the email say again?" She shows me her phone, and I roll my eyes, pointing at the Grand *Salon* across the hall. "And yes, I think Violet is cute, but her attitude sucks. She acts like she has better things to do than be a deb."

"Um, maybe she does. Being presented to society is essentially an archaic, sexist tradition."

I shoot her a look. "Yet everyone's dying to be part of it. Including you, Ms. NOLA Royalty," I remind her. "Besides, if she doesn't want to participate, cool. But the whole debutante-loathing angle . . . a bit much. You don't have to love the concept, but at least be polite and lie. Really not that difficult."

Piper glances at her phone. "Hold up. Read this." She tilts it my way. "Seems someone has a different policy about lying."

I scan the Under the Gown post from five minutes ago. "Wait. Is that . . . *Lily*?" The girl in the photo is pressed against a wall, lips locked onto a guy with roaming hands, but I recognize the tattoo. It's a bright red balloon that Lily, our sorority sister, had stenciled on her hand after a hell week dare to tat an image from the last movie we'd seen. Hers was *It*. Guess Pennywise the clown would be a pretty shitty thing to have haunting you.

"Holy crap . . . that guy. He's president of Crescent Club." Piper taps the screen with her French manicured fingernail. "I got paired with him at the summer mixer. For a bachelor, he's literally a decade older and not even remotely attractive."

I read the post:

U-G-L-Y. Lily has no alibi. Here's a tip for those who want to stay off this page. Pick a different hotel than the one you're practicing at. It can't be a walk of shame if you never actually leave. Right, Patrick? Oh, and congrats on the engagement!

"Dude, no way." Piper clicks on his tag, quickly navigating to Patrick's profile where there's a photo of a cute brunette flashing her diamond ring. "Poor fiancée. Sucks he's cheating. Also, a pretty shitty way to find out."

I pull her phone closer. "Look at those buttons in the corner. Someone took a photo from inside an elevator and sent it in, but why would UTG post it? I thought the whole point of that account was to elevate the debs and showcase their parties. Everything was flattering—until *this*."

Piper and I scroll through past posts to make sure we didn't miss anything. Looks of the day. Dress inspirations and throwbacks to last year's parties. "Who knows. Maybe it's extreme karma or payback for them cheating, but one thing is certain. *I* am not down for a public shaming in this century."

I open the door to the salon. "Awkward," I whisper, as we steer past groups of girls in Lululemon leggings huddled excitedly over their phones. A few guys are also gathered, laughing and high-fiving, each trying to out *bro* the other.

Shaking my head, I scrawl our names onto a clipboard and scan the room for somewhere to sit. Leslie is in the back of the room with Willa Kennedy and a few other St. Claire alumnae, but when I wave, she turns her head like she doesn't see me.

Rude.

Finding two empty seats near the front, Piper and I sit. "Welcome, ladies and gentlemen. I'm Sims Charbonnet, floor chairman of this year's event—excuse me, can everyone put their phones away and listen up?" He waits for the room to quiet. "Before we get into the ins and outs of the presentation, I have some exciting news about a new protocol we're implementing this year. We've kept it hush-hush, even from esteemed members." He smiles sheepishly at several guys seated in the front row. "So, without further ado, I'd like to introduce this year's chaperones who shall hereafter be known as your *den mothers*."

Whispers ricochet through the crowd.

He taps the microphone. "As I was saying," he snaps, "these

ladies have graciously volunteered their time to assist with your debutante efforts, not only at our event, but every sanctioned party or deb presentation throughout the season. Trust me, things will flow much smoother with their knowledge of and dedication to our sacred traditions." He fumbles some papers, then continues. "Ladies, will you please stand as I call your name?"

Piper mouths *lame,* and I nod in agreement.

He reads off a list of ten or so names and assorted women pop up like excited jack-in-the-boxes, waving and smiling, each followed by a round of applause. Most appear to be in their early to late forties, meticulously dressed in chic dresses and heels—no doubt, prior debs—but the last two blondes, Sara and Sloane, look young enough to pass for one of us.

I lean into Piper. "Think this is what Eli was talking about?"

She shrugs, but I'm sure it is. Ever since we received our invitations, Eli has given us grief about being debutantes, and game night on campus last week was no exception. After making us swear we wouldn't say a word, he shared what Cooper had told him about Cresent doing things differently this year to keep the girls "under control." Eli knew the comment would annoy us—exactly why he told us—but when I pressed for an explanation, he admitted to not knowing much more. Just that it had something to do with a club member being stalked by a girl who hadn't made the cut.

While Eli's laid-back personality doesn't gel with the deb scene, his brother is quite the opposite. Cooper loves reaping the rewards of parties, premium booze, and eager-to-party girls. Exactly why he's not only a member of Crescent Club, but apparently has enough clout to be privy to their protocol before the rest of the club members. Because the fact that this staunch, nearly a century-year-old organization is making a change to their holier-than-thou traditions *is* a major deal. It means either this girl who was snubbed had truly been a nightmare, or there's a lot more to the story than being shared.

But . . . *den mothers*? Girl scouts we are not. Besides, where were these seraphic den mothers when UTG decided to play show-and-tell with Patrick and Lily?

Sims prattles on, "Practice won't last long. Hour tops for you ladies. Gentlemen, you'll need to stay to go over a few details after our run-through." He pauses. "One more thing. Everyone, pay close attention. Name cards for each deb's parents are labeled on the chairs surrounding the dance floor. Make sure your guests are accounted for and the spelling is correct. During your presentation, Patrick will announce your names as you enter the room. If there's a pronunciation error, please address it with him *now*, not later."

"Doubt that's all Patrick wants to address with us," a girl blurts from our row as we head to find our designated escorts.

Everyone laughs.

Poor Lily.

She's a few girls in front of me, head down, body droopy, like she wants to sink into the fleur-de-lis carpeting and disappear. Glancing around, I spot Patrick, who is busy chatting it up, but even from here, I can see his neck is scarlet and mottled. Though I have no respect for cheaters, I feel the tiniest shred of empathy for the guy. Sure, he's a player. But because of Under the Gown, his fate is now publicly tragic. Not only will he probably lose his fiancée, he'll most likely be canceled. From the club. Hell, maybe the whole NOLA social scene.

Minutes pass, and everyone seems to be matched up with their escort, listening to the instructions as best as they can, given the circumstances. It's simple. Walk in a square. Curtsy at all designated spots, especially in front of your parents, then move on. Pretty much the same routine we've done at countless other society events.

As we line up for our first run-through, Sims's voice booms. "It seems we're missing a few of our members. If anyone feels confident enough with the routine, could you pair up with a deb whose partner is not here? Um,"—he glances at his page—"there's a total of seven girls without escorts."

Tuning him out, I snap back to attention when I hear the name *Violet*.

Scanning the ballroom, I spot her in a bright green sweatshirt with black leggings tucked into her cowboy boots. But before I can catch her attention, Piper pokes me. "Dude, you're like an owl on steroids, screwing your head around for that girl. Could you be a tad less obvious? She doesn't sound like the *nicest* person. Why are you crushing so hard?"

I mull over her question. Sure, Violet was annoyingly sarcastic at Leslie's luncheon, and she'd probably rather be anywhere but here, but maybe that's why I'm intrigued. "Sorry, Pipes. Never been one to turn down a challenge. Wish me luck."

Turning to my escort, a Mr. Chuck Spencer III, I assure him I know the routine, but that I'll be bowing out to help a deb. Then I dash off in Violet's direction.

After several minutes, Sims taps the microphone again. "It appears everyone now has a partner to work with, but please, don't hesitate to reach out to a club member should you need assistance."

Switching off his microphone, he storms in Patrick's direction with a pissed-off look on his face, which is not surprising. Like I figured, there seems to be a line of people gunning for their president.

I nudge Violet's shoulder. "You should be thankful I came to help. Consider yourself lucky."

"Yeah, maybe, but I certainly can manage on my own." She shakes her head and hooks her arm through mine. "Not exactly brain surgery."

"True, but if you don't practice, how will you teach your boyfriend later? You don't want him to look like a total ass, do you?"

Leading her to the first yellow *X* taped to the carpeting, I tap my foot.

"I don't have a *boyfriend*." She yanks me downward as she sweeps through her curtsy.

"With such graceful moves, I can't imagine why." I shake out my jammed knee. "And you don't have to do the whole sweeping thing before going into the curtsy. Your gown will hide the move and your shoes."

"Oh? Dated a Carnival queen, did we?" Her green eyes snap. "Bet you help all of your girlfriends practice."

"No, but you're partially right." I drop into a corrected version of the curtsy, happy to show off my moves. "May I present Ms. Clarke, former Queen of Krewe of Athor." I grin. "And I *don't* have a girlfriend."

"That's why I said girlfriends." She hisses the *s*. "Apparently, you have quite the reputation."

"What?"

"When my friends saw the photo of us at the luncheon, they may have warned me."

"Is it possible your friends aren't being honest? Girls are known to spread inaccurate gossip from time to time."

While the small-town aspect of a city like New Orleans can come in handy for networking, it can bite you in the ass when you try to land a new date. Especially when there's a rumor circulating that you're back with your ex.

"I think this one is spot on, considering you *dated* her."

I pull her to a stop. "Wait—who?" Glancing around, I expect to find Leslie peering from the sidelines, but Violet points to a short blond.

Casey? "I don't know why she would discredit me. We went on *one* blind double-date, and she spent the whole night schooling me on my bowling technique, which made zero sense, considering her balls all went into the *gutter*."

She smiles. "Something tells me you're a whole heap of trouble."

"Maybe. I don't know." I shrug. "Did it ever occur to you that I came over here for a purely platonic reason? I'm a friendly person. Surely your antisocial behavior and complete distaste for the only thing we share in common checks off a box on my college bucket list for the friends I hoped to meet."

"Do you know what's on my bucket list?" She reaches up, hand skirting past my neck, then she tips off my hat. "Teaching manners to those who should know better than to wear a baseball cap *inside*." She grins.

I like her.

"Fair. So, what are the manners on asking for your phone number?" Retrieving my hat, I put it on backward and out of reach of her aggressive hands. "That way, if you have any further questions about practice, you won't have to get it from your very biased friend group."

"And if I don't have questions?"

"Oh, some people like to hang out, eat food, or watch a movie. Really, I'd be up for anything." While I'm trying to appear nonchalant, I know this is the part where I'll either sink or swim, so I take a deep breath and hold out my phone. "If you'd prefer not, I'll go lick my wounds in the corner. But let me know early enough so I can heal for the presentation. I'd hate to look ghastly in my photos."

"Says the girl wearing a hockey jersey with a Tigers baseball hat." Her eyes travel the length of my body. "Aren't you supposed to be Miss Dream Barbie Debutante?"

Shaking her head, she snatches my phone.

"Hey. They make a sports edition of Barbie, you know." Taking my phone back, I text my number to her before I realize she's beaten me to it. I smile at the crocodile emoji she sent herself. "*I'm* trouble?"

She laughs, and for the first time since we've met, she seems to be enjoying herself. Which is great. *Really, really great.* "Keep it up, and I'll send Under the Gown a post that you're bullying me," I tease.

"Oh God—the post about Lily." She frowns. "I don't know her, but ouch."

"Awful they cheated, but I assumed the worst I'd have to worry about on that account was an unflattering photo." I make a silly face. "Nothing harsh like that."

When I escort her to the last *X*, she bites her lip and glances around. "Do you think that's the worst it will get though?"

She looks frightened, which is weird. "It's an account *for* us, not against us," I say, hoping to reassure her, but I have no idea why she's so freaked out. I mean, sure, today's post was cruel. And maybe a bit more menacing than your basic, bitchy gossip for the two involved, but it seemed like an isolated dig at Patrick for doing something really shitty.

At least, it did to me.

"Look around." Her voice drops. "All these girls and guys. Pretty sure they all have secrets. I doubt it will be the worst they post. And if it isn't, who do you think will be their next victim?"

CHAPTER 5

DAY OF CRESCENT CLUB PRESENTATION
NOVEMBER 22

If holidays were ranked, Thanksgiving would land near the top of my list, considering I can chill in pj's in my favorite chair, watch football, and recover from any number of food comas. Plus, I love to cook. More specifically, to prep. But do I like it enough to start at nine in the morning? That would be a resounding no.

"You can finish later, honey." My mother's voice soothes from the other side of the island, but I'm already hunched over, slicing onions, trying to blink away the tears pouring from my eyes. "You're always a big help, but this"—she gestures around the room —"way above my expectations."

Waltzing past the containers of chopped vegetables, ready-to-bake dishes covered in foil, and a growing list of instructions taped to the oven, she smiles. "It's a *lot*, Ainsley."

"I don't have makeup until three and hair is at five. That gives me an hour to get ready for Crescent. More than enough time. Besides, if I leave this to you and Dad, we'll starve."

The worst part of this presentation is the fact that Crescent is one of two clubs that host their presentations on the eve of Thanksgiving, aka Blackout Wednesday. Only tonight, there won't be anything close to blacking out. At least, not before the presentation. And since Thanksgiving is tomorrow, and I'd prefer to eat without barfing, not after, either. But even though I must curtail my cocktails on the most notorious drinking night of the year, it's not enough to sink my mood.

Dancing around the kitchen, I pause when my mom eyes me suspiciously.

I pop out an earbud. "What?"

"Nothing honey. It's just nice seeing you this excited."

"And I hope to stay this way. Mom, please make sure everyone is on time tonight."

Fanning her face with a potholder, she scoffs. "We've never been late to a single one of your events. Why would you think we'd do so tonight?"

"Because you have been late." She starts to protest, but I hold up my hand. "The summer mixer. It might not have been mandatory, but it still mattered."

There's no way she's forgotten that my father came home in scrubs, and when I demanded he change into an actual suit, he took so long, we ended up meeting him at the bar. Which was more than late—*he missed the whole thing*.

"He was on call." My mother morphs into defend-Dad mode. "Would you prefer he refuse emergency neurosurgery and be on time?"

Draping the kitchen towel over my face, I sigh. "Am I not allowed to lodge one complaint or want my family to be present *and* on time for an event without you laying a guilt trip on me about my selfishness causing some poor person to die?"

"I also wish your father was around more, but he did get his shift changed for tonight."

"Yes, Mother, I know. He's told me multiple times. And I'm really not trying to be a nag, but I worked extremely hard to get here."

I motion to the photo gallery of young me at numerous social events on the walls. I had participated in most of the subdeb events thanks to Piper's parents inviting me into their sacred social sanctum. And though I wasn't supposed to know Piper's dad was a bigwig in one of the most prestigious carnival organizations in New Orleans, without his influence, I probably wouldn't have landed on the radar of any debutante club, despite my dad being a well-respected doctor.

To these clubs, it's not how successful you are. It's about old money, decades-in-the-making family status, and lineage. Or, in my case, being lucky enough to have a best friend with those qualifications to take me along for the ride. "You realize being presented helps you meet important people, right?"

Crossing her arms, she gives me a look. "When did you start discounting other people, Ainsley?"

"I didn't mean it like that. It's just *these* people . . . look, never mind."

There's no use debating this with my mother. We moved from Chicago when I was in fourth grade, and I only landed at St. Claire's—one of the largest deb feeder schools in the city—due to a referral from a fellow navy doctor who worked with my dad. So, despite having attended the right school for years, I've always felt like an outsider.

Like I had to do more just to measure up.

And honestly, I don't know which is worse. Being oblivious to the New Orleans pool of social elites, or having one toe in their water, perched on the sidelines, always waiting for your chance to be invited in.

"Honey, we appreciate the honor of this occasion," she says, "and the others over the years. Didn't your father wear those embarrassing white tights and shrimper boots when he was king? I'd say that was more than a sacrifice."

"It's okay, Mom. Come mid-February, you guys won't have anything left to sacrifice. I'll either have made enough connections to succeed in this city, or I'll become a spinster, plucking herbal remedies in the swamp."

"Masquerade!" My brother's voice filters through the house, followed by his lanky body dancing into the kitchen. "It's hilarious how dramatic they make these events. Can't wait until I get to be one of those creepy lieutenants wearing Dad's curly white wig and big-ass boots."

"That was for Athor, a Carnival ball, dumbass. Besides, you have to be *invited*. Good luck with that." I aim a diced bell pepper at his head. "Also, why are you not helping me cook?"

"Dad can get me in," he taunts, ignoring my reference to his obvious neglect of anything kitchen related. "Who do you think signed you up to be queen when you were a mere infant, *Ass*-ley?"

"More like lower school, but okay." I make it rain peppers.

"Stop, jerk. Besides, if Dad doesn't have enough pull, I don't care. Every event is the same. Girls in giant white dresses and gloves, prancing across the dance floor. Not to mention the zillion times I've had to watch you parade around in that awful wedding dress. Hate to break it to ya, sis. You look more like you're haunting the house as a jilted bride than some snooty society girl."

He knocks my shoulder on the way to the fridge, taking a sip from the milk carton. "Besides, Mom says I don't have to help cook because I suck at it."

"That you do. But FYI, I parade around to make sure my heels are high enough that I won't trip. It's normal to work hard for things you want. Maybe you should try it sometime."

He sticks his tongue out, and it spirals me further into sibling rivalry mode. "Mom. Tell him to stop infecting the milk." I point at his indiscretion, and she shrugs. "If this family isn't sexist, I don't know who is. How do you expect him to get better at cooking if you never make him try?"

"Having you and Luke together in the kitchen on a normal day is a nightmare. I refuse to tempt fate on an important one like this."

He flips me off behind my mom's back. "Yes, Ainsley. Be a good girl and listen to your mother."

My mom shakes her head. "I'll finish up, Ainsley. Why don't you take a nap, so you can be well-rested for tonight?"

Slapping the kitchen towel down, I sigh. "I will. If you make sure he doesn't eat everything before it's cooked. And please, be ready for seven."

I shoot a final glare at my brother. "That includes you, Mr. Spandex Pants. Pretend this is one of your wrestling matches. Maybe that will set a fire under your ass."

Even silenced, my phone illuminates the bedroom, flashing possible morse code messages of doom, but I refuse to pick it up. I don't want to read anything that could wreck this evening. Then again, it could be something important. Like a change of ballroom for tonight's presentation. Or Violet.

The thought nearly propels me to check my screen, but I'd have a better chance of falling asleep than receiving a text from her. It's been days since practice, and since I didn't want to appear desperate, I vowed she'd have to make the first move.

Yet even that thought is filled with its own set of worries. Sure, I want her to text. I really do. But at the same time, I hadn't dated anyone serious since Leslie, and the concept of a new relationship makes me queasy.

First, I'm way too busy.

Second, maybe I'm reading into things, but I'm starting to worry Leslie might actually want to date again. While the thought is a stretch, considering she broke up with me over a text, of all things, it could explain her recent mood shifts.

Even if I wanted to get back together, which I don't, it had taken us separating for me to realize the truth. While Leslie claimed our relationship wouldn't work with us going to separate colleges, the truth isn't that we couldn't make it apart. It's the being *together* that seemed to bring out an insecurity in her that had often left us in tears by the end of the night.

A bright red flag. Especially when she drank.

Shaking off the thought, I call Piper to remind her of our makeup appointment. Before I can say a word, she bombards me. "Did you *not* open the TikToks I sent?"

"Hello to you, too," I say, pressing *speaker* and speed-reading through her unopened texts. "What am I even looking at? Is this some mystical charge-your-crystals-by-the-moon crap? Did you not learn your lesson with those Voodoo love incantations?"

"It's no woo-woo crystals," she sniffs. "If you had bothered to listen, you'd know it's about meditative breathing. And how intensive practices of silence in environments with good energy can reflect back on your physical health and skin."

While Piper babbles, I fiddle with an old Camp Briarwood lanyard hanging on my bedpost. Though we'd met in lower school, we always landed in different homerooms, which kept us from bonding until we were assigned as bunkmates at summer camp. That first evening, I heard Piper sobbing over the mosquito bites riddling her body, so I spent the rest of the night pulling out clothes from my duffel bag, trying to rig a bug-proof costume for her.

We've been inseparable since.

"Are you saying I interrupted your meditation, therefore, I ruined your *skin* for tonight?" I try to rationalize her pseudo-science explanation. "Is this an overall thing, or are you trying to harness the moon's light for a certain someone? Like *Jamie*?"

"You're the one who invited him to be my date," she says. "But if you must know, I'm this worked up, so I don't end up being trolled by Under the Gown. After Lily's *Scarlet Letter* moment, I'm not taking any chances. Nor should you. Remember the stories about the shit that went down at some of the presentations? What if it's true? What if this site—"

"C'mon, Piper." While there'd been vague urban legends that floated around high school about disasters during prior deb seasons, we'd been to a ton of presentations with zero catastrophes. "I know of one *actual* incident," I say. "Which, according to Laney, wasn't a big deal."

"Oh, when was that?"

"Ashley's debut. Don't you remember?"

"Her sister? Yeah—no. We were barely out of middle school. I have limited recall of anything that occurred during the braces-and-acne years."

"Or maybe because it *wasn't* that memorable, but let me refresh. So, according to Laney, Ashley was next to be presented, but the girl ahead of her—I don't remember her name; I think it started with an *O*—tripped on her dress and was so embarrassed, she ran away without finishing her presentation. The end."

"I kind of remember hearing that," Piper says. "Embarrassing, yes. Epic disaster, no."

"Exactly. It could happen to any of us. If it does—which it won't—you better not run your ass away. Smile and keep going. Besides, UTG is new. Those rumors are old and probably false. So forget about that account and concentrate on your debut and Jamie. Besides, *I* asked him because you were too chicken. Did you or did you not need a date?"

"Yes, but—"

"But nothing. I'm your best friend, Pipes. I know how much you like him. Plus, I felt bad leaving him out. Especially with Eli escorting me. How many times did Jamie remind us at game night how great he looked in a tux?"

"A lot."

"Right. Plus, he's cute and cheats at Clue. What more can you ask for in a guy?"

Though Piper won't admit it, I know she's psyched about going with him. It's probably the actual reason she's nervous, and not because of some lame account that after the Lily incident had returned to showcasing daily deb events.

Either way, I have no intention of letting that gossip-fest account wreck my evening.

"Funny you'd pick my future boyfriend's potential by the degree he's capable of cheating. Not to mention, Eli's right. Someone *did* steal the cards, and you knew it." She sighs. "I don't meddle in your love life. Why can't you allow me to make the same poor decisions?"

"Because you deserve better. If I don't vet the people you date, you might get back with John from Calc, who wears Crocs as his primary shoes."

"Says the one who won't allow herself a real relationship to avoid possible hurt feelings down the road."

"Yeah, yeah. Maybe work on meditating some more and *not* projecting," I sniff. "I'll see you later. Love ya."

"Love ya, too!"

With a few hours to kill, I drive to my own personal nirvana to soothe my nerves. Lowering the music roaring through my headphones, I hand Charlie five bucks to let me into the Grand Slam Batting Cages. Unlocking the rusty lock on the chain-link gate, I head to the back of the cage, extract my lucky bat from my backpack, and set the batting machine to fifty miles per hour. While I've mastered greater speeds, it's not the time to chance a black eye.

Holding my bat steady, I wait for a ball to let loose.

CRACK! A single—*not terrible*.

Shaking my arms out, I feel the tension leaving my body.

When Luke started playing baseball as a kid, our family was transplanted into Little League World to help with practices. But after he traded baseball for wrestling, I remained obsessed with sports. In high school, I played anything I could fit into my schedule. While I was more than decent enough to compete, for once, winning wasn't my first priority. Having my name on a team roster offered an opportunity to be part of something bigger than myself. Not only did I fall in love with the camaraderie, sports became my way to fit in. As long as I tried my best and showed up for practice, I was treated as an equal.

So here, at these beat-to-shit batting cages, even when I perform poorly, it's an easy way to get that feeling back. It's the reason I chose physical therapy as my major. Only me being me, I had to up my own game. With an end goal of becoming a PT for a college or pro team, not only will it be a reach, it's nearly impossible to land on my own merit, despite what my dad thinks.

I need connections to boost those odds.

And that mission starts tonight.

Especially since I haven't heard back from Laney or Cooper.

I have no plan C or D.

"Come on, Max, gimmie an easy one!" I yell at the dilapidated pitching machine, and the groan of the wheel catches. Tipping my helmet, I adjust my bat and *smack*. The ball blurs into the back of the farthest net. "That's what I'm talking about!"

If things go this well tonight, I'll be one happy debutante.

CHAPTER 6

THE DAY AFTER CRESCENT CLUB PRESENTATION
(THANKSGIVING DAY)

Despite the horror of the last twelve or so hours, there are things to be grateful for this Thanksgiving. Because as much as no one would dare admit, I'm sure everyone feels lucky that whatever fate cursed Alexandra Williams did not come knocking on their door last night.

Sounds cruel, but it's true.

No matter how shitty your life is, death is the one thing that can give you a wake-up call, and if anything good can come of her passing, it's that. One week ago, had anyone asked me what fate could be worse than tripping in front of five hundred pairs of eyes, I would've sworn up and down no better answer existed.

A girl had to die for me to know better.

I attempt to force down another bite of sweet potato casserole, but the memories hit.

When everyone realized they were dancing on the same floor that had just hosted a girl's final moments, gasps filled the room,

51

tears were shed, and a cloud of white silk dispersed into a hundred directions. But today, well, that silk has been replaced with sweatpants, hoodies, smudged mascara—even on my mother—and subdued conversations.

I put down my fork, push my plate away, and excuse myself from the table to go change for an event I never thought would be part of my or anyone else's deb season—*a vigil for a dead debutante.*

Crescent Club seems to be in full damage control mode with its hastily thrown together afternoon memorial for Alexandra, and though I've been trying to block the flashbacks of her last curtsy, it's not like I can miss it.

After doing my best with a funeral aesthetic, I head north up City Park Avenue and turn into the double-sided, horseshoe entrance of the New Orleans Museum of Art, continuing until the sound of amusement park rides overtakes the music in my car. Parking under the shade of a moss-draped oak, I follow the ensemble of people wearing black, chastising myself for being stupid enough to wear heels to an outdoor event.

Shifting my weight to my toes, I skirt around muddy recesses, relieved when the sturdy bite of concrete scrapes against my soles. This area is usually occupied by those having picnics or boiling crawfish. Today, it's serving a loftier purpose. Guess it's the only place the club could secure on a last-minute basis.

"Here." Madison K passes me a stubby white candle. "So terrible what happened. I can't believe someone our age had a heart attack."

Teenagers don't have heart attacks, I think, but who am I to challenge Alexandra's cause of death? "I guess a heart attack can be misdiagnosed as fainting from nerves, like everyone assumed," I repeat what my dad said over breakfast. "It's just . . . unlucky. Or rare. Whatever you want to call it."

"A tragedy is what I call it." Madison K raises a tissue and blows her nose.

"You guys weren't presented at Crescent, but um, you *know* Alexandra?" I ask Madison J and N who stare like I've grown another head.

"Did you not read the post we sent to Under the Gown?" Madison N frowns, picking at the melted wax on her candle. "It doesn't matter if we didn't know her. We feel horrible about what happened, so we asked the guys if we could pitch in to help commemorate her life. She's still one of us, right?"

"Plus, we were there. Jesus, Ainsley. I was seated not far from where she fell. It was horrible. She looked like she was about to cry." Madison J screws up her face like she's trying to force out her own tears.

The other two grab her hands.

"That's weird. I don't remember seeing any of you at the front tables. Or even at the event, for that matter." I cock my head, trying to look past the crocodile tears for a shred of the truth. "Considering I stood front of the stage; you'd think I would've noticed." I sink my fingernails into my palms as I wait out the Madisons and their tier-C theatrics.

"People forget things during traumatic events, Ainsley. It's been proven, time and time again." Madison K wields her candle at me. "Besides, why are you being so rude? We're trying to do something nice for Alexandra. I don't see you doing a thing."

"How would you know? Because I didn't post it? Or check on whatever the other debs are up to after this traumatic event?" I close my eyes and, once again, Alexandra's bloody smile haunts me. Along with the thought that had I not been so worried about myself, I might have realized her condition was dire.

While I had tried to wave people down, I basically said nothing. Did nothing. Then went back to partying the night away.

"I think it's nice y'all volunteered," I snap, "but also think you want to get noticed, no matter what stage you're on." I point at the weeds around us. "Maybe save your need for attention until that poor girl is at least in the ground." I pivot. "Please, excuse me."

Side-stepping between familiar faces, I'm relieved when I find Piper and Jamie.

Piper grabs my hand. "Did we just hear you chew out Cerberus?" She smiles. "You okay?"

"Not really. Since apparently I was that *loud* and *harsh*, but thanks for giving me a heads up about the vigil." I fiddle with the ribbon holding my ponytail high. This morning, it was the only way to coax my over-sprayed hair into a conservative look without washing it, yet now, it doesn't matter. I could've left it unkempt and wild to mirror my current personality because I just bitched out the Madisons at a dead girl's vigil for no particular reason. Other than them being their true selves, which, in reality, is nothing new.

"They deserve it," Jamie and Piper say in tandem.

I shake my head. "Nah. Not today."

"If they weren't walking around, asking everyone to post testimonials on Under the Gown as a way to pay their respects, maybe I'd agree. But they are, so I don't," Piper fumes. "Do you remember when Ms. Susan gave that weeklong seminar on eating disorders in ninth grade, and we had to watch that depressing *Lifetime* movie where the girl never got well?"

I don't know where she's going with this, but I nod. "I remember being too terrified to look at the calorie count in my food for like a year."

"Exactly. But do you also remember the Madisons started a Healthy Choices Club the next day? And, despite designating themselves as the poster children of body positivity, they went behind Rebecca Sloan's back, calling her Shamu every chance they got. Until she switched schools. When she left, guess they needed a new person to nickname." She pauses. "That would be me."

I stare at Piper. While I vaguely recall the Shamu part, I can't believe she never told me she was bullied by the Madisons. Not that it surprises me. Holy angels, they are not, but leave it to my best friend, who *is* an angel, to help me feel better about being an outright bitch.

"You're making my high school sound not that bad," Jamie adds. "And it was . . . *bad.*" He does a double take at the Madisons and shakes his head. "Total try-hards."

"My point is," Piper continues, "they've been chewing on a mean bone their entire lives. You did the world a favor putting them in their place. Cochairing an event for heaven doesn't get you a foot out of hell. Least, not in my book." She sighs.

A telltale sign she's done with this conversation.

"In case you're interested," her eyes brighten, "your girl is over there, standing by that mildly familiar basketball player in the plaid sports coat. If I weren't intimidated, I might have gone over and said hello. Do it for both of us."

Caving to Piper's suggestion, my heart canters as I slide next to Violet. "Mind some company?" She shakes her head. "You didn't tell me you were coming. I could've picked you up or something."

Playing with the cuff of her long-sleeved black dress, she looks up. "Could say the same to you." She dabs a tear from her face. "Then again, I should've known you'd be here. Even if this is macabre, I can't imagine you'd miss a *debutante* event."

Wow. She's back on the insult train. "Did I do or say something wrong?" I stare into her watery eyes that refuse to break away, until at last—I concede.

"I don't know. Did you *do* anything at all? Did anyone here even speak to Alexandra?" Violet motions to the crowd. "An awful lot of people who I'd bet never met or cared about her when she was alive. Just saying."

I toe the mud with the point of my shoe. "No. I didn't know Alexandra. Not personally. I never saw her at any of the parties, so we weren't officially introduced," I admit. "But I *was* at the presentation, Violet. And during cocktail hour, I lent her some face powder in the bathroom. A den mother said Alexandra needed a touch-up, so I gave it to her. She thanked me, and that was it. Either way, it's awful what happened to her. I came out of respect. Is that a sin?"

Before she answers, another conversation bleeds into ours.

"You think this will mess up *my* party? No way can I cancel. It's a week away. Plenty of time for people to move on, right?" a girl says, in deep conversation with a guy standing next to her.

Violet's face reddens, and she huffs loudly, but the two continue.

I touch her shoulder, aching to give her a hug, but it's neither the time nor the place. "Take a deep breath. It may help," I say, glaring at the gossiping couple, trying to force them away with my eyes, but it doesn't work. "It was a horrible accident, but like it or not, those two are right. People will move on. Alexandra was a debutante. I'm sure she wouldn't expect the whole season to be canceled."

"Of course. Everyone is so worried about the *parties*. Oh, wait —I know. Why don't we throw a funeral party?" Her voice raises. "Want to know why you never met her, Ainsley? Her name wasn't on the list."

I tilt my head. "What list?"

"Like you don't know what I'm talking about. The Master List. The one with the debs' addresses and the calendar to keep track of the parties." Violet talks with her hands. The more excited she gets, the faster they flutter. Right now, she looks ready to take flight. "It's one thing to be a debutante. Quite another to be *invited* to the private parties. A rigged system that appears to be inclusive, when really, it's the most exclusive thing around. Guess if you're an outsider, you're conveniently left off because, as you know, if you're not on the list, no invites."

"I—uh, I don't—"

She puts her hand up to signal she's not done. "It's a pretty devious way to control the system when a girl has enough family connections to make her debut, but not enough to land her on the A-listers' private circuit. So, no. You never met Alexandra at any parties because she wasn't invited."

"You're blaming me for a *list*?" Not only is her suggestion off-base, I have no clue why she's going all full-blown conspiracy theory over a basic component of the season. Of course there's a list with the debs' addresses. And since it's nearly a prerequisite for a family member to host an event to honor their daughter during the season, there's also a calendar to prevent one party from conflicting with another. Essentially, it becomes a debutante's bible to plan our schedules and outfits accordingly.

I, for one, would've never been able to plan my wardrobe for the season without it, and I hadn't heard of names being left off. But Violet wouldn't know that because she never bothered to ask. "You're clearly invited to the parties, *Anderson*," I say curtly.

Her face wilts, and, instantly, a part of me wants to apologize.

But I don't. I'm far too angry.

"Maybe, but the truth hurts, no?" she claps back with an ironed-out voice. Like she's steaming out her emotions to further stiffen her words. "In fact, I'd bet a huge sum of money if I approached anyone here, they'd spin the same sad story. *We feel so bad about Girl X*"—her voice raises—"who they never knew or cared to know. So, let's light candles at four in the fucking day, so we can move on, guilt-free, to the next party. At least own up to your attitude."

"I'm sure you have boatloads of cash to bet with, but FYI, I'd pay any sum to get that girl's bloody smile out of my head. Sorry for wanting to do something to move on with my life. Or for *not* having the rest of this month ruined."

I shove my candle into her hand. "How about you go light all the hypocrites on fire for the both of us? Maybe burn down the whole list? That way, you don't have to own up to your truth. Because last time I checked, your name is at the top of that damn thing. I'm sure your family is hosting some epic bash. Tell me: Was Alexandra on *your* guest list?"

Her face blanches. "Wait, Ainsley—"

I hold my hand up. "I know you're upset, but I don't recall signing up to be your punching bag. Catch you around."

Starting my car, I tear out the clamshell parking lot, churning up a white cloud of dust as I veer onto City Park Avenue. No way can I go home. I'm too upset. Besides, my mom is a human radar detector of moods. I'd never survive her interrogation.

Two blocks later, I hear an odd sound. Switching off my radio, I slow the car to listen.

Thwack, thwack, thwack.

I speed up, but my steering wheel stiffens.

Is it the road?

Too many potholes . . . *shit*. Had I driven through one and popped a tire?

Pulling over to the side, I park and survey the perimeter of my car.

Something silver glints in the sunlight. Leaning down, I touch the shiny object, but draw back when I realize a knife is speared through the rubber of my now deflated tire.

It's eighty degrees outside, but a chill sweeps through my body.

Last night, Alexandra nearly died in front of me.

Now this?

Who would do such a thing? And why?

How can they stand in the sun without the plastic melting off their bones?

Fake, fake, fake—every last one of them.

Wearing black as if there's something or someone to mourn. It's just a fucking dress code, but of course, no self-respecting deb would dare deviate from the fashion norm. Or not follow the orders of a simple email or social media post to fit into whatever sardine can they're expected to be pressed into.

"Poor Alexandra!" they moaned, crying their Rougarou tears.
Not like they care.
She's just another pretty figure in a music box that got shut too hard. Too bad for this one; her tiny foot got snapped off in the process.

But shouldn't she have outgrown that silly music box?
Or recognized her act was finished and done her best to leave the stage gracefully?

Dying isn't a good look on anyone, but if we're being totally honest . . . it was mighty fun to watch.

CHAPTER 7

Pacing the cracked sidewalk, I wait for someone to answer. "Roadside assistance. This is Charles. How may I help you?"

"Hi, Charles. This is Ainsley Clarke. I need a spare tire. Mine, um, see, it popped. My family has an account." I nudge the knife with my heel.

"No problem. I've pulled up your account, and you are, let's see, near City Park. Can you verify this as your location?"

"Yes. I'm near the entrance to Tad Gormley Stadium." Scanning the street, I'm overcome with a thought that whoever knifed my car may still be lurking around. *Shit.* Why did I throw away that can of mace?

"We've dispatched a driver, Ms. Clarke. Until he arrives, please stay on the side of the road, and move an adequate distance away from your car. Do you feel like you're in a safe location?"

I nearly laugh. *Is anywhere safe these days?*

If a ballroom of crowded friends and family can become a conduit of death, I guess standing on a public street after having your tires slashed would be a resounding no. "I guess," I lie, glancing down the Avenue.

There are cars. People jogging. Walking dogs. Strolling babies.

How can someone get away with this when so many people are out and about?

With Charles on speaker, I open our group chat and gasp.

There's a flood of photos with thirty or more slashed tires.

Whoa.

Maybe I should be relieved I'm not the sole target, but honestly, it's ten times creepier. Someone intentionally slashed our tires at Alexandra's memorial, which makes this a deb-specific act. Not just some random, out-for-a middle-of-the-day slasher.

My phone alerts me to a new Under the Gown story.

Clicking on the circle, I read the caption:

To those at the vigil, perhaps you need to pay a heftier fine for your indulgences to keep your sins at bay? Seems someone isn't happy with your good deeds.

Are they suggesting this is our fault?

That's more than a thousand levels of messed up. Once again, this site has morphed from deb-positivity to deb-shaming. What in the actual fuck? I can't believe I'm thinking this, but I wish I was back at school, safely tucked in math class, where my biggest problem is trying to stay awake during lectures instead of standing atop this screwed up world where everything that shines is definitely not gold.

Being at college the last two days *is* comforting, considering the tragedy of my last week at home. There are no surprises in algebra. Just forty students sleeping in a giant auditorium-style classroom where I show once a week for "football math." At least, that's what it's called, since a good percentage of athletes pick this class for easy credits. But with the rest of my heavy course load this semester, I have no need to seek a greater mathematical challenge. Easy credits make my GPA look fantastic, plus it keeps Shelbi off my ass to keep my grades up. With her main concern in life being to maintain boasting rights for Lambda Mu as the sorority with the highest GPA, not like I need her nagging. I reside in the body and brain of the world's most agonizing taskmaster—*myself.*

While this class doesn't require a swath of brain cells, it does offer time to focus on the few electives I'm allowed as a freshman. And if the snoring student behind me ever woke up, he might spot the thick kinesiology textbook I'm poring through. Not like he'd care. Or the teacher, to be honest.

"Yo." A voice jars me from my reading as the adjacent chair creaks under the weight of a beefy guy lowering himself into the seat. "For someone who has their phone glued to their hand twenty-four-seven, you're sure impossible to get a hold of."

His hand covers mine, capturing my phone underneath, and the vibration from his delayed text rattles my desk. "What do you need, Brady?" I slide my hand and phone away. "*I* was on Thanksgiving break. Like the rest of the campus."

"Yeah, cool, but I tried leaving you a message at your sorority house. Only some half-deranged chick yelled at me for standing too close to the stairs. She also refused to take my note, so here."

He passes me a crumpled pamphlet taken from inside his hoodie, and I laugh. "That had to be Shelbi," I say, "and I don't live there. I'm a freshman. Plus, guys aren't allowed on the second floor of sorority houses. Shouldn't you—" I was about to say *know that?* but Brady isn't a frat guy, so he probably doesn't.

"Never mind." I smooth the yellow flyer. It says *Rugby Club at the Quad* with today's date and a soon to be approaching time stamped below. "This is in two hours." My voice raises. "You do realize I'm not a *real* trainer?"

"Totally. But you need practice, and we need a 'medical supervisor,' so the club won't get canceled," he explains. "Besides, who lets you in Friar's every weekend without paying a cover?"

"You do, Brady. But only because I beat you in a Rock, Paper, Scissors Tournament . . . *drunk*." I remind him. "So, you're an ethically questionable bouncer that's better at keeping your word than not getting injured every other game?" I raise an eyebrow.

If I agree to this, it means my off period (aka lunch) will be spent hovering over his team of unofficial jocks once a week. The ones who try out for the sanctioned clubs, but fail to make the cut, so they create a dumbed-down beer league in its place. But kudos to them—can't say no to that.

I sigh.

"Yo, yo. That's your defeated sigh. Guess I'll see you there, yes? Up high." He knocks my fist, then rises from the chair. "Answer your phone next time, and I won't have to ambush you in class."

Can this day get any worse? Shit, it can. Sorry universe. Please don't kill someone else just to teach me another lesson in humility. Or reinforce the reason that I shouldn't feel sorry for myself the way I presently do. But is it selfish to worry why Violet hasn't reached out? Or feel sad that she didn't? Then again, maybe I'm just überpathetic for checking my phone every hour for texts that will probably never be sent.

To make matters worse, I keep feeling like I'm the one who should apologize to *her* when she bitched me out. What if I just texted to see if her tires were also slashed? Would that be stalkerish?

Shaking the idea out of my head, I peruse my unread messages:

PIPER

Have you checked Under the Gown????

If you didn't, I'm ordering you to do so now!!!

This is insane.

Against my intuition, I open the app, scrolling past pictures from the vigil and sappy quotes that have probably been stolen from a Pinterest board to make it seem like they give a crap about Alexandra. Landing on their most recent post, there's a photo of a lock dangling on a red ribbon stretched between two tree branches.

It's a new week, ladies! But first and foremost, our greatest condolences! RIP dear Alexandra! By now, I hope everyone is safely back at college, away from the extravagance and tragedies of this past weekend. But being your friendly neighborhood peddler of words, I figured I'd offer some help.

How about a party exclusively for the girls who exemplify the ideals of a perfect debutante? Should you qualify, not only will you have an awesome time, but in grand New Orleans tradition, this party comes with lagniappe.

Send in a request with some scoop, and I'll invite whomever you specify as your very own VIP guest. What's the point of networking if I can't serve your connections up to you on a party platter?

WTF? Another party? I text Piper.

A

Think it's legit?

PIPER

?? They'd lose followers if it's BS. I don't need a VIP guest. I have Jamie.

A

They could have great connections. It might be worth it.

The ellipses on my screen start and stop. Start and stop.

PIPER

Be careful what you wish for, Ainsley!

I set my phone down and rest my head on my laptop. When I showed for math, I hoped for peace. Not another freak-out over messing up my chances for the future once again.

But I don't know if it's *real*, or even what that means any longer.

"Stop moving." With a vice grip on a rugby player's leg, I tighten an ace bandage around his ankle. "You can't play anymore. We have ice in the cooler. I can get you set up—"

"I'm good, thanks." Number fifteen bolts from my bench, sprinting back into the crowded quad to rejoin the game. It's the fourth person I've iced, wrapped, bandaged, or warned, and then they totally ignored my advice. While I wouldn't mind being a human Band-Aid dispenser for an actual team I could list on my resume, this isn't close. Unlike Laney, who *is* working for a real team, and still ignoring me for some unknown reason.

Which means if I want to turn my luck around, I may need to get on my knees and beg her to help me get that reference for my application. While I'm totally willing to stomach the humility of that action, it will require me enduring rants about her team, which, I hate to admit, may be way more painful.

Sure, I'm stoked for the position she's landed. It's awesome. Just not so much for me.

Oh, you're majoring in physical therapy? Like Laney Wilson, right?

The first time someone asked, I brushed it off. But it's getting old. Though I'm not jealous, I'm starting to feel, I don't know, left behind. Freshman year is like one giant ocean with ten thousand tiny minnows all trying to make their way upstream. And the truth is, that stream will narrow. While I don't mind the journey or the work, sometimes—like now—I can't help but think, at any given moment, I may lose my way.

Even deb season, which was supposed to be an opportunity to dazzle some VIPs with my achievements, is turning out to be a mini lesson in survival. So far, I've been featured in two questionable posts on that moronic account, met zero VIPs, witnessed a death, and had my car sabotaged.

Way to go, Clarke.

Then again, if I get picked by UTG for their party, it may make up for last week.

I could request a head coach, physical therapist, or any number of football legends currently or previously on the team's roster. Really, any player could offer tips on my future profession or help vouch for my character for the internship.

My mind reels with infinite possibilities, but a yell on the field snaps me back to the present. Perusing the field for collisions, I find none.

I open my app, and pause on the DM screen for Under the Gown.

It can't hurt to ask.

What if I simply request a good word be put in for me regarding the internship? Then I won't need to bother Laney or worry about being indebted to Cooper, which would alleviate twenty pounds of stress.

A

I need a fast track in with someone in charge of our NFL summer physical therapy internship. Is this doable?

No reply.

They could be offline? Or maybe they're laughing at me? The first fool to fall for their post.

My phone vibrates and I jump. It's flashing Violet's name. Do I answer?

"Hello?" I smooth my voice, trying not to betray the twist of emotions inside me.

"Hi. I'd say it's me, but guess you know that," Violet says, but she sounds weird. Maybe even nervous, if that's possible.

"Well, did I make a good decision . . . answering?" I ask.

"I hope so. I mean, I'm glad you picked up, but first, let me apologize. I lashed out at you, and it was misplaced. The vigil felt like some reality show episode, and it made me angry. I'm sorry I lost it. Alexandra was a family friend, you know."

No, I don't know. Nor do I know what to say now. All I know is when my own grandfather died, it was beyond painful to stand around, getting the same tired platitudes. *Sorry for your loss*, blah, blah, blah.

"I was wondering, can we talk in person? I'm still in town. My classes don't start until midweek, and I just got done with this whole family get-together." She pauses. "I could really use a friend, Ainsley."

"Of course, um, yes. But I'm at school. Unless you feel like trekking up to Baton Rouge, you'll have to settle with FaceTime." I wince as the scrum collapses, and a boy takes a cleat to the face. "I hate to do this, but I really have to go. Looks like I'm about to be picking grass out of some pretty bad facial wounds. Text me in two hours."

"Wait—drop me a pin. My driver will bring me to you."

Clearly, she's joking, but I drop the pin just in case.

I hear her before I see her.

"You really weren't kidding about the facial wounds."

Holy shit, she's actually *here-here*.

Dragging the jersey I'd been using to shield my face from the sun, I run my fingers through my wind-whipped hair and tug down my shirt. "Yes, I, uh, help this team." I laugh. "Actually, I'm kinda being bribed by a player to do so. He's the only bouncer who lets me in the bar we hang at without a cover and doesn't bust me for my fake ID. That and job experience, of course."

I pat the bench next to me, stunned by the tingly feelings coursing through my body. She drove all the way to Baton Rouge to see me. Technically, her driver did, but still, I'm flattered. "Wanna sit?"

"Sure." She eyes me warily. "No blood on your shirt, or anywhere else? I'm not up for any second-hand infections after the week we've had."

Sighing, she collapses next to me, her long leg brushing against mine.

"Rude, as always," I say, subtly checking for blood. "How did you get here so fast? Do you also own a helicopter? I hate that drive, and I live here."

She laughs. "That's because you're spoiled. Everyone from New Orleans thinks a forty-five-minute drive is *long*. In Dallas, or pretty much any city, commute times are an hour at a minimum."

"Says the girl with a driver at her beck and call," I tease. "But you're originally from here, so stop hating on us locals. We need to stick together."

She smacks my arm. "I lived in New Orleans until middle school. My family's land is in Texas, so they uprooted us, midsemester, though we kept a home here. And I have a driver because I don't have my car here, smartass."

"We would've gotten along so well in high school had we met," I blurt without filtering.

She tilts her head. "Yes—maybe? I *am* happy to see you. Even if you're mildly infectious. I kinda miss your obnoxiousness."

"I thought you missed me for twenty-one better reasons," I say, before remembering why she's actually here. "Seriously,

Violet. I'm really sorry. I didn't realize you and Alexandra were close. Guess that's how you knew about her not being on the list?"

"Yes and no." She sighs and leans her back against the concrete wall. "Technically, we weren't good friends. Our families are business associates, and when I was younger, we used to hang out at work conferences and stuff. Being the same age and bored with our parents, we'd take the money they doled out to keep us occupied and go cut up." Violet fiddles with her necklace.

Maybe that's why I didn't recognize Alexandra. Are they both Texans?

She continues, "I didn't know about issues with the list until Leslie's luncheon. I overheard her gossiping about some girls being presented, but not on the list. She mentioned Alexandra. When my mom and I were emailed it, we assumed it had addresses for all the debs and club members. Guess I didn't look hard enough to notice her name missing."

"Not your fault. At least someone in your family knew to send in the fee for you to be included."

Her forehead creases. "You have to pay a *fee?*"

I wave my hand. "Not the point. It's twenty dollars or so to cover administrative costs, but now that I think about it, none of my deb packets included the contact information. Piper ended up giving it to me, so I guess it's something you're just supposed to know. Like a word-of-mouth thing. Or some inner knowledge locals are born with." I laugh, but Violet looks more distressed.

"Which obviously, I'm *not,*" I add. "My invites arrived so late, my photo and bio didn't make the deadline for the special deb issue of the newspaper. A bit humiliating, but guess if you don't know the rules or you're a late invite like I was, it's easy to see how you can get accidentally left off."

"Or more like *on purpose.*"

Though I'm still not buying into her silly list theory, I feel bad seeing her this worked up. I squeeze her hand, then immediately worry—what if I'm trampling her boundaries?

"Shit, sorry." I pull my hand back, but she catches my fingers, interlacing mine with hers. And we sit, holding hands, both probably thinking about Alexandra and her final moments alive.

At least, I am.

"Kinda freaky she had a heart attack at nineteen, right? My dad said conditions like that are usually congenital, impossible to predict. That it's never suspected until it's too late." I scan the field, then continue, "Besides, I'm sure some people's intentions at the vigil probably were shady at best." I think of the Madisons. "But I didn't go for that reason."

Violet looks up. "It doesn't matter. They still *showed*. Better than no one. I was just angry at everything, everyone." She tightens her grip. "My family forced me into this debutante mess, and, as you know, I was furious from the get-go. Then Alexandra's accident happened, and when that stupid puppet show of a pity account Under the Gown started trolling for likes, it pushed me over the edge. Again . . . sorry."

"Will you please stop apologizing? I never thought I'd say this, but I actually prefer your cold sarcasm. It lets me know I haven't been zapped into some alternate Violet universe." I nudge her and she laughs. "Seriously, you're good in my book. Besides, your driver picked the perfect time to bring you. Anything is better than toddler-level rugby."

Her face brightens. "Ooh—I know the perfect way to make this up to you." She nearly jumps off the bench with excitement. "FYI, we do not own a basketball arena. But we do own an ice rink. A professional hockey rink."

My mouth drops. "Are you serious?" I yell. "Please don't make promises you can't keep," I say. "The thought alone is enough to propel me through the rest of this dreary quarter. Hell, I'll even go to algebra every day."

"You sound like a toddler on a sugar high. Good Lord. Should I prepare for you to be this loud at the actual game?"

"Guess you'll have to wait and find out."

"I can do that." She snuggles closer.

"Hold on." I pull out my buzzing phone. It's a reply from Under the Gown.

> Consider yourself in the fast lane, Ainsley. I think you'll love your special guest. But don't forget, you must submit a worthy secret for final approval.

"Who is it?" Violet asks.

"Piper," I lie, tucking it away. "Tell me more about this hockey rink. Can I buy a new jersey?"

CHAPTER 8

STALLIONS HOCKEY GAME
DECEMBER 2

Standing before the clothes rack I'd purchased for deb season, I flip through the garment bags labeled for each function. Only this event is not on my calendar. Therefore, I have no idea what to wear.

When my Ring app dings, I tap *speaker*. "Come in, Piper. Door is open."

"This is some *Fifty Shades of Grey* shit. Ya know that, right?" She eyes me as I switch gears and begin rifling through my closet.

"Stop saying that. It makes it sound weird." I fling out a coat, and it settles over her protesting face. "Besides, it's just a date. Oh, shit. Piper—is it? She never said the actual word *date*."

"Pretty sure it's a date if she's picking you up on a private plane to attend a hockey game in Dallas at the Anderson Arena. In case you're unaware of that fact." She smirks, apparently pleased with her vast knowledge of the Anderson enterprise.

"Thanks for making me feel worse," I say, throwing out four

options for her to consider. We narrow it down to a pair of black jeans, motorcycle boots, and a maroon V-neck, or a checkered skirt with dark leggings and an oversized sweater.

"I can't believe you're this nervous." Piper points to the skirt, vote cast. "I thought you buried your feelings where no girl could exhume them."

Piper loves giving advice about my relationships, despite her not being even close to the Dalai Lama of the dating world. Though I am hoping she'll have better luck with Jamie. Guess time will tell. All relationships start out like a fairy tale. It's the endings that don't always include a happily ever after.

"It going to be so awkward," I lament. "People are hard enough to predict in normal settings, let alone this."

When Violet first mentioned the game, I thought she was joking, until she texted to see if I was free for the weekend. Then she transferred a ticket into my digital account for the game.

Piper hands me the chosen outfit. "You don't have to plan every second of your life, Ainsley. Just go with the flow." She waves her arms like an auto dealer blow-up figure.

"I *do* have to plan every moment," I mumble from beneath the sweater, as I struggle to pop my head through. "Know why Leslie was the longest relationship I've ever had?"

"Because you *liked* her?"

"No. Because she liked me more than I liked her."

Piper gives me a disapproving look.

"Hey, I *liked* her. I'm not that big of an asshole, but I don't know how to do anything without planning, without knowing, I'm two steps ahead of the game." I slide into my leggings. "What are the odds of a high school relationship working out? Terrible, right?"

Piper nods.

"So knowing we'd eventually break up, I didn't want to invest my whole heart, you know. And good thing, since she axed me."

She grimaces. "Yeah, she may not have handled *that* in the most considerate way. But your life's not a chess match." She settles on my bed. "What's the worst thing that can happen if you have an awful date? You get to see a live hockey game, yeah? I can think of a thousand worse fates."

Goosebumps erupt on my arms.

Alexandra was certainly handed a worse fate. And ever since her vigil, I've felt like the world's been sending me these cryptic, billboard-sized reminders to stop complaining because surely when she woke that morning, she never realized—*it was her last.*

Piper's right. I need to calm down and enjoy the freaking game.

Anything else that may or may not come my way will strictly be a bonus.

A private plane certainly qualifies as a bonus. When Violet left instructions to look for a guy holding a sign with my last name, it's exactly what I did. Now, I'm following Sign Man, sneaking photos along the way.

Climbing the stairs of the sleek jet, I enter the cabin and update my Snapchat with a picture of its dope galley and oversized camel leather seats. "Here I thought you were going to stand me up."

"V-Violet?" I bash my head into the low ceiling.

With her long legs sprawled across two seats, she's jamming to the beat of whatever song is streaming through her earbuds. "Y-you didn't say you were going to be on the flight." I rub the throbbing spot above my eye.

"I told you to *meet* here. I figured you'd realize I'd be here too." She walks over and pulls me down to her height, checking my forehead for a wound. "While I appreciate making an impression, I certainly didn't mean to concuss. I'll get ice. Sit."

I do, and she does the same.

"I assumed you bought me a ticket, if that's what you do for these things." I make a circular motion with my hand. "I just never thought . . ."

My words trail off when I notice how close she's sitting.

That her lips are millimeters from mine.

". . . that I wouldn't mind forty extra minutes with you?" Finishing my sentence, her eyes flicker over me. "I think that's a burden I'm willing to bear." She skims her fingers over my face, my lips—

"Um, ma'am, will this suffice?" A flight attendant holds out an ice pack, and Violet jerks her hand away. I don't know if she sent out some cryptic bat symbol, but somehow, this lady knew to appear with ice, and at the worst possible moment ever.

Thanking her, I take the bag and turn to Violet. "I wanted to bring you flowers, but I didn't know if there was anywhere to keep them, so I improvised." I open my purse and pause. "Close your eyes."

"A surprise. Perfect." She's being sarcastic, but she shuts them anyway.

I pull out the beanie with my college logo emblazoned on it and hold it upside down, so the coin I've brought will remain in the middle. "Alrighty. Open."

She looks at the beanie and the coin, then back at me with a blank expression.

"You're probably a Cowboys fan, which leaves only college football for me to indoctrinate you into, but your college isn't known for football. Even if they were, the Tigers are superior to any college in the SEC. At least, to me they are." With my heart thumping, I point at the coin. "That's a one-dollar Louisiana coin with a magnolia on it. So technically, I brought flowers, albeit minted in metal."

"Aw, that's so—"

"Wait, there's more. Please direct your attention to the Sharpie writing on each side."

She flips the coin over. "Plan F and Plan H?"

"Yes. Plan F is for *far, far away.* Which means I'll try my best to take you far away from anything that bothers you. I may not own a *plane,* but don't underestimate me." I turn the coin over. "And Plan H is for *hugs.* A bit more self-explanatory. Did you know it's scientifically proven that a hug can reduce stress *and* boost your health? Which, by the way, I give the best hugs. So, you're welcome."

She is unusually quiet, and I start to freak.

I should've cleared this with Piper.

Why did I ever go rogue on a gift?

"For someone with an iceberg on their head, you're far more charming than I gave you credit for. Thanks. I'll hold you to both plans."

Taking my hand, she guides me to the row where she'd just been sitting. There are scattered papers and an open notebook perched on the tray. She motions to the seat beside her, and I sit.

"What's all this?" I ask.

"Homework." She frowns. "I'm doing a double major. Business and law. Which means double the work. We can chat while I go through it, but if I don't finish this stack"—she pats the taller pile—"the ones in my backpack will bury me."

"That's insanely impressive," I say, but I'm thinking *so are you.* "While I'm known to put a lot on my plate, even I don't have the courage to try something that tough."

"Not really my choice. Every Anderson needs a business degree, but if I also get a law degree, I'll have the necessary tools to fight the masses." She raises an eyebrow. "Here to further their legacy, ya know?"

"You don't get a say in what you study?" This time, I frown. "Or what you'll eventually *do*?"

"A partial say. It took a ton of convincing, but I'm minoring in environmental studies. Get it? The exact opposite of what my family pays attention to. Fracking and oil spills aren't generally considered environmentally friendly. Not like they care."

Playing with the seat button, I push recline, happy to kick back. "I may have Googled your family, full disclosure." I hope she's not mad that I snooped, but she waves her hand dismissively. "So," I continue, "they're titans of their industry, but maybe stepping on some smaller ants?"

It's the kindest way I can let her know I've read the article accusing her family's company of poisoning a nearby lake surrounding a protected area of endangered species. The same article Piper told me about where a town of local workers boycotted their newly built warehouse that took the place of a dozen mom-and-pop shops. Maybe the Andersons aren't supervillains, but they seem wealthy enough to sway anyone required to get what they need out of the land, a town, or an ocean filled with vulnerable marine life.

"Quit trying to be nice. The plane's not bugged," she says, but glances around. "At least, I hope not. If it is, I really don't give a fuck." She sticks her finger in the air, essentially flicking off anyone who may be watching. "Besides, you're a pitiful liar. Your smile gets all wobbly."

Leaning forward, she sticks the back of her pen into the crook of my lips. "And Ainsley, I also read the news. Unfortunately, I get to hear their side of things over dinner." She pauses. "When I visit."

"You're not like them at all, are you?" I nudge the pen out of the way and retract the seat. "Why not do something else?"

"If I don't stay in, who fixes their mess? It's a family business. That means no new blood can come in and change the way they do things."

As we start to descend, I stare out the window, watching the buildings enlarge. The cityscape is glittering, and I almost miss what she's saying.

" . . . and I'll become an environmental lawyer and use that annoying business degree to profit from anything, except for any creature's pain and suffering."

"Seems like a solid plan," I say, thrilled to learn even a shred more about her. Because like I promised Piper, I'm trying to soak up every second of this experience. The flight. Her eyes. And the fact that this awesome girl likes me enough to invite me into her world, even if it turns out to be just for this night.

"You make my goal of getting a Super Bowl ring working as a physio for a certain NFL team seem incredibly meager."

She laughs. "As if they'll ever win a Super Bowl in this century."

"Don't be a hater. Are you sure you're from the South because you certainly don't possess any hospitality?"

"We'll see about that, say, in twenty minutes." She leans into me and points at a large, domed building below. "Because we're about to be in there. I think you might change your mind, eh, Tiger?"

On the balcony in the Anderson suite, I gush, "You're my absolute favorite person, like ever, but please don't tell Piper that." With a mouth full of popcorn, I grip my signed hockey stick. "I can't be bought, but if I could, this certainly is the way to do it."

"Oh? You're clutching that stick pretty tight for someone who can't be bought."

Not only are we in her family's suite, she's managed to wrangle nearly every signed and coveted fan merch for me. It's so much, she's presently wearing a signed jersey draped around her own shoulders simply because I can't fit another thing in my swag bag.

"This stick is signed by *him*." I point at their star forward. "Anyone with eyeballs and ESPN highlights knows how priceless it is." I place it carefully in the seat next to me. "If NOLA had a hockey team, I'd so be gunning for that job."

"After grad school, you could certainly look out of state. Texas isn't far."

Texas? Hmm. I don't know if she's flirting or trying to make friendly conversation. "Let's see. I know exactly one person in the great state of Texas. *You.* But I've busted my ass to make as many connections as I can at home. If you uproot me, not only will I shrivel from lack of importance, this whole deb thing will be for naught." I sigh dramatically.

"So it's not the archaic traditions that have you obsessed with deb season, but the dusty old people pulling the strings? How reassuring." She claps as the Dallas goalie catches a slapshot in his glove.

"That's a trip! Are you kidding?" I jump up, but Violet tugs me back down. "Sorry." I blush. "And yes, I'm a bit more interested in who is attending the parties rather than the actual *partying*. You lived there. You know how small the city is. In size and mindset."

"You're willing to admit the system is small-minded, yet you still love it? I don't get it."

Sure, the concept is outdated. And sexist, if you look at it from a modern point of view, but in reality, it's not hurting anyone. Exactly the opposite. Deb season is big business for the city. People spend thousands of dollars on new wardrobes, and the parties provide jobs for a whole assortment of industries. A win for the families, the girls, and the city, but I'm not about to give a monologue on the pros of deb season at a hockey game with a girl who seems to like me, but despises the whole concept.

She continues. "Not to mention that inane Under the Gown. It embodies the attitude of everything I left behind."

She's right about the account and, maybe, a few other things. "St. Claire's was the same way," I admit. "You need to know someone to get in, donate enough money to put your name on a building, and have a three-generation lineage to be relevant."

"Oh, which building is yours?"

"Ha—none. My father funnels his philanthropic efforts into a research center that studies the neurological system of a fruit fly." I laugh. "He's not into the whole private school dogma. But Piper . . .

she's another story. Her dad knows how to play the game. Their family has several wings dedicated to them. Full disclosure, she's the reason I got invited to the subdeb events in middle school. Which, as you know, puts you on the radar of the deb circuit. And led to me annoying you at a boutique party." I pause. "Then it landed me here."

"So, the big white dress . . . more like a date or job interview?" She looks the slightest bit annoyed.

"Not the date part. Though I'm glad *this* happened."

The last thing I need is for Violet to think the reason I'm interested in her is because her family is affiliated with a team. While my goal is to network with people in the industry, I'd never leverage this or her family to my advantage.

"I'm curious. Why not try out for any of these sports you're so obsessed with?"

"Those genetics were kinda passed to the male side of my family. My annoying brother, actually. I'm hardly skilled enough for college sports."

"I don't know. I've watched you move. You're very *agile*." She runs a finger up my arm, and I nearly pass out.

She's hardcore flirting, which is awesome, but I'm way too nervous to reciprocate in her family's suite. "I, um, used to want to be a neurosurgeon like my dad," I say, trying to keep the conversation flowing in a neutral direction. At least, for now. "I talked incessantly about it, about going to Yale. You know, the whole child prodigy thing."

"What happened, Dr. Clarke?"

"I grew wise enough to realize I *wasn't* a prodigy. Would've been kinda soul crushing to spend eight years in med school only to be told I didn't have the skills to make it as a brain surgeon," I say, and her smile droops. "Hey, it's okay. I picked a medically *related* field. Besides, I must have something going for me if I ended up here, getting showered with gifts by my Sugar Momma."

"Shut up." She elbows me and her phone buzzes. Swiping on the alert, she frowns. "Seems someone else is watching the game." She tilts her phone my way, flashing the latest UTG post. It's a blurry photo of a flat screen with our faces in the far-right corner.

"We're on ESPN? Who has the bionic eyes to tell that's us? We're literal ants."

I glance at the Jumbotron. A girl is shaking her head, mouthing: *He's my brother.*

The Kiss Cam, ugh, but even more worrisome—*is there any place Under the Gown can't infiltrate?*

Maybe Piper and Violet are right to be concerned.

When the Kiss Cam zips away, Violet says, "It appears that post alerted my best friend Blair, who is at the game." She motions to her right. "The next suite over."

In the adjoining balcony, a guy decked in head-to-toe Stallions gear is hanging onto the railing, shouting, "Yo, Violet. Introduce your date."

Others start to wave and hoot while Violet furiously texts. "We probably have a solid five minutes before we're bombarded." Her face flushes. "Sorry."

"No problem. It will make it fair when you get to hang with my friends, who'll likely prove way more dysfunctional." Though Violet has been to two deb events and met Eli, Jamie, Leslie, and Piper briefly, she hadn't really had time to interact with them.

I hear booing, so I scan the rink. "Did I miss a bad call or something?"

"Not a bad call." Violet points up. "That."

Our overblown faces are on the Jumbotron with the words: "Kiss her! Kiss her!"

The camera zooms in for a tighter shot, and Violet turns to me. "Do you want to ignore it?"

"Not really," I say, waiting for her reaction.

She leans in closer. "Is that because you've been swayed by all this hockey gear, or you actually like *me*?"

Placing the popcorn box in front of us, I seal my lips over hers. And she kisses me deeply, passionately, then pulls away. The crowd goes crazy. But I'm still reeling from the intensity of her kiss to care how dumb I may or may not look, because I like her.

I really, really like her.

But Piper's wrong. This feeling . . . it's the worst.

CHAPTER 9

PIPER RICHARDS'S & AINSLEY CLARKE'S
DEBUTANTE LUNCHEON
DECEMBER 9

It's the morning of our boutique luncheon, and I'm perched at an unset banquet table, running through a checklist to ensure everything will go off as planned.

Table arrangements—*check*.

Playlist—*on*.

I scan the menu: grillade and grits, beignets, crawfish Monica, étouffée, Caesar salad, puffed potatoes, jambalaya, fried catfish, and a very special dessert. All I have left is to triple-check the substitution menu with the chef for those with allergies or gluten and lactose intolerances and review the seating arrangements for our eighty-four guests.

Then, it's game on.

Taking my eyes off the diagram, I try to recall who currently hates whom. "Does anyone know how to remove curses?" I yell to

Leslie, who is not only being cool, but graciously volunteered to help us set up, along with Jamie, and a here-by-force Eli.

"No," Piper and Leslie chime in unison while I stand. Then pace.

It feels like Piper and I have waited a lifetime to cohost this event, but today, all I can think about are the million and one things that could go wrong. "No such thing as curses, Clarke," Leslie says, balancing two floral arrangements for the head table while Jamie trails behind, carrying a set of smaller, matching vases.

Meanwhile, and true to form, Eli is sprawled across three chairs, napping.

I love him dearly, but he is a certifiable slug.

"You *do* realize where we live?" I ask, voice catching. "One of the most haunted cities in the country."

"If you're that superstitious, why choose The Monteleone? One of *the* most haunted hotels in the country," Jamie asks, catching Piper's glare, turning three shades of red. "I mean, it's a beautiful, haunted hotel. With great historic value. And ghosts can be friendly, right?"

"I don't care about ghosts. They're invited, for all I care. I'm talking about an actual *curse*." I flash my phone with Under the Gown frozen on its screen. "Willa was just released from the hospital. The second deb in less than a month who's had something awful happen. Let alone the curse that is this page."

Opening an Under the Gown post is like playing Russian roulette. There's a chance the post may be flattering, such as the epic video from Sharla Gutiérrez's deb party at the Civic Theatre, or the complete opposite—yesterday's post about Camille Thibodeaux cheating on her SATs for Duke. If that rumor mill is even half correct, not only will Camille be booted from Duke, she'll be lucky to get into any college.

"Willa is a Kennedy. Isn't that a curse on its own?" Eli asks, arising from his makeshift jacket-and-sweater cocoon. He sits up and peruses his phone. "Besides, she's alive. Says here it was just an allergic reaction."

"*Just?*" I shake my head. "Anaphylactic shock is quite deadly without immediate treatment. Look it up."

"She's not a real Kennedy, dumbass," Leslie clucks at Eli. "But come to think of it, Willa's had more than her share of bad luck since we were kids." She looks at Piper. "Remember when she sat on those fire ants during the lower school field trip?"

"Yaaas," Piper says. "Ooh, and the Girl Scouts camp out in middle school when she came home covered in ticks. She also got caught in a rosebush patch during Gardening Club. Ms. Peters had to chop off a section of her hair just to get her out. Lucky for her, she'd already taken senior pictures."

I chew my bottom lip. The photos of Willa getting jabbed with an EpiPen two days ago are plastered all over Under the Gown. "Still weird. Look." I flash the additional images at Leslie and Piper, who continue to work. "Pretty shitty thing to post, considering her luncheon was ruined. According to this, it was due to a kitchen staff mix-up with an order from the public dining room. What if something like that happens today?"

Piper shakes her head. "It won't."

"How do you know?" Willa and I were close in high school, and while the post says she'll be fine, I can't help worrying about her or any other potential disasters in the making. Initially, I had shrugged off Piper's concern regarding deb season, but after everything that's happened, I'm truly starting to think that maybe our season has its own Macbethian-style curse, but aimed at the debs.

"Because *you've* checked our menus a hundred times. Everything will be perfect," Piper says.

"Remember Carnival season 2020?" Eli whistles the *Twilight Zone* tune. "That whole year was hexed. Riders fell from floats. People got rolled over. Maybe your season is like that?"

"Not reassuring whatsoever. Thanks, Eli." I sigh.

He waves his hand. "Chill, Clarke. Nothing is gonna happen. Not with all your helpful den mothers." He laughs, knowing how I feel about the childish supervision aspect. "They've been clucking around, sweeping the area for proverbial mines since I got here." He bats his snow-cone tie out of his face. "Besides, Cooper just texted. He's in the freight alley with your photo booth. So relax, and um, try to have fun."

Pulling out a flask from his jacket, he salutes Piper and me, then takes a sip.

"Yes, Ainsley. Please take your own advice and stop prophesying doom on our party," Piper chastises. "Listen to Eli, who, for once, not only is saying something reasonable, he's actually gotten his brother out of bed on a Saturday to help with *our* party. Imagine that." She flips a name card up and proceeds to the next table.

Speaking of Cooper, I need to talk to him, though now is probably not the best time with everyone bustling around. Though our parents chose to host a boutique party—a private event that doesn't require inviting the whole cast of debutantes, plus-ones, parents, and club members—it still amounts to a lot of people who could listen in on a conversation not meant to be shared in public. Or ever.

Someone taps my shoulder, and I turn.

It's Violet. Giving me a kiss, she pushes a strand of hair out of my eyes, her warm fingers sending shock waves down my spine. "Wanna go on the balcony for a sec?" It's like she can sense my stressed-out mood without me saying a word.

I nod, and we head out the door and onto the balcony that overlooks the French Quarter. It's been a week since the hockey game, but we've spent nearly every evening since on FaceTime, doing homework, or just sitting in silence, content to be in each other's company.

I loop my arm around her waist and pull her close. "Thanks. I needed a break, but now that you're here, everything's perfect."

"I wouldn't have missed it for the world, though you may get sick of me soon."

"Doubtful. But please tell me again how you convinced your family to let you spend the majority of your Christmas break away from Texas?"

"I simply reminded them I'd be participating in more of these precious events. And that I'd actually attend the one they're hosting for *me*." She wiggles her eyebrows.

This is news to me, but when I glance through the window, I notice an uptick in the number of waiters bustling about. "We better get back," I say, leading her inside. "But hold that thought because I need to hear all the details about this party of yours."

"You're having a *party*?" Piper shrieks after we nearly collide into her and the large *Welcome* sign she's toting. "Did I get an invite? Or did Ainsley already get us booted off the list?"

"Everyone's invited," Violet assures. "It's the one listed on that *calendar*"—she hisses the word—"on December 28. I requested my name remain anonymous, but your invites are in the mail."

She grabs a stack of name cards and waves them in my face. "I can help if you tell me where they go. Oh, and heads up. There *is* a specific dress code for my party, so have fun shopping."

I stare at Violet. "You're having a *theme* party? On purpose?"

"My parents were going to host a party, one way or another. I may have chosen a theme to annoy them. You know, my own personal satire. Not like they'll put two and two together."

"Mind telling your good friends the theme?"

"It's a secret." She grins. "At least until the invites arrive. I don't want to ruin the surprise."

Leslie, who's also been helping with name cards, slides between us. "Uh-oh. Someone's lost their charms if their *girlfriend* won't tell them her theme ahead of time."

I can't tell if she's being bitchy or I'm just hypersensitive from the stress. I check for Violet's reaction, but she appears nonplussed, texting away on her phone.

Seconds later, she glances up. "Blair's here. I need to meet her out front because she could get lost in a shoe box. Back in a flash."

I had met Blair at the hockey game, and I'm more than thrilled she could attend. Not only is she nice, Violet will have a much better time with her best friend here, considering I'll be busy hosting.

Giving Violet a thumbs-up, I check the list one more time. Here's someone who won't be attending. *Laney Wilson.* Who I'm now certain is purposely ignoring me, though I can't worry about that.

Not with guests arriving.

"This is so nice!" the Madisons coo, as they make their way to their seats—at the farthest table I could assign them to. Returning their smiles, I turn my attention to Violet with Blair in tow.

"Thanks for inviting me. This hotel is dope," Blair says, leaning in for a hug. Bubbly and sweet, she's nearly the polar opposite of Violet, whose charms are more subdued and buried under her beautiful surface.

"You know what they say. 'Everybody is nothing until you love them,'" I quote Tennessee Williams and her mouth drops open.

"*The Rose Tattoo*, right? Are you also an English major?"

"God no." I laugh. "But I did take Southern Writers senior year. And Violet may have mentioned you were a lit major. Figured you'd appreciate knowing the Monteleone is an official literary landmark. If you get a chance, try to poke around after the luncheon."

"That's epic. Now, I totally love you." She looks at Violet. "Considering I haven't heard one positive thing about the NOLA deb scene from *her*, this is a welcome surprise. I'll definitely hit up the concierge for a tour. Thanks."

I can only imagine the tales of woe Violet concocted to entertain Blair, though in all fairness, we've had more than our share of tragedy. "One more thing. We're cheating seasons today by serving king cakes for dessert," I say, and her face goes blank. "Carnival season. It doesn't kick off until Twelfth Night . . . um, January sixth to be exact," I explain. "We were able to get our hands on some early. Make sure to snag a slice. Totally delish."

When Blair shifts, I spy Cooper grabbing a drink, so I excuse myself. It isn't the perfect place to talk, but considering everything that has gone down, I need to know if he plans on holding up his end of our bargain.

I exit the ballroom, dart down the hall, and slide next to him on the inclined ramp leading to the garage. "Hey, Cooper."

He wheels around. "Ainsley. W-what are you doing out here?"

"I um, I wanted to thank you for setting up our photo booth, and—"

"Don't tell me you left your party to thank me? Little bro already did that. Mission accomplished."

"Alright, Cooper. I didn't come out to thank you, but I am grateful for the help. I came because I-I wanted to know—"

"Know what, Clarke?" His dimples deepen.

Leave it to Cooper to make me feel worse than I already do, but here goes nothing. "Am I or am I not getting an invite to The Mystic Maskers?" There, I've said it. I uttered what few dare to say aloud.

Placing his finger over his lips, he glances behind us. "I'm afraid I don't know what you're talking about, *Ms.* Clarke." He winks. "Remember, good things come to those who wait *and* don't ask too many questions. Now, get back inside and be a proper deb instead of a bratty, nosy one."

Whistling, he heads for the valet, while I return without an answer and my dignity knocked even further down than I thought it could go.

This so better be worth it.

. . .

After appetizers and the meal are served, Piper and I make rounds, visiting guests, handing out monogrammed swag bags.

When I return to my table, Blair is happily gobbling down her last bite. I reach across the table and tap her hand. "I'm glad you could join us. It's not as large as some bashes, but I'm guessing you know that, considering our mutual friend is probably throwing *the* event of the season." Since Violet is not in her seat, it's my chance to pry. "Have you bought your costume by chance?"

She grimaces. "I swore on my life not to give spoilers, but if you happen to go shopping before the invites arrive, think flashy. Maybe, um, the eighties."

"I heard that!" Violet says, bustling back, scooting her chair next to mine. "Whose side are you on, blabber mouth?" She shakes her finger at Blair and her cuff sparkles.

I grab her hand, ogling her jewels. "I've been meaning to ask, what's with all the green? Your bracelet is stunning, of course, but I don't think I've ever seen you *not* dripping in emeralds or a green outfit. Is it because of your eyes?" I smile.

"Family color," Blair interjects. "Ever seen the Anderson logo with the star in the background? The paint store in Texas named that color Anderson Green."

"Ah, so the family rebellion stops when it comes to jewels?" I taunt.

"My grandfather picked these pieces when I was born. From what little I remember, he was one of the thoughtful ones. He died when I was young. So these"—she fingers her bracelet—"serve as a reminder that even Andersons can be kind."

She lowers her arm, and I'm left speechless over her moment of honesty. "I guess you take after him then." My stomach twists and a rush of heat spreads across my cheeks. "Um, you two order drinks. Dessert will be served shortly. We"—I kick Piper under the table—"need to check on something really quickly."

Piper gives me a look, but follows me across the ballroom. Once inside the bathroom, she leans against the marble counter, arms folded, while I inspect each stall for possible occupants. "Dude, what's wrong with you? Why did you drag me in here?"

"I think I'm having a panic attack." I clutch at my neck. "She's terrifying."

"Who?"

"Violet," I say, catching a glimpse of my scarlet cheeks in the mirror. "She's being so nice, so honest. It's freaking me out, Pipes." I try to catch my breath, but my lungs feel hollow. Like air isn't making its way down my throat. "I think I might pass out."

Steadying myself on the counter, I breathe slowly through my nose, and after a few minutes, the terror starts to subside. "Whenever she tells me something really personal, I get this weird spasm." I press on my stomach. "Right here. What do you think is wrong with me?"

"Not to be cliché, but I'd say butterflies in your stomach, aka nerves. Though yours seem a bit . . . extreme. More like hornets." She laughs. "Either way, it's not that strange. You like her, right?"

I nod. "But what if I'm not good enough? Or I run her off because I'm the worst when it comes to being open with anyone that isn't, well, you or Eli." I pause. "It's not like I don't want her around. I feel worse when she's not. Damn it. It's so confusing. I wish I could just back over this feeling with a truck."

Piper grins. "Ooh, you really *like* her. Guess all that flirting and the kiss really paid off." She gives me a hug. "You'll be fine. It's supposed to feel this way when you date someone you care about."

"Well, it's horrible." I shake out my hands, hoping to dispel the remaining tension in my body. "Is this how you feel with Jamie?"

She nods. "It's not *horrible* if you remember that they are worth dealing with a bit of initial nerves. Violet probably feels the same way. Give yourself and her a break."

"Fine. But this sucks, sucks, sucks," I chant over the sound of plates clattering outside. "Okay, I'm better. Let's get our asses out there to see who gets the baby."

A line of waiters in tuxedos weave through the dining room, holding platters of purple, green, and gold king cakes as Piper and I return to our table.

"Ains," Eli yells from his seat, holding up his phone. "Check Insta. Now!"

Not again.

I pull up Under the Gown's congratulatory post, tagging Piper and me with a photo from our table. One where Violet and I are deep in conversation. Though I expected pictures to be posted tomorrow via the social columnist who had just photographed the event, I never imagined Under the Gown would get a hold of them before lunch ended.

I don't know who's behind this post, but whoever it is, they've just made our private affair very public.

Another great party, courtesy of the Richards and Clarke families. Looks like Ainsley Clarke may be playing for keeps this time. I'd raise a hand to her, but I think a few of us would rather use one particular finger.

BTW . . . Laney sends her regards.

"What the hell?" I seethe, while Piper climbs on her chair, waving her phone, asking who posted the photo.

Violet leans in. "Just another bitchy post from UTG. It will be off everyone's radar by tomorrow morning, tops. Or until they roast their next victim." She puts her hand over mine. "Don't let them get under your skin."

Digging my fingernails into the back of my neck, I zone into the sensation of pain to block the anger that's building. I'd just recovered from one panic attack. Now, I'm on the verge of another.

Glasses jangle. Plates clatter.

Each amplifying the sound of the other, but at least they're serving the cake.

I need to focus on the positive. Maybe that will distract from the carnage that is UTG.

At least until I can get my shit together.

When a piece of cake is placed in front of me, I thank the waiter and lift my knife to carve into its delicate fluffiness. Before I can finish the task, Violet waves her hand in front of me. "Stop. I think you got the baby. Look." She points with her knife.

Sure enough, a flash of pinkish-white pokes from beneath the purple section of icing, and I beam. "This is the best luck I've had all day."

I start to slice, but my knife refuses to cut through the cake.

I move an inch away and try again. Still, a no go. "*Baby*? More like Godzilla."

Changing my strategy, I slice along the top of the cake, removing inch after inch, until the cinnamon speckled crumbs begin to disappear. "Oh, my God!"

I push back, pulling Violet with me as our chairs clatter to the floor.

"That!" I point. "It's a fucking finger." Bile rises in my throat as I stare at the ringlets of flesh and bone that peek out.

The hell?

My mind reels as I try to process what I'm seeing, but all I can think about is the UTG post.

This is no accident.

A young blonde den mother appears at my side. "Ms. Clarke. I'm so sorry. This is simply unbelievable." She looks at the cake, then reaches for my hand. "Come with me." Nodding, I follow her into the hallway. "I'm Sara, by the way." She guides me over to a velvet bench in the hallway, motioning for me to sit. "Are you okay?"

I shrug. "That was seriously messed up. Who would do such a thing?"

She pats my arm, making me feel bad for ever knocking the whole den mother thing. It's surprisingly comforting to have someone here who not only knows the ropes, but can relate to the amount of stress we go through to host one of these events.

"I wish I could answer that, but I can't," she says, her eyes darting around the hallway. "But that's why we're here. To make sure nothing goes wrong. Guess we failed you."

I offer a weak smile. "No one could have known *that* would happen."

She stares at me like she wants to say more, but instead, we both start laughing. "Guess you're right, but hey, we have a party to salvage. Take as much time as you need to pull yourself together. I'll go help Ms. Richards clear the room and settle your guests. In the interim, is there anything else I can do?"

"Yes," I say. "Call the police!"

CHAPTER 10

"When's the last time you saw Laney Wilson?" Officer Jones holds his pen, midair, ready to scribble in his small black notebook.

"At the summer mixers, several months ago. I tried contacting her a few times since then, but she never responded." I glance at the empty room and my table, where the confiscated plate had prompted Sara and two other den mothers to help Piper whisk our guests into the Carousel Bar for after-lunch drinks. Yet, here I sit, giving a statement, wondering if I'm going out of my mind, or had I really and truly nearly ingested a human finger that could or could not be connected to Laney Wilson?

"Did you think something was peculiar?"

The detective coughs, and I flick my eyes over his slightly bulging eyes and grayed, unkempt facial hair. "I'm sorry, what did you say?"

"I asked if you thought it peculiar your friend didn't contact you?"

"Not at first. She'd been posting and stuff, but then she didn't show for the Crescent presentation and missed all the parties since." I frown in symphony with the drooping of his mustache.

The detective seems bored. Like I'm some airhead debutante prone to hysterics. "I'm aware how insane this sounds, but Laney went MIA, and suddenly there's a human finger in my cake. Which happened literally minutes after a message was posted to Under the Gown, saying Laney 'sends her regards.'" I sigh. "Oh, and something about everyone wanting to give me a particular finger."

"Yes, the um . . . finger. We plan to run forensics. Could've been a cooking injury or simply a prank. Girls your age, in the middle of pageant season—"

"Debutante," I correct.

"Right, sorry, *debutante* season. Isn't there a possibility this is from some mean-spirited girl? Someone perhaps, who didn't get an invite to your fancy soiree?"

I'm not naïve. Things like that happen. In high school, during the endless rounds of sweet sixteen parties, the St. Philomena Academy girls got into a trend of sending RSVP cards with the words "No Thanks" written in bold to the parties they deemed unworthy of their attendance. In return, those spurned girls often hosted a revenge after-party to get back at them. Annabeth Taylor hosted a "Girls Just Wanna Have Fun" theme which no one knew whether it was a bitchy dig about sexuality in general or making fun of how sexually active the girls that rejected her party were.

According to Violet, the mean-girl antics are still alive and well.

I shake my head. "I don't think this fits their MO." Because, honestly, I don't. I can't imagine any of the girls I know going within ten feet of a severed human finger. Not to mention how they'd ever come to possess such a thing.

"You said a message tipped you off? On social media?"

"Yes. On Under the Gown."

"Who does the account belong to?"

"I have no idea."

He looks up. "You said you follow them, correct?"

Before I can answer, he yawns.

"Yes," I answer, harsher than before, because this is a waste of my time. "It's a page for debs participating in this season. We follow it to keep up with the news."

Or gossip, I think, but don't say it. "Even if you disregard the content of that post, it's the timing that bothers me. Seconds before we were served the king cake with the finger in it, they posted a comment that mentions Laney, who hasn't been heard from in weeks."

I bounce my white linen napkin on my knee.

"I understand your concern, Miss Clarke, and I assure you, we'll run tests on the finger and look into your statement regarding Ms. Wilson." He stows his notepad in his jacket. "Until then, why don't you try to have a good time with your friends? There's ample security at the hotel and with the high chance of this being, um, just a well-timed joke, you shouldn't waste the day." He gives me a once-over. "Or that dress."

I suddenly wish I had a coat large enough to drape over myself because I'd just spent the last twenty minutes as a *talking dress*, for all this detective cared.

"Thanks for your time," I snap, rising from the table.

My heels clack against the hard marble of the Monteleone lobby as I rush away, only to collide into the back of another gun-toting man.

His partner? No way will I go through this a second time.

"Miss Clarke?" The dude fumbles with his cap, unveiling a mess of blond hair and a round baby face. He blushes. "I know you've spoken to Officer Jones, but if I can be of any assistance, please let me know."

"Ainsley." I stick out my hand. "And thanks . . . Officer *Roy?*" I recite his nametag, wincing when his face brightens. Now, I need two coats and an exit plan, unless . . . I glance over my shoulder. "Honestly, I'm a bit freaked out. Could you stay to keep an eye on our party? I'd feel much better knowing someone capable was on guard in case that creep is still lurking around."

"I don't think that's possible. As soon as I finish up my notes, we're set to leave. Much to Officer Jones's dismay, I'm not as fast as him. Besides, your king cakes weren't made at this hotel. Correct?"

"Of course not. They're from Mae-Mae's bakery. Why?"

"Officer Jones believes somewhere at that bakery there may be a cook with a missing finger." He grimaces.

Like I suspected, the other policeman had decided this was a simple prank or accident, rather than consider my account of the incident. Which doesn't make a bit of sense. If this were a prank, who would've had the time or opportunity to insert a corpse's finger into our cake before the waiters served it *and* make sure it was served to me? Unless it *was* a waiter, which seems highly unlikely.

Piper and I had orchestrated our share of pranks over the years, but even our worst has never reached this level of debauchery.

The cop leans closer. "I can take a bit longer if you're that nervous. There are worse things to get yelled at over." He winks.

He's taking the bait. *Perfect.*

"I'd hate for you to get in trouble." I touch his shoulder and smile, hoping it will pay off. "But if you really want to help, could you call me if you hear anything? See, the girl I'm worried about, um, Laney, she's a good friend, and I won't be able to sleep until I know she's okay."

I lay it on thick. Even if Laney *is* ignoring me, if this is what it takes to get him or the other detective to check into her welfare or figure out who sent me a cut-off finger, the flirting is worth it.

Holding out my hand for his pen, I scribble my number down. It's a long shot, but much better than having to call stuffy Officer Jones.

"Great, I'll give you a call—"

"For a progress report, correct?" I cock my head. While I'm purposely flirting, I don't need him harassing me for a date.

"Of course. You're a sweet girl, Ainsley." He taps his pen on the paper. "I'll do my best to help. Go enjoy the rest of your party."

It's been eight days since I've heard anything from the police and the radio silence is driving me crazy. I don't know what to do, or who to take seriously, and it's been rough, considering I've had to attend a dizzying number of lunches, teas, and even another presentation. To say my mind's elsewhere is beyond an understatement. And since Under the Gown hasn't responded to any of my messages, but still posting regularly, it means—I'm being ignored.

There's only way to distract myself. My favorite holiday.

"Is there a reason your ass keeps lighting up?" Violet trails behind, dodging fake Santas and store attendants handing out coupons. "And why did we come to this mall during one of the busiest weekends ever?"

Before I can answer, my phone rings, and it's Officer Roy for the fourth time. "It's the cop from my party. I gave him my number," I say, trying to text back a cordial reply when I actually want to curse him out.

"And?"

"He's asking if I like Indian food. Or if I'm free to eat said Indian food with *him*."

Daggers shoot from her eyes.

"Whoa, V. I asked him to call when there's progress on the case. Not like I could charm decrepit Officer Jones. This dude is my best shot."

"Is he cute?" Violet asks.

"Not as cute as you." I hold my hand out, waiting for hers to slip into mine. "And I asked you to come because if I don't concentrate on something besides the fact I almost ate a human finger, and that finger *may* or *may not* be Laney Wilson's, I just might cry. Again."

"Yes. That is a problem, but I'm sure they've checked on her whereabouts by now." She pulls a trapped section of her hair from under the strap of her quilted Chanel backpack. "If you don't mind, can we not talk about that today? I'm as stressed as you over these horrid events, but we're supposed to be having fun. So, back to the subject at hand, yes?" She eyes the crowds warily. "You don't seem like the type to last-minute shop."

She's right. I'm not the type to last-minute anything. I detest surprises, and if an event isn't inked onto a schedule or immortalized on my digital one, it doesn't count as being worthy of attending. "I've had my Christmas gifts since August. They're even wrapped," I admit, smiling over her baffled expression. "What? If I can get things done early, I do. But it never hurts to triple check. Especially since my extended family has invaded my home this year. While I love them dearly, especially my great-grandfather, his eyesight is failing, and he makes you sit right next to him. Then he tells the same stories, over and over. Normally, I'm patient, but right now, on top of every other reason, if you make me go home, I truly will cry."

"There are better ways to pass the time, Ainsley."

I raise my eyebrows, and she scowls.

"Not like that, perv."

"Can't say I didn't try," I say, and she swings her very expensive backpack into my ass.

After hitting a few stores, we take a breather in the Canal Place Food Court to fuel up for more shopping. "I'd happily trade places with you," Violet says, scarfing down a mouthful of fries. "At the Anderson home—filled with relatives with *impeccable* eyesight— they still do their best to make me cry." She snatches a fry from my pile after polishing off her own. "Ooh, maybe I can use that lucky magnolia coin you gave me to make me feel better."

"Hey, why don't you spend Christmas evening at my house?" I blurt, panic surging when she stops eating, midfry. "After everyone finishes celebrating with their families, we meet at my house to compete in these crazy, winter backyard games. It's become a tradition and you're more than welcome to come. Heck, invite Blair. When we're done, we watch movies and make hot chocolate. Super low-key," I say, while I'm dying fifty deaths.

Who invites someone they've been on fewer than five dates with to *Christmas*? She probably thinks I'm strange. Clingy. Or worse. Though I did mention inviting Blair. Maybe that made it sound less intimate?

"Winter games, eh?" She smiles.

"And hot chocolate. Or you could just go with plan H and accept a hug. Seriously, I won't be offended if you have plans."

I'm offering her an out, but she shakes her head. "No way. I'll definitely ask Blair. Her parents are going abroad for the holidays, and she was thinking of spending the rest of break with me in NOLA anyway, but you'll have to put her on someone else's team." She pauses. "Are there teams? Because she's tragically bad at sports. All of them."

When we're done, we empty our trays, and she grabs my hand. "Let's go in that store." She points. "This year I may actually have something to shop for."

CHAPTER 11

CHRISTMAS DAY
DECEMBER 25

Standing in front of our Christmas tree, I nudge my brother. "If I wanted to take a photo with someone who possessed the same brain capacity as Frosty the Snowman, I'd go outside," I say, batting his hand away from prodding my ribs.

"There's no snow, genius." Luke blows a piece of fluff off the garish sweater our aunt gifted him, looking me over. "Hey! Why aren't you wearing *your* sweater?"

"Because I used my brain and said I'm allergic to wool." I flash my cheesiest grin.

"Wait!" my mom yells. She waves my dad over. "Honey, why is this thing recording instead of taking a photo?"

"Liar," Luke whispers.

"Obviously. But no way am I letting Mom post a photo of me in that thing."

If my mother and father weren't two feet away, for sure, a fight

102

would ensue, but for now, I'm safe. Plus, I look way better than my brother. A big win in my eyes.

After hours of family bonding, I announce my exit. "Love all of you, but I've been playing the same game of Scrabble with Gramma Gertrude since this morning. Every word she picks is *not* an actual word, and I'm done. Plus, I need to help set up our games."

I point at my brother. "Oh, and Luke. I told Gramma you'd take my place. Don't keep her waiting, you hear?"

Outside, Rudolph's nose is set for badminton, the shields have been placed next to the beanbags for cornhole, and a giant net added behind the Christmas tree for slapshot.

I congratulate Piper, Eli, and Leslie on a job well done.

"I refuse to pay for your neighbor's window again," Piper says, pink beanie bouncing. "And the hot chocolate is sufficiently spiked. Maybe too much. Not sure."

She offers me a cup. One swig later, I'm coughing. "You think?"

"I may have added a bit more brandy than usual."

"Tastes perfect to me," Eli says, glancing down the driveway. "Whoa, we have guests. Wait—is that Violet and Blair? *The* Blair from your luncheon? You never told me she was coming, Ainsley." He whips a hand through his hair.

"She never mentioned either were coming." Leslie shoots me a bitchy look.

"Blair's staying with Violet over break to help out with her party, so you're welcome, Eli." I grin at him and turn to Leslie. "I didn't know I had to preapprove my guest list with you, Les, but FYI, Jamie will also be here in a few minutes. What's wrong? Worried you're going to get your ass kicked by the new competition?" I tease, but she doesn't laugh.

Though Leslie and I had seemed to be back on the good-friend train, clearly I'm wrong. Not only are her mood swings giving me whiplash, I don't know what to do or say to ease the tension. And anything I do say seems to piss her off further.

Violet greets me with a hug, as her eyes skate across my backyard. "Quite a setup," she says, while I survey her outfit. She's wearing a green skirt, leggings, and a maroon turtleneck that matches the ribbon looped through her hair, and looks adorably Christmas cute.

Eli returns with a welcome drink for Blair, and Piper and I exchange smiles. We've never seen him fawn over a girl like he's doing with Blair, even in high school, and we couldn't be happier.

After Jamie arrives, I recite the rules for the holiday-inspired badminton. "Random Christmas songs will play. If you don't know the lyrics when it's your turn to hit Rudolph's nose, you'll have to take a shot, don the antlers, *and* play the remainder of the game with your nondominant hand."

"I call Ainsley, first game," Leslie says.

I mouth *sorry* to Violet, but she waves her hand, like, *no big deal.*

When Blair volunteers to play the music, Eli passes Violet a racquet. "Guess it's you and me. I don't intend to lose to Ainsley. Hope you brought your A-game."

"Of course I did. I'm an *Anderson*, after all."

During our first game against Piper and Jamie, we rack up several points. When Piper flubs her lyrics, she downs her shot, but pouts when she has to put on the antlers. Jamie flicks her headpiece. "I think you're doing amazing. Plus, you look pretty hot as a reindeer."

"Enough with the PDA!" Leslie yells, rolling her eyes. "Serve the ball so we can destroy!"

Piper and I exchange what-the-hell looks.

Leslie's always been competitive, but this is a bit much. When the game ends, she squeezes me in a victory hug that lasts way too long. *Here we go again,* I think, pushing her off playfully, but she looks pissed. Perfect.

The next game we're pitted against Eli and Violet, and before long, we're tied. That is, until I fumble the lyrics of "Santa Baby."

Leslie turns my way, eyes blazing. "Are you *trying* to let her win?"

I lower my racquet. "Whatever stick is up your ass, it's starting to annoy. Chill the hell out. We've got this."

Turns out, we didn't.

Bowing to the victors, I grab Violet's hand and pull her over to our firepit. Sprawling on a chaise, I snuggle against her, pressing my face next to hers. It's the first chance I've gotten to be with her tonight, and already I feel my body relaxing. Not simply because she calms me, but I can't take another moment of Leslie's negative vibes.

I need to find out what her problem is, once and for all, so I make a mental note to text her tomorrow.

After we finish our hot chocolates, we return to Eli explaining the rules of cornhole to Blair, while holding the cardboard shield he fashioned out of Miller Light boxes stolen from Cooper's vast stock.

Violet bumps my shoulder. "Are you going to be my knight? Because this shunned mistress may actually need defending with all the shade Leslie's been throwing." She nods in Leslie's direction, who appears to be slamming her fourth, maybe fifth drink.

"It's not like that with us," I say. "I mean, it hasn't been for a while. I want you to know that."

"Better make sure *she* knows that," Violet says, refocusing on the game as the timer counts down. "Besides, I plan to win this."

When Violet scores the winning goal, I give her a high five, but Leslie storms the court. "Now I know why you're so perfect for each other!" she yells. "You both love to play games with p-people." Her voice slurs, and she nearly trips.

Piper rushes from the sidelines. "C'mon, Les. I think you've had a tad too much to drink."

"Who cares? How do you expect me to tolerate *this*?" She jabs her finger in the air. "You're a sucker, Clarke. Little Miss Anderson shows from out of nowhere, and you fall under her spell just like that." She snaps her fingers. "You don't know a thing about her. I bet she has more secrets than she can afford c-closets."

"That's enough." I wrap an arm around Leslie's shoulder and steer her through the yard, ignoring the looks on my friends' faces. "We can talk tomorrow, Les, but I'm calling an Uber. Hopefully you'll feel better in the morning."

She knocks my hand off. "Fuck off, Clarke. This is your fault."

"My fault?"

She's breathing hard, trying to stay vertical. "You keep showing back up, but you don't want to *be* with me. I thought you didn't want a relationship, but this whole time, you've been gaslighting me!" She stares in Violet's direction. "Why do you have to flaunt her in my face?"

"I'm not. Didn't we have, like, twenty conversations on how we function better as friends than partners? And that was way before I met Violet." I rub my eyes, exhausted. "I'm sorry you and I hooked up a few times after we broke up. I thought you were cool with an occasional thing. I thought we both were cool with it, as long as neither of us was in a relationship. But now, I am, and—"

"Ever think it's the only way I could keep you in my life?" she blurts, and I jump back.

I've never seen her this angry.

"But you don't care about anyone but yourself because who could possibly be good enough for the girl who has to win at everything?" she fumes.

She's pissing me off, but I know any defense on my part will only escalate the situation.

"Les, clearly, this is my fault," I say. "I'm sorry I hurt your feelings. It was never my intention." I reach for her shoulder, and again, she slaps my hand away. "You've always talked about your numerous dates and . . . I was happy we could still be *friends*. This has nothing to do with you not being good enough."

"You're right. This"—she gets in my face—"is not about me! How many presentations will it take before you find something new to perfect? Hmm? You did this in high school for homecoming court. Then student council. Anywhere you could control the narrative. But you know what your problem is, Clarke? Deep down, you'll never be good enough for yourself."

That's it. I'm done.

"Go home, Leslie. Text to let me know you got there okay, but you need to sleep this one off." I fling the door open to the Uber that's pulled into our drive.

"Merry fucking Christmas, Clarke!" she screams as the door closes, and I'm left standing in the driveway, too stunned to move.

Leslie's been a part of my life for as long as I can remember, in one form or another, and I never wanted that to change, but I can't let her drunken rage ruin my evening.

"Is the Grinch gone?" Standing on her tippy-toes, Piper peers over my shoulder.

I nod. "She needs to sober up. Guess the brandy did her in," I say, trying to lighten the mood. "So, what did I miss? Am I beating everyone as usual?"

"Negative. You and Violet are tied," Jamie says, "but since the last event is solo, either of you can take the whole enchilada." He grins. "As expected, I'm in last place."

"But you're first in my heart." Piper swings her arm through his.

"You're only one point ahead of me, Pipes." Jamie laughs.

"But I'm first in your heart, right?" She stares, waiting for his answer, while I hold my breath. If he doesn't respond, she'll die of embarrassment, and I'll, I'll—

"Of course you are," he says, and I exhale.

The last thing we need is another lovers' quarrel.

"Yeah, well, me and Blair, we're kinda in the middle," Eli says. "Certainly worse places to be stuck, right?" He ruffles her hair and looks at me. "Oh, and I bet fifty bucks on you being victor, Ainsley. No offense, Violet."

"None taken," Violet says, as I hand her a pair of gloves and point at the tree.

"You have thirty seconds to shoot as many targets as you can. Simple."

"*Simple*? Shooting hockey pucks at a Christmas tree?" She shakes her head. "Also, how worried should I be about Leslie?"

"In what way?"

"In a way where you bolt back to your old girlfriend, instead of the one with multiple closets." Her eyes sparkle with defiance, but her tone is more subdued.

"Are you saying you have closets full of secrets?"

"Who doesn't?" She shrugs.

"Fair. Let's make our own bet. If I win, I'll escort you to your party as an *official* date. And if you win, you can—"

She presses her lips against mine. Though startled, I cup the back of her neck, pulling her to me, and we kiss.

"Ainsley! Stop!" Piper booms. "I bet on you also. You're going to make me lose."

We pull apart, and I pick up my hockey stick. "I didn't *lose* anything yet," I say to Piper, then turn back to Violet. "And *you* . . . if that kiss was part of your strategy, looks like you'll be paying the angry Piper her money while I win this."

Before Jamie can blow the whistle, Piper throws me my phone. It's probably Leslie, which I plan *not* to answer, but I check to be sure. "Oh, merry Christmas to you also, Officer Roy."

I wriggle around Violet while he explains he has an update on the case, but before he goes any further, he says he'll need my pledge of confidentiality. It's a bit odd that he's trusting me with private information, on Christmas at that, but hey, it's what I'd been hoping for.

"Hardly in my best interest to repeat anything," I say. "Not with sites like Under the Gown trolling for scoop."

"Okay. We have a deal." He continues. "I've recently learned that the Wilson family filed a missing person's report on their daughter, um, Laney, weeks ago. After extensive digging, as embarrassing as this is to admit, it seems the report was never logged into the system. We're in the process of correcting the error, but I thought you might like to know your hunch was correct."

His words swirl in my brain. "Did you say the police department *lost* a missing report on a teenage girl? Like, no one's looking for Laney?"

He coughs. "Errors happen. Exactly why I hope you recognize the delicate nature of what I'm sharing. Heads could roll if this gets out. Including mine."

"And Laney can lose her life, since apparently, no one's looking for her. But sure. Swore I wouldn't say anything. Thanks for the update." I hesitate. "Wait. What about the—the—"

I can't even say the word.

That's how far I've pushed the memory down in my brain. Just the thought makes me nauseated all over again.

"The what, Ainsley?"

"The f-finger." There, I said it.

"I'm afraid there were no reported accidents at the bakery. The lab is still working on a DNA match, and"—he lowers his voice—"we're hopeful it won't be a match. But there's always that possibility."

I hear his name being called in the background. "Gotta run. Stay safe, and have a merry Christmas, Ainsley."

He hangs up.

CHAPTER 12

While it was surprising how few law enforcement personnel wished to talk to me, considering I almost ate a human finger hidden in a king cake at my party, there are even fewer who would admit I was right that something was amiss when Laney Wilson went MIA from debutante season.

What shocks me most isn't that something else went wrong with our cursed season. It's that someone deliberately buried Laney's missing report, and if that's true, what else could our fine men in blue be hiding? Officer Roy said it was an error, but I don't believe in blatant coincidences. Debutantes appear on Under the Gown for breathing incorrectly, so it's only natural to assume word of a *missing debutante* would make headline news on every media platform. Especially UTG.

Only, it hasn't.

Nor has anyone offered a reasonable explanation as to how or why I was given a cannibal cake by chance, yet most have the nerve to parrot—*don't worry*.

I wish I could do that. But I can't. Because in addition to my missing friend, I feel like I've had a target on my back this entire season. At this exact moment, it happens to be coming in the form of another UTG post.

As we await the Anderson party, why not slow things down and play a little Ainsley Bingo, courtesy of her Broken Hearts Club?

How many of you can cross off bowling or baseball game dates, or our actual *debutante* in exchange for brain cells?

Seems a few will be wearing déjà vu to this party.

***Been there, don't want to be with her again*—courtesy of our favorite troublemaker.**

Freaking Leslie!

God help the woman who dates her next. The amount of scorched earth she's trying to shovel my way is beyond astronomical, yet UTG seems more than happy to assist with her maligned efforts.

The post is followed by digs and comments I read until I can't digest another horrid word. Diving into bed, I spend the rest of the day moping. Even Piper's offer of a *Pitch Perfect* marathon isn't enough to move me.

After a fifth call from Violet, I pick up.

"I was starting to think you didn't have enough *brain cells* to operate a phone."

"It's not funny, V. I don't know half of the people posting these mean comments. Let alone why it should be newsworthy."

"I'm sorry." Her voice softens. "I called to check on you, not annoy you further. But since you generally respond better to sarcasm, I figured I'd give it a whirl."

"You do realize I'm being date-shamed by half of our social world? Besides that, I'm afraid to eat any food I haven't properly smashed with a fork, just in case it has body parts inside. Not to mention, I've been effectively silenced from asking too many probing questions about Laney from our seemingly inefficient police department."

"I can bring you soup. That's easy to sift through." She lists off a litany of other translucent foods, which I decline.

After Officer Roy had instructed me *not* to tell anyone, I immediately relayed the phone call to everyone in my backyard, swearing them to silence. I wasn't trying to get him in trouble. I just figured if anyone could help Laney, we were her best shot.

So, we devised a plan.

Eli agreed to track down Laney's boyfriend, Hunter, while Piper and I tasked ourselves with discovering why Laney's family was staying quiet. I briefly considered telling my parents, but decided against it. They'd pull me from all debutante-related events, leaving me with zero to go on. No leads. No intel. I'd be cut off from helping Laney and all the other reasons I wanted to participate in the first place.

"Ainsley, you okay?" Violet jolts me back to the present.

"Sorry. I spaced for a sec, but stop worrying about me. *You* have a party to oversee." I glance at the black sequined dress I'd chosen for her party, hanging on my garment rack, shoulder pads and all. "*Dynasty* is one hell of a pick, by the way, even if your family doesn't get the jab. Kinda feels like we're already living one of their episodes. I mean, who has enough power to shush a family like the Wilsons from not going public about their daughter's disappearance?"

"I thought you said it was a police error?"

"*Officer Roy* said that. But if your daughter went missing, wouldn't you be talking to the police every day? Doing neighborhood searches? Hell, putting up signs? Something's off, and I don't think it's just some random-ass clerical error."

"See how smart you are, Ainsley?"

"Ha, ha."

She's quiet for a moment. "How do you know her family cares to look? There's also a remote possibility they did it to cover their own asses. You can't make assumptions on how someone will react." Her voice tightens.

"Are you serious? I've been to Laney's house tons of times. I know her mom, dad, and older sister Ashley. They're great people. Besides, what parent wouldn't care about their missing daughter?"

"Mine."

"You're joking, right?"

"Wish I were. When I was younger, I threw a major temper tantrum when I found out my parents were too busy to attend my cello recital. Days later, when they tried to drag me on their business trip, I said I was too busy to make the flight. I sat on my suitcase, determined to stay until someone apologized. Or I don't know, said something."

"I'm sure they—"

"They left me."

"Shit."

"It's okay. I wasn't *totally* alone. We have maids and such, but I cried the whole night. Then my sister came over the next day to give me some advice. She said while our family was important, individual Andersons only hold as much value as they can offer to the organization. She said maybe *I* didn't have the heart to go along with our name."

"That more than sucks," I say, wondering how her family could be that cruel. "But it's not true. You have a spectacular heart I'm quite fond of. And your family—sorry to say this, but—they sound awful. Just because you live in their mansion full of mirrors, doesn't mean it reflects you. You're none of those things."

"I think you used up all your brain cells on that one." She laughs. "Ooh, is that on the bingo cards? Swoon-worthy quotes by Ainsley?"

"I'll never live this one down." I sigh. "But hey, you made me laugh."

"Yes, I did. Mission accomplished. Now that I know you're okay, I need to get this diva ass ready. The amount of hairspray and makeup needed to pull off this aesthetic is quite scary. Oh, and my driver is picking you up at seven. Don't send any spoilers of your outfit. I want to be surprised. Text if you need anything."

"Yeah, yeah. In the interim, I'll be bingeing more *Dynasty* reruns to learn how to properly cope with an eighties fashion disaster. Maybe the shoulder pads will heighten my false bravado instead of my anxiety. See you soon, *date*."

I'm not lying about *Dynasty* because I need to screenshot the way they do their eye shadow to show my makeup artist. Besides, it will prove way more productive than prepping for a mental breakdown, though at this rate, that might not be a bad idea either. Especially since Piper's gone rogue—planning a tandem ensemble with Jamie—and I've been left to fend for myself on just how much eighties could be considered overkill.

Eli sends a snap of his white tux with a skeleton emoji.

I get it, Eli. You hate the decadence, but it sure didn't stop him from agreeing to be my plus-one as an excuse to hook up with Blair.

He owes me. Big time.

At seven prompt, a black sedan pulls into my driveway.

When Eli and I arrive at Violet's house, my fake-eyelash-adorned eyes widen.

Though I'm familiar with most Garden District homes, I'd never noticed this one. Tucked behind wrought-iron gates, strings of lights crisscross the yard tethered onto massive oaks. Pulling Eli along, we sidestep the cracks in the flagstone walk as music pours from behind the twenty-foot front doors. At the entrance, greeters hand out flashy sunglasses and fake smoking pipes.

Taking both, Eli and I step inside, but the decadence doesn't stop there.

I pause at a display case filled with glittering costume jewelry—I think it's costume?—in the foyer. A line of girls are waiting to pick out a piece to wear into the party, so we skip it and make our way into the main room. Massive is not an adequate descriptor. The ceiling nearly stretches to the sky and a wall of glass overlooks the backyard with a pool covered in plexiglass to serve as the dance floor.

Waitresses with feathered hair and lamé dresses pass out caviar in martini glasses and small bottles of Cristal, which Eli is more than happy to snag. Everything glitters, including the *Security* arm bands on the bodyguards weaving throughout the crowd.

Not only is the decor killer, Violet isn't taking any chances. Smart move.

"Miss Clarke?" A guard taps my shoulder. "The lady of the house asked us to inform you she's upstairs. First room on the right." He points to a curved staircase.

I bid Eli a temporary goodbye. *Time to get the girl.*

When I make it to the top landing, I stop to adjust a slipped strap on my gold heel. A door creaks. I glance up, and Blair's hair fills the open doorframe. "Oh, my gosh!" she blathers. "You look a-mazing! How did you manage to pull that off while I look like a Dallas Cowboy cheerleader reject?"

She twirls me, squealing, while I strike dramatic poses.

When I left my house, I swore I'd have fun, and with these vibes, surely, it won't be hard. Violet says she doesn't care about her party—and may be throwing it for purely spiteful reasons—but her name is attached to it, and I only want the best for her. Though I hope she'll have fun too, the way the last few parties have gone, I'll settle for zero injuries or fatalities.

That alone will be a win.

"Krystle Carrington is perfect for you." Violet's silken voice raises goosebumps on my arms. When she steps around the corner, I see her and *holy shit.* She's wearing a green bandage dress that plunges at the neckline with a giant diamond necklace filling the space where fabric should've gone. Her black hair is half pulled back with equally large emerald earrings peeking out.

"I'm speechless," I gush, and her Ruby Woo colored lips arch into a smile. With heels on, she's closer to my height, so she easily grazes my cheek with a kiss. "This party . . . it's insane. You might not care, but if you do, you more than nailed it."

"When I commit, I kinda go all out. Besides, I had to meet your standards. Considering how great you look, hope it lives up to your hype."

Whether she wanted the party or not, she seems to be reveling in the gilded vibes. She's dynamic, sparkly, and it overwhelms me in the best way possible. No one can top this party. At least, not in my book. And that's saying a lot, considering it hasn't officially started.

"Is Eli here?" Blair blurts, breaking my lustful trance.

I drag my eyes from Violet. "Yes ma'am, he is. Fair warning, he looks like a large fridge in a bow tie. If y'all are ready to go down, we can find Piper and Jamie too. I'm dying to see their costumes. Piper's kept it a secret, which is not an easy thing for her to do."

"You two go. The spotlight, um, not my thing." Blair flees from the room.

I turn to Violet. "Am I missing something?"

"I'd tell you, but it will ruin the surprise. More fun to see your face. Escort me, please." She holds out her French-manicured hand, and we link elbows, heading to the entrance of the staircase.

The music cuts off. Someone taps a microphone.

"May I have everyone's attention, please? It's my distinct pleasure to welcome our guest of honor for the evening, my daughter, Miss Violet Easton Anderson!"

Her dad. Shit.

Peering over the rail, I spot the resemblance. If I wasn't nervous before, it's been amped one thousand times. "I'm going to kill you!" I whisper through my staged smile. Being in the limelight is something I know how to *do* or *fake*, whatever the occasion calls for, and right now, guess I have to fake it.

Before we hit the last step, I turn to her. "I thought you hated being in the spotlight?"

"People will talk, one way or another, and they're already talking about you. This makes a much better storyline, don't you agree?"

I shake my head, trying to ignore the throng of people and her dad burning a hole through my mile-high shoulder pads.

Only Violet doesn't stop. She promenades past her father and her mother, who is tracking our every move. As we weave through the crowd, compliments roll in. "Such a cool party. Thanks for inviting us!" the Madisons gush, once again, nearly indistinguishable in their coordinated dresses.

"Violet, this party is the bomb. And Ainsley . . . love the dress. It's fitting, you playing mistress of the house. I doubt Leslie will like that lipstick, though," Madison J says, pointing at my cheek.

Whipping out my phone, I rub at the red lip imprint, and Violet laughs. "You let me walk down like this?"

She laughs even harder.

"You've already made the story for Under the Gown; why stress?" Madison K interrupts. "Ooh. Let's take a photo. Everyone smush in. Hurry, I wanna post it."

Biting back curse words, I cringe when she hands a guest her phone.

Pulling Violet closer, I force a smile until flashes go off. "Can't tell if you're naturally mischievous or you've got a closetful of jealousy over those bingo cards," I whisper.

"Didn't you hear? I have enough money to buy as many closets as I want. Now, let's have fun."

It's impossible not to spot Eli. Bopping around on the dance floor with Blair, Piper, and Jamie, he waves as we make our way over.

"Christ on a cross, you actually wore *cheetah*!" I yell to Piper over the music.

She shimmies my way. "I did. I'd say you look pretty great yourself, but I just posted that exact sentiment on UTG. I was worried you wouldn't make it. Glad you did. Way to stand up." She gives me a high five.

"Couldn't exactly miss her party." I motion to Violet with my chin. "Rather be distracted here than sitting at home going stir-crazy."

"Ooh, speaking of that, I may have found something out. Actually, Jamie did. Switch partners." She pushes me toward Jamie, and we collide.

"Holy shit, Ainsley," Jamie squawks, as I steady myself with his arm.

When the music segues to a slower song, I loop my arms around his waist. It will be much easier to talk this way. "Piper said you found something. Spill."

"When we were going through the names of girls being presented, I recognized one." He pauses. "Riley Coyne."

"What about her? We went to school together." I think for a moment. "Why does her name suddenly seem so familiar, like, *not* in a high school kind of way?"

"Maybe because Chief *Coyne* is the head of the Orleans police department." He glides us over to the edge of the dance floor where it's not as crowded. "That's Riley, right?" He nods at a group of girls. "Short brown hair. Giant white hat."

"Yes, but you really think she knows something?"

"If anyone should be aware of a missing classmate, it should be the police chief's daughter." He leads me to a nearby table. "One way to find out. Bring her a drink." He snatches two radioactive-colored shot glasses from a passing waiter and hands them to me. "Be gone with yourself."

Time to find a third partner.

"Riley, hey!" I hug her. "Haven't seen you since, what, graduation? Way too long. How are you?"

"Wow—Ainsley. I was just thinking about getting in touch. Saw you on Insta, and thought, I need to text that girl for brunch. Guess we can skip the brunch part, now that you're here." Smiling, she takes the shot. "Cheers to old friends?"

"Of course." I down the drink, wincing when my throat sizzles like hellfire. "Remember when we did those shots at Muses each time we caught a bedazzled shoe?"

She nods. "How could I forget? When I beat you, you were the sweetest thing. You gave me our whole haul of shoes the next day because you felt bad that I threw up all night."

"While there may not be shoes to compete for, I bet I can drink you under the table now." I throw down the challenge, and her face brightens.

"Deal. Okay if I post?" she asks.

My reputation is already in tatters. "Why the hell not?"

"You're so on." She dashes off to find a waiter while I grab a Solo cup from a buffet table, pouring the next shot into the glass to keep up with Riley. A shot or two later, she says, "You know, I love your friend"—she points at Piper—"but she looks like a walking Cheeto!" She slaps a hand to her mouth. "Oh, fuck. Please don't tell her I said that!"

Apparently, she's drunk enough to tell the truth.

It's go time!

"I'll hide your secret if you tell me one." I hand her a water, absconding the next shot so she won't get too drunk to talk. "Before

I forget, have you seen Laney? I ran into her parents a few days ago, and they were saying some crazy-ass shit."

"Like what?" Her voice cracks.

"They asked if I'd seen her. When I said no, they said she was supposed to be at Hunter's, but they hadn't heard from her." Of course, I'm lying my own red-lipstick mouth off. "They also mentioned talking to *your* dad. The whole thing sounded super sketch. Honestly, I've been trying to get in touch with Laney, but she hasn't answered my texts either. Guess when they said all that, it kinda freaked me out."

Riley's nostrils flare. "Laney can't do a thing without making a scene. I could kill that girl!" She sips the water, grimacing. "Uh—gross. Why does this taste so bad? Must be the cheap shit!" She scowls at the drink. "And Laney is fine; stop stressing. She and Hunter have been fighting, and I may have suggested she skip the Crescent presentation and go on vacay with him in Georgia at his family's timeshare. That's what he wanted to do, so she did. End of story."

"It's been more than a weekend, Riley." I frown. "More like a month, and her parents seemed really stressed. Aren't you a little worried?"

"We've been texting, like duh. I told her to call her parents, but she's afraid they'll freak out once they realize she skipped school and deb events for Hunter. She told them she missed Crescent because of Covid. I don't know what other lies she's concocted, but rumor is, her parents despise Hunter. Like a lot. None of my business, though."

"She may want to do more than that, considering they filed a missing person's report. I mean, how is that not news?" I hold my breath, waiting for her answer, but she doubles over, laughing.

"You wanted a secret? Here it is." She motions me closer, cupping her hand over my ear. "Since I'm the police chief's daughter, I may have mentioned that the perfectly *live* and *well* Laney's missing report would screw up *my* party. Hell, maybe all of deb season. Especially since she *isn't* missing. So, until Laney decides to crawl home from her faux honeymoon, my dad says he'll keep the lid on it. Since he knows she's fine and all."

Is she saying all it took to call off a police investigation is one pint-sized girl currently singing "Come on, Irene"?

Guess Eileen is busy.

It takes everything for me to play along with her charade and not go off on her. "I won't rat her out, but if Laney stops texting, you need to tell your dad, okay?"

She bobs her head. "I promise! Scout's honor."

"You'll also tell me, right?"

"Gotcha, boss." She salutes. "I need to find my friends. A few minutes ago, your girlfriend kept giving me the evil eye. I don't want to end up in her dungeon or something. Text you later! Thanks for the drinks—love ya!"

I find Violet inside. "Hiiii," I drawl, slipping my hands around her waist and kissing her cheek, motioning for Piper to come closer.

"Are you back for good this time, Nancy Drew?" Violet asks.

"I hope. Unless you have a hidden staircase I need to worry about. But even if you do, it will have to wait. You guys won't believe what Riley just told me."

"Please tell me I've been a stalker for a good reason," Jamie says, dabbing his forehead with Piper's sweatbands.

"Things are definitely getting weirder as debutante law states, or whatever is cursing us dictates," I say, repeating the tale Riley just spun to my amazed friends.

"Let me get this straight," Jamie says. "She got her dad to put a gag order on Laney's whereabouts, so her season doesn't get canceled?" He swears. "One thing for girls to go crazy over this shit. Quite another to do something *illegal*."

"You think a police chief would call off a search just like that?" Blair snaps her fingers. "Yeah—no. She's lying."

"He is her dad," I say. "And, according to Riley, Laney's been in constant contact. If this whole ran-away-with-her-boyfriend story is a farce, she needs to go to Hollywood because she sold that shit. Hard."

"I told you Hunter said Laney wasn't doing Crescent. Guess that's why," Eli reminds me, spinning a neon glow stick around his neck. "Maybe her story is legit. A terrible misuse of power, yeah. But good news, no doubt."

"I don't know. Something feels—"

I stop talking because Piper's eyes are wide and she's staring at her phone. Which means whatever she's looking at—she's not happy.

Under the Gown.

I reach for mine, but Violet beats me to it. "Guess you're not the only target for the night." Her face pales. Tilting it my way, a photo of a young Violet stares back. She doesn't just look young, she looks scared.

I scan the title:

V is for Violent! Check the floorboard before you leave, folks.

CHAPTER 13

"I'm going to fucking kill her!" Violet screams, scanning the room for whomever is unlucky enough to meet her gaze.

"Who? What's this about?" I ask.

Blair shakes her head and mouths: *Later*.

"Leslie! That's who! *She* got this posted. I know it." Violet rips herself from my arms.

I have no idea what's going on, but I'm not about to keep standing here, being the last to find out. "Violet, wait—"

"I should've known you'd find another way into the party after I threw you out, you low-lying rat." Violet's in Leslie's face, chest reddening, while Leslie's smile widens.

Did she have Leslie thrown out? And if so, when?

"Rats have nothing on how sneaky you are," Leslie claps back. "Showing back in town, acting like Miss Innocent. As if!" Snorting, she shoves Violet backward. "Kicking me out of your party is a small power play for you. Thought you wielded more power than that."

I grab Violet's hand. "Don't," I say. "There are a thousand cameras waiting to document your reaction."

"I don't care!" she yells. "This psycho dug into my medical records, which is illegal!"

"Watch who you're calling a psycho, *psycho*. Besides, Under the Gown posted the news, not me. I believe your anger is misplaced." A crowd starts to gather, but Leslie seems to revel in it. Her voice raises. "I bet you have a therapist or two who tell you that quite often. No wonder your parents were hellbent on you being presented. Guess they're trying to give you an opportunity to wipe your white padded room clean."

"Shut your mouth. You don't know a thing about me!" Violet warns. "Do you routinely look into the past of anyone who pisses you off, freaking stalker?"

"Clearly, someone knows a thing or two about you, Princess," Leslie says. "Don't hold *me* responsible for a bunch of concerned citizens."

While I don't understand what's going on, one thing is obvious. Violet believes Leslie has leaked her medical records to UTG. And since Leslie's parents *are* doctors, technically, she could have access, and after the way she's been acting, maybe motive.

It's out of character for Leslie to act this brazen, but even more mind-boggling to think she could do something this cruel or use her parents' connections to violate someone's privacy. Then post it.

It doesn't sound like something she'd do. But if not her, who?

Either way, I can't just stand here doing nothing.

I step in front of Violet and face Leslie. "Whatever you did, I'm asking you to stop. You've caused enough damage tonight."

"*You* caused that damage." Leslie jabs a finger into my chest. "This is a consequence of *your* actions. Did you think I'd be okay letting you make me look like a fool? Just to show off your new play toy. One who's crazy enough to have me ejected from a party I was invited to, by the way."

"I'm not playing," I warn Leslie. "You may have been invited, but this is Violet's party. And whatever you fed to Under the Gown had to be strategically planned. No way is it a coincidence it got posted the night of her party."

I'm trying my best to keep my cool because the crowd is growing. And like I told Violet, a million ears and phones are ready to document anything that goes amiss. I need to get Violet out of here. And fast.

"Whatever you did, I hope it's worth it." I grab Violet's hand.

"Worth what?" Leslie spits back.

"Helping me realize that you're a mistake." We lock eyes. "You were never played a fool, as you like to pretend. But I do regret that we ever dated. I don't want you in my life anymore, as a friend, or otherwise. I hope the mountain of trouble you just shook falls on your side, sooner rather than later. Remember, karma's a bitch."

Violet and I dash upstairs, but before I say a word, she ushers me out of the room. "I need a minute, okay?"

Is she kicking me out because she thinks this is my fault? Because technically, it is. I knew something was off with Leslie. The way she's been so flirty, so possessive. I should've addressed it right after Christmas, like I intended.

I'd kicked the hornet's nest. And it ended up stinging Violet.

Had I not wasted time feeling sorry for myself over that petty bingo post, I might've realized that if Leslie fed UTG gossip about me, surely she wouldn't stop there. The one thing I know about Leslie—*when she gets pissed, she gets even.*

Yet, here I stand, ambushed by the most predictable answer, doing nothing. While I couldn't stop a girl from having a heart attack or an allergic reaction, or figure out who sent me that grisly finger, I can try to stop this.

Navigating to my direct messages on the app, I click on the sinister account.

A

> What do I need to do for you to take down the post about Violet?

A chat bubble appears.

UTG

> The Maskers party is soon. I know you're invited. Find me a better story. We'll be in touch.

How do they know about Maskers? And even if they do, how do they know who *is* or *is not* being presented? Because even when you do get an invite, you're thoroughly vetted before they allow you into their folds.

I know this because Cooper has finally come through.

I received an invitation to be presented by The Mystic Maskers.

Arriving last week via private email, the only way I could read it was through a double authentication process. When it finally opened, I had to sign a nondisclosure agreement before reading a single word. After I viewed it, the whole thing vanished.

Talk about some Skull and Bones shit.

I still don't know when or where it's being held, but at the bottom of the email it stated that all debutantes would receive notification within a forty-eight-hour window of the exact time and location.

Not only is it rude to speak of, it's social suicide to post about it.

What choice do I have? I need to help Violet.

I hit send.

A

> I'll get you a story, but the post comes down. Now! And you can't upload it again if I don't find something you like. Deal?

UTG

Done. Can't wait to see what you wear.

I just signed a deal with the devil.

"Excuse me." Violet's dad pushes me aside, entering her room, before I can say a word.

I press my ear to the door. "It was your idea for me to have this party!" Violet shouts.

"I wanted you to fit in with your peers, though it seems, once again, you've found a way to ostracize yourself." His voice is just as loud as Violet's. "Your mother's so embarrassed, she's already in the car. We're going back to Dallas on a red-eye. I suggest whatever damage control you need to do, start now, young lady."

I back away as footsteps approach, eyeing her dad as he leaves. He appears to be in his early fifties, with a perfectly tailored tuxedo and green eyes that match hers. Good looking, yes. Intimidating, hell yeah.

I knock softly. "V, can I come in?"

When the door opens, she's standing, red-eyed and sniffly. "Could've just taken a page out of my dad's book and barged in. I'm sure you were close enough to get an accurate read on the situation."

"Yes . . . he, um, sounded a bit upset." I bite my lip. "And I'm, um, really sorry about Leslie. If I'd reached out earlier, she might not have gone after you," I say, not sure Violet's heard a word since she's paced three circles around the room. "I didn't expect her to do something like that. Not to you, at least. I'd do anything to undo it."

"Didn't you hear? She said she's not the only one who knows." Violet stares at me, her normally vibrant eyes, watery pools. "Someone told her to look into my background."

"But who? And why?"

"My family has a lot of enemies. Unless your ex has a history of breaking a metric ton of red tape, someone tipped her off. How else would she know my medical history was a risk worth pursuing?"

Hanging my head, I wish I could disappear. *This is my fault.* "I've seen her be vindictive, but never on this level. I can't imagine getting someone's records from a different state is an easy task."

Violet sits on the bed. "They're not from out of state. They're from here." A tear slides down her face. "Did you *not* read the post?"

"I didn't." I cross the room and settle next to her, suddenly exhausted. "Whatever she posted, I'm sure it's not something you want anyone to see. I can't stop others, but I don't want to read some tabloid level of shit about you."

Violet wipes her face, leaning into me. "Doesn't matter. I'd show you the post, but UTG removed it. They sent a DM saying they may have crossed a line. That they didn't know it would generate so much traffic. As if," she huffs. "Am I supposed to be grateful they apologized? There are probably enough screenshots to keep the rumor mill circulating, but I guess it's better they took it down."

I sigh. They might be lying, but at least they've honored their promise.

For now.

"Do you want to tell me what it said?" I slip off my heels. "Otherwise, I don't care to know."

"If anyone should know, it's you. My sister was right. I didn't manage my family's legacy well when I was younger. I may hate the limelight now, but I used to hate it even more. The importance of our name. People making instant assessments when they realized who I was, instead of getting to know *me.*" She picks at a sequin on my dress while she talks. "It made me sad and bitter. I think I had more therapists than friends. Except for Olly."

"Olly?"

"My Great Dane. He was gray and sweet as he was big. My

parents let me get a dog because they thought he would be a good companion. Naturally, I picked the most obnoxious choice. Loud. Clumsy. But so loving. I let him chew on my notebooks after class, just so I could say my dog ate my homework. And I'd bring back the shredded notebooks as proof." Her face lights up as she reminisces.

"I'm glad something filled the obnoxious role in your life before I came around." I nudge her playfully.

"I suppose it's a trend. Though I hope you don't have the same fate as Olly."

I stiffen. I don't want to hear the rest of this story, considering her hesitation, and the fact that she's looking everywhere but at me.

She inhales. "See, these girls at school made it their mission to pick on me. Maybe they were jealous of the attention the principal and teachers paid me, hoping to get another wing or library donated, but one day they decided to mess with my piano before a recital. I guess they wanted me to sound like an idiot in front of everyone, including my family. When I did play, everything was off-key. I was mortified. I knew it was them, so I said I'd bring Olly to school and let him eat them up. When they started laughing, I knew something was wrong."

"Tell me this isn't going where I think it is." I catch her hands between mine, and she looks up with a sad smile.

"Like I said, Olly would eat anything. Packages delivered inside the gate had to be scooped up by our housekeeper. Which is why it was bizarre when I got home and found a box full of half-eaten cookies with my name on them. Olly was hunched in the corner of our living room, foaming at the mouth. They poisoned my dog for the fun of it."

"That's horrible! How can you look bad if that's what this is about? They should have gone to jail! They're animal abusers!"

"I know, but thankfully, he didn't die. We made it to the vet in time, but he was never the same. It messed up his health big time.

When I realized they sent the cookies, I went berserk. I went to school and threw anything I could get my hands on. I shattered a window. Gave one of them a bruise from a thrown math book." She smiles at that part. "The girls told our principal I was insane. They said they sent cookies to *congratulate* me on my recital. That it was probably the chocolate that caused my dog to get sick. They were lying, of course. To top it off, none of the shit they did at my recital was ever brought up. Their families were also rich, so my word meant nothing against a bunch of battered-looking girls."

She glances up at me. "I got expelled. And sent to reform programs. Anger management. Mood stability classes. If you could throw money at it, I went. Which means my record looks a whole lot messier than I'd like."

"You think someone tipped Leslie off about that? And she turned your files over to Under the Gown?" I ask. "Are these girls still around? Are any of them debs?"

"One lives here. The other sheep moved away. I don't think it was her though. I ran into her a while back, and she apologized. It seemed genuine. She said she still felt guilty, after all these years." Violet flops onto the pillow.

"Guilty enough for me to *not* throw another item her way?" I squeeze her hand.

"Please, no more fights. It's not worth getting in trouble for me."

"Trouble seems to be finding me these days. What's one more mishap? Besides, I don't think a better excuse exists than *you*." I wince over the serious tone that came out.

Will I push her away?

Hoping to lighten the mood, I say, "What's the plan? We can't sit in bed all night. Is there some hidden library with a door that can lead us outside without being spotted in this ginormous house?"

"Afraid not. And I'm sure you heard my father. He wants me to do damage control. Which means I need to go back downstairs and be a very scary bitch."

It doesn't sound like the best idea to me, but who am I to contradict her father? "Okay, whatever you think. But fix your makeup so you look less sad, and a hell of a lot scarier."

I pull out a tissue from the box on the bedside table, dabbing at the runny mascara under her eyes, and her lips crook into a smile. "What?" I try to pull away, but her head dips closer.

"How sorry are you, really? About this Leslie mess?" Her lips are millimeters from mine.

It's a strange moment for her to be romantic, but the heat between us builds. "I'll do anything to fix it, *trust me*." I stop short of telling her what I'd already done to try and wipe the bad parts away, because if I don't find a story at Maskers, she could be thrown right back into the fire.

"If I ask for your help pissing her off, will you?" She practically purrs.

"Won't that pan out badly for both of us?" I raise my eyebrows.

"Kinda fits with my *Dynasty* theme, no?" She trails featherlight kisses along my jaw. "We've had the extravagance and drama of a *Dynasty* episode. We're just missing an integral part of what makes that show fun."

"Which is?" I wince as she nibbles at my neck, the smallest prick of pain, easing into a kiss. It hurts, yet feels good at the same time.

"Sex." She pulls away and I groan.

"Here?" I croak. "Violet—"

"Never mind. This will do." She eyes my neck proudly while I poke at a throbbing, tender spot. "Nothing will enrage Leslie more than seeing you like this. Trust me, I'd be furious."

I rush to the mirror. "All this is about getting back at Leslie?" I try to temper the hurt welling up inside me, cursing as tears brim under my perfectly lined eye makeup. "I guess I deserve it. Getting you involved in my mess."

"The thought that it will bother her *is* quite satisfying." Violet stands behind me, repairing her battle scars from earlier. She pulls out her phone. "Say cheese."

Holding the phone above us, I reluctantly strike a pose, my mind reeling as she texts. This is a side of Violet I've never seen, and hopefully won't, ever again. When she finishes, I say, "If you're trying to talk me into *not* being upset about being used as a rope in you and Leslie's tug-a-war, it's not working."

"So . . . post it?" She flashes the photo of me bearing several giant hickeys on my neck. The caption reads:

VIOLET

I must've left my secrets under a different house. The only thing I've been hiding in this house is a girlfriend. Eat your heart out, Broken Hearts Club.

Maybe I shouldn't be that mad. . . .

"Is this for show, or is it real? Because my answer will seriously change depending on your response." I place the phone on a side table, worried a stray finger might hit *post* before she answers.

"Consider it me asking if it can be real?" The playfulness in Violet's voice is gone. "Unless your answer is no. In which case, yes, this is my master plan against Leslie."

I sigh. "I've made headlines enough times today. Fuck it."

I hit *post*. "The things I do for you."

I had spent the last several years prepping for this moment. Dreaming of the people I'd meet. The parties I'd attend that could put me on the path to success. Making me feel like I truly belonged. I'd used every moment of downtime to plan how my presentations and party should play out, down to the tiniest detail, but never in my wildest nightmares did I imagine a season like this.

Sure, I met Violet, and hopefully, she'll be my one glittering spot of this season, but that verdict is still out. I have about a half dozen more parties to attend, a Carnival ball, two more presentations, and oh, let's not forget, I'd just signed myself up as UTG's newest junior reporter at the most exclusive debutante ball of the season.

Extra. Extra. Read all about it! Ainsley Clarke is in way over her head!

What better way for me not to worry about literal finger food, by putting myself on the societal chopping block. As long as that finger doesn't belong to Laney Wilson and she really *is* somewhere happily nesting with her boyfriend, guess I should stop sweating the small, gory stuff and count my blessings.

Like the way Violet is looking at me now.

Like she wants to kiss me for real this time. . . .

CHAPTER 14

JANUARY 4

Turns out, when you pick an option destined to spawn a shit-fest, it may be the best possible counter to preexisting problems. When Violet posted that I was her girlfriend, Leslie didn't melt into a nondescript puddle, but it sure did quiet things down.

With a brunch at Commander's Palace and an epic New Year's Eve party for ten debutantes behind us, it seemed to be enough for people to start gossiping about something other than the trouble Leslie stirred for Violet at her *Dynasty* party. And though that event fast-tracked my relationship into the dating lane I'd hoped we'd reach via a natural course; I really can't complain.

Apparently—Piper can.

"I can't believe *I* had to find out on UTG. You'd think you would've given your best friend the scoop, but no. The only bat signal I got was those giant-ass purple marks on your neck."

She grabs a book from the fiction section of Books-a-Million and huffs.

"I found out the same way," I remind her. "But I won't go anywhere with you again if you continue to complain every time I bring her up."

"Can't you let me be dramatic over something *good* for a change? I've been practically living with a cross around my neck due to the wild-ass luck that keeps following you around. Did I tell you my mom thinks you should get your house blessed?" She passes me the book, a silent recommendation of what I should read next, and plops down beside me on the bench.

I turn to face her. "In case you haven't noticed, none of that luck is stemming from *my* home. So, please, tell your mother I was baptized as a child, and I doubt more holy water will stop the bitch pack following me around with chopped-off fingers, bingo cards, or Leslie." I groan. "It's only been a week, but even I'm tired of seeing myself online. Why do people care so much?"

"Because you're dating Violet Anderson. Not to mention that certain rumor going around that you had sex with her in the middle of her party. Quite scintillating news." She rolls her eyes at a woman snapping her head in our direction.

"I did no such thing," I hiss. "Besides, who are you to grill me about my love life? You and Jamie have been—"

"Did you say *love*?" She giggles. "Besides, we've just been talking."

"*Talking*?" I raise an eyebrow. "You seemed pretty close at Violet's party, but if you don't want to kiss and tell, hey, I respect that. Unless there really has been no kissing? In which case, I can ask Eli to give him a nudge."

"Don't you dare. Eli is as obvious as you are obnoxious. He needs to worry about Blair and leave my relationship alone. Me and *Jamie*,"—she blushes over mere mention of his name—"are in a nice, peaceful place."

"Peaceful, hmm? Can I borrow some of that for this weekend?"

She shakes her head. "Yeah, about that. I love you, but I'm still jealous you were invited, and I wasn't." She elbows me. "Though that jealousy has been tempered due to the insane task you've been assigned by the tyrannical overlord of debutantes." She sighs. "Figure anything out yet?"

When Under the Gown played hardball in exchange for taking Violet's post down, there was no way I could sit on their request without telling someone. That someone, of course, became Piper.

Pushing her book choice aside, I get up to search for a more interesting title. Anything that can distract me from my own whodunnit of a life. "No, Pipes, I have no clue how to pull this off. I don't know who is invited, what the party entails, or how I'm supposed to get a story out of there. I just got the email yesterday with the time and date. Did you know they send a car for you as another layer of secrecy? All I can hope is that some drama unfolds, like it's been apt to do, and I can hop on the scoop before someone else does."

If I can't, Violet's post could resurface, she'll be miserable, and I'll be at fault. *Twice.*

"How would *I* know about the car? And since we're being honest, who did you sacrifice to get invited? Maybe you're the one who's been tampering with Voodoo incantations," she jokes, but I know Piper, and she's waiting for a truthful response.

She, more than anyone, knows how hard it is to get presented by The Mystic Maskers, and I'm sure she's curious why they picked me. And I want to tell her the answer to that question, but I can't. Not yet.

As if telepathically summoned, Violet appears, holding two Starbucks, saving me from Piper's grand inquisition. "For someone who reads voraciously, why do you look so stressed over the book selection process? Here, maybe this will help." She hands me a hot chocolate.

"I can't seem to find anything interesting," I say. "Maybe one thing, but it's not in these books." I poke her, and she blushes. Of course, it's a lie—not the part about her—but I can't admit that I'm freaking out over some *Eyes Wide Shut* ball which, for all societal purposes, does not exist. Much less that I'm invited. Or the real bombshell . . . that this weekend, I may ruin someone's life with gossip fed to that awful site.

We find a table to sit at, and Eli returns from upstairs, immediately snatching Piper's book. He reads the title, then returns it. "Way better than what Ainsley probably picked. She reads old-people books."

"Is it my fault I like to gain *knowledge* from the books I choose?" I sniff. "And not waste time on that comic book garbage you read."

"Hey now. Don't trash my books. If you took the time to look at a graphic novel, maybe you'd gain an appreciation for a culturally important art form."

"Don't bother trying to convince her," Piper tells Eli. "I'm sure her bucket-list guest appearance on Jeopardy will be historic, given the random knowledge she's amassing."

"We do owe her the tiniest shred of credit," Eli says, grinning. "Without her vast knowledge of randomness, we might not be alive." He slices his finger through a scar running across his eyebrow.

Violet's eyebrows raise. "Do you also box in your free time, Ainsley?"

"Nope. That's from a minor wreck we may have had during driver's ed. From what I recall, I think *you*"—I point at Eli—"were in control of the wheel at point of impact."

"True. But thanks to your extensive knowledge on skidding, I turned the wheel in the right direction, instead of killing us. Besides, you two had your share of adding dents to that jalopy."

Violet sighs. "Please tell me you guys didn't wreck your driver's ed car?"

"We kinda did. Apparently, facing death together forms unbreakable bonds," I say. "Speaking of bonds, who do you think is going to be our next *official* couple? Blair and Eli? Or Piper and Jamie?" I grin mischievously.

"You're such a troll." Piper flashes her fake, toothy smile.

"I bet on Piper and Jamie," Violet says, sticking out her tongue at Eli. "Jamie's way too lovestruck to *not* seal the deal. Ooh, maybe we can double date?" She leans over and kisses my cheek. "I've heard about your infamous Clue games. I definitely want in. How about this weekend?"

Nearly spitting out my hot chocolate, I stare at Piper—*Help!*

"No can do," Piper says, swooping to my rescue. "I've been summoned by our sorority she-beast to help with a toga party for incoming spring pledges. It's not as big as fall rush, but since I'm Shelbi's biggest GPA disappointment, I'm it." She scowls, selling the excuse hard.

While it's not an outright lie—Piper is helping at the party—she knows where I'm going, and it's nowhere near our sorority mixer, so I'm more than grateful for her save.

"Greeks doing Greek mythology. How original." Violet turns to me. "Are you going?"

"Me? Yes, I'm, um—"

"Dressing as Narcissus," Piper interjects again, smoothly navigating through the lie. "Naturally."

"And I'm Eros." Eli puffs out his chest. "I hope it's okay I asked Blair to come? Of course, you're more than welcome to join. They put me in charge of making the jungle juice in their designated trashcans."

Holding my breath, I pray Violet will not take Eli up on his offer. If she does, I'm sunk.

"Thanks, but I have to get an early start for my Wildlife Restoration project, and I was afraid Blair would be bored all day, so cool," she says. "Sorry to miss out on trash-flavored drinks, but you,"—she flicks the top of my baseball cap—"don't stay in love with yourself for too long. I detest competition."

"You're not missing much. Trust me." I'm relieved she declined his offer, but my guilt far outweighs any sense of relief.

I'm a liar. And I suck.

CHAPTER 15

THE MYSTIC MASKERS BALL
JANUARY 6

After donning my fifth white silk gown and gloves of the season, a black limousine arrives.

Fifteen minutes of a soundless ride later, it deposits me at the *aquarium*? Not exactly what I expected. A nondescript building hidden behind ivy-covered stucco walls was more the image I'd conjured in my mind, but maybe that's the point? Considering it's the official start of Carnival season—Twelfth Night—with more than a few debs participating in the court of a Carnival krewe across town, it offers the perfect foil to host a super-secret event.

But now that I'm here—*alone*—I feel even shittier.

Once inside, I wiggle my phone out of my small cocktail purse. "Luke, I genuinely would've eaten you in the womb if it were possible," I seethe over the phone, pacing in front of twelve unfazed African penguins, blinking sleepily behind their display glass. "I have a calendar. A physical chunk of paper that is magnetized to the fridge for the express purpose of being a reminder of my events."

"Chill out, Zombie Deb. It was a last-minute thing, just like your recent addition to said calendar. We didn't have a spot in this tournament, then a school dropped out after their team got food poisoning. Rumor is, there may be scouts," my brother boasts.

"Did it ever occur to you *I* may like at least one parent to show at *my* event? I'll probably be the only idiot at this thing without a family member."

"It's one of many boring presentations. Don't you have a zillion more?"

"I do not, idiot. Don't you have a trillion more wrestling tournaments? Same sweaty guys in gross, tight spandex."

"Way different. I'm trying to get recognized to nail a scholarship."

"You're doing the same thing as me. Just a different path with an end goal of opening doors to opportunities we wouldn't otherwise have. How do you not see that?" I lower my voice as an older couple strolls past. "Besides, my events can help Dad. If he were to get in tight with the CEO at NOLA General, it could put him on the map next time they elect the neurology head. Or he could mingle with a pharmaceutical exec and land a drug trial for those stroke victims he's always talking about. My events help all of us. But somehow, my family is the only one in New Orleans that doesn't grasp the necessity of networking with A-listers."

"Sorry to burst your puffy-white-dress bubble, but not everyone wants or needs to be an ass kisser to get ahead, Ass-ley. Stop trying to shove your uppity scheme down our throats."

"Okay, Mr. Clueless, but please tell *my* parents they're missing out on seeing actual sharks. Wait—there goes a fat manta ray that moves just like you on the mat. Slowly."

I hang up before his curses hit my ear.

"Excuse me, ma'am?" a man in a sleek black domino mask that matches his tuxedo calls out. "You *do* wish to be presented tonight, correct?" He points at my phone, shaking his head, like I've committed a cardinal sin.

"Sorry. I had an urgent family matter. No further distractions, I promise." I fiddle with my mask. "Those penguins are so cute."

"You'll have plenty of time to take in the exhibits later this evening. Please come with me." I follow him down a long corridor. "You're not supposed to be out and about, where guests can see you before the presentation."

I'm already making waves.

"May I take that?" He points to the large envelope I was presented at the door.

"Of course." I transfer it to him, and we wait at the end of a hallway where voices leak from behind a closed door.

He reads the crimson inked letters aloud. "Ms. Ainsley Prescott Clarke," then pulls a key from the envelope.

How did I miss that?

I follow him to a table with a dozen ring-sized boxes. Each box has a miniature gold lock. After a minute or so of trying my key, one clicks, and he extends the box. "For you, Ms. Clarke."

Nestled inside is a silver fox charm, childlike in design, save the glittering diamond eyes. "It looks like the Animal Crackers collection by Mignon Faget," I say, since I own several other charms my dad has gifted over the years.

He smiles. "It appears the fox is an appropriate choice for you, Ms. Clarke. While I can't disclose vendor sources, it was commissioned especially for this event."

He pulls the charm out of its box, which is attached to a delicate silver chain. "Each debutante is gifted an animal based on a quality we admire in that girl." He pauses. "May I?"

"Oh, sure." Holding up my hair, I wait as he fastens the necklace. "Are you going to tell me that reason, or is it another secret?" I don't know what character trait I possess that reflects a fox, but hey,

I'm certainly flattered to have it as my spirit animal. There are far worse creatures I could've been assigned.

"We don't present debutantes by their names; however, it is listed on the program next to the symbol of the animal you represent."

This is different.

"Don't worry, you'll be allowed to use your actual name after the presentation. It's a well-received tradition for Maskers to introduce their debs silently and symbolically."

He checks his watch, like he's done with our conversation.

"Okay, thank you so much. I'll just head in—"

"Your phone, please." He holds out his hand, and I freeze.

Why does he want my phone?

"I'm sorry, Ms. Clarke. No one's allowed to have a phone or camera at the presentation for the safety and privacy of our club. I'm afraid it's a nonnegotiable policy. Especially due to the postings on social media. We've been made aware of a certain account that is particularly interested in the affairs of our debs. Therefore, please keep in mind the nondisclosure agreement you signed. We hope you'll abide by our rules."

When I don't release my phone, his smile tightens.

How will I message UTG if I don't have my phone? Let alone take a photo or record anything for their story.

Months ago, all I wanted was to be a part of this Maskers Ball, yet tonight, the idea of having to participate without an agenda is more than a problem.

It will sink Violet.

"Okay. When and how do I get it back?"

He slips my phone into a lockbox, snapping it shut. "At the end of the presentation. There are tables at either side of the exit. You can retrieve it there." He holds the door open. "Have a lovely time, Ms. Clarke."

Once inside a small room off the main terrace, fifteen girls in white gowns give me the once-over. Each dons a mask and necklace, properly showcasing their assigned animal from the exclusive collection.

"Talk about cutting it close," a girl says to another, loud enough for me to hear. While it's bitchy, I know if things hadn't taken a turn to the deadly, I'd probably be in her same mindset. Checking out other girls' dresses. Fretting over my own. Planning how I should pace my drinks, so I could have fun, but not too much.

Those things no longer matter.

My stakes are much higher.

For me, for Violet, and whomever else I choose to throw under the bus tonight.

I run a hand over my tightly wound, twisted updo and catch a dude with a bear mask, staring. His mask is deep brown with a texture that resembles fur, but once the mask hits his nose, the design changes to a set of faux, pulled-back lips with a row of giant, pointed teeth.

Sinister as shit—*jeez.*

"Family call," I say, trying to explain my late arrival to the bear. I can't see his face, and since every other guy in the room is also in a black tux, there's not much to differentiate one dude from another.

"Do you approve of the fox I picked for you?" The bear steps forward, using his finger to trace my necklace.

I hold my breath, standing stock-still.

Holy hell.

"I seem to remember a certain young lady who liked to steal cupcakes from our backyard. Like a fox in a henhouse. When I saw the charm, I couldn't resist."

"*Cooper?* Oh God, it's you." After all these years, I should've recognized his voice or his eyes, but I didn't. Of course, when I finally received the invitation, I knew he had nominated me, but I never expected him to be my escort.

Not that anyone knows what goes on at Maskers.

He flashes a toothy grin that reminds me of Eli. "Yep. The one and only. Pleased to be your escort." He bows. "After all the strings I pulled to get you in, I'd expect you to look much happier."

"I am. I'm really, really happy. Thank you so much." I try to reassure him. "You didn't tell anyone, right?"

"Like my precious brother? Negative. As I told you before, we're only allowed one nomination. If Eli was privy to that, he may have ratted you out to Piper. He tends to babble when he drinks, but I don't have to tell you that." He cocks his head, pointing to the table of champagne. "Care for a libation?"

"No . . . well, actually sure." While I didn't plan on drinking, it may help calm my nerves, and right now, I can use all the help I can get.

Cooper resembles Eli from afar, but while Eli looms over me at six feet, Cooper is a few inches taller, and—though I'd never tell Eli —a bit more handsome. Over the last few years, I never knew for sure if Cooper was part of Maskers, but I confirmed my suspicions after spotting their symbol on his law school notebook.

Though no one is supposed to know about their symbol *or* the club, girls pass on that knowledge to friends during hushed whispers at school. So, once detected, it was game on. Any encounter with Cooper out of earshot of his family, I'd drop hints about nominating me as a deb for Maskers. I did it the entire year. And the year after that.

And here I am.

"Cheers." Cooper hands me a flute of champagne and we clink glasses. I down it in one gulp. "Jesus, woman. Good thing I brought extra." He smiles mischievously, and suddenly I feel like I may barf.

"Thanks," I speak basically to my second drink. "Cooper, I'm not trying to keep this from Eli or Piper, I'd just rather them not know *how* I got in." He gives me a look, like, *sure*, but I go on. "See, one day, during lunch at St. Claire's, a classmate mentioned that her father—former coach of NOLA Hurricanes—was getting a sub to coach against Arizona so he could attend a *secret* ball. She made a big deal about it. Said several bigwigs from our pro and college teams attended, and I knew it had to be Maskers. I figured if that were the case, surely, it was *the* deb event I needed to be presented at to make connections within the NFL, NBA, or any other relevant sports franchise."

"Don't have to convince me, Clarke. I get it. Why do you think I stay involved with this crap?"

"Possibly because of what we share in common?" I say, and he tilts his head. "We both like pretty girls."

He laughs. "I've never had a problem in that department, in case you haven't noticed." He winks. "Besides, quit worrying. Piper will probably move to Texas, or somewhere like that, to get a job in petroleum engineering. But you and your sports gig . . . definitely could pay off locally. So, yes to your underlying question. Most of the movers and shakers in the NOLA sports world *are* members and attendees of Maskers."

He adjusts his bow tie and checks the time on his Rolex. "Where was I . . . oh, yes. Wanna guess how I landed my summer job with McEllen Law that led to my recruitment?"

I nod. As long as Cooper is talking about himself, he's happy. Which means he won't want to bail before I can finish what I came to do.

"I prevented a drink from spilling on my future boss's daughter before the presentation. And bingo, I was a shoo-in. I'll be a full-time associate this May if all goes as planned. Like I said, this ball is the crown jewel of the deb world and, basically, our city."

That's another thing Cooper and I have in common. Ambition respects ambition, and he's certainly no slacker. Completing his undergrad at twenty, Cooper was accepted into an accelerated law degree program, and now, nearing twenty-three, his future is golden.

"I know why I'm here. I just feel wretched being so dishonest." Wringing my hands, I feel more than wretched. I'm terrified. Not just because I'm lying to my best friends *and* girlfriend. If tonight doesn't go perfectly, I'll have a whole societal firing squad ready to riddle me with the world's-worst-person, most-disloyal-friend, and dishonest-girlfriend bullets.

"Here. Have another drink, or put your glass down," Cooper says, but I tap my glass, and he fills it to the brim. When I finish, he takes it from me, grabbing my gloved hand. "Where are we going? Wait. Are we d-dancing?"

His strong arms pull me forward. "Cooper, we'll look crazy."

"Hence the masks, Clarke. Nobody knows who we are. We'll be *anonymously* crazy." He hums an obscure tune while shuffling us around. "Your mask is boss, by the way."

"Thanks." After a few minutes, I slip into his easygoing mood as we waltz around the tiny pocket of space we've created. I do love my mask. It covers half of my face in an ivory metal lace pattern that hovers over my cheek, then climbs like ivy over my right eye.

"You're one of the last to be presented. Dance to your heart's content," he says.

"It's not in alphabetical order?" I ask because if that's true, I might not have time to execute my strategy. I figured I'd hunt for scoop after being presented, but if I'm last, it could cut my free time in half.

He shakes his head. "The club assigned the order during a drab meeting I never paid a lick of attention to, so don't ask the reasoning behind it. All it meant to me was I'd need to find some-thing for us to do while we're back here." He stops. "Glad I picked you, Clarke. I doubt Piper dances this well. Nor is she as hot."

He tightens his grip around my waist, and I grind my teeth while we dance. I have no plans of shit-talking my best friend. Nor do I want to be here as his *date*, if that's where he thinks this is going. "I'm stepping all over your feet, so doubt I'm as good a dancer as you claim. You always were the flatterer, eh Cooper?"

"Ooh, my little fox has fangs. I'll make sure not to forget that." He grins. "C'mon, Clarke. Lighten up. Since the champagne is obviously not working, I may know a way for you to have a better time."

Warning lights flash in my brain, screaming *don't ask*, but I must. It could be the lead I'm searching for. "Oh? How exactly is that?"

"I may know a certain guy, girl, or group who can hook you up with something a little stronger than alcohol. That is . . . if you wanna swim with the great whites."

"Great whites?" I tilt my head.

"Yes. A little white powder to help power you through these shark-infested waters. Some of my friends did lines beforehand, and a few girls brought extra. May not snow in New Orleans, but we sure know how to make our own," Cooper whispers, like the walls have ears, or more likely, cameras. Which is certainly a possibility, considering the nature of this organization.

"I appreciate the offer, but not my speed," I snap. Then again, this is exactly what I need for my story. A high-society secret club where its debutantes don't just dress in white, they make sure to powder their noses in it.

With scoop like that, Violet won't be the top story of UTG ever again.

"I have to run to the bathroom. Be right back, okay?" Untangling myself, I dash off, brushing past the domino-masked guy and into an exhibit while searching for a bathroom.

I hear a ringtone. *Is that a phone?*

It sounds like it, but how? And where? I see no one. Just me and one angry puffer fish. But the ringing continues, so I stalk around the room until the flashing, blue-white screen of a cell phone catches my attention.

It's perched atop a *Fun Fact* sign explaining how the toxins of the puffer fish work.

Should I pick it up? Bring it to the table guy? I don't know how anyone got past him, but if it doesn't stop, someone may hear it and try to bust me for it.

Shit.

I pick it up. *Unknown Caller* lights up the screen.

"Who's there?" Domino-mask shouts from down the hall.

Double shit. "Hello?" I pause until the echo of footsteps disappears.

"Yes, hello. Who's this?" a voice questions.

"I'm a . . . the owner of this phone," I lie. "May I help you?"

"I'm sorry, this is *my* phone. I lost it earlier with my kids, and I really need it back. We're from out of town, and it contains our travel info. I've tried ringing it dozens of times to get someone to pick up. So, thank you."

"Yes, well, I-I, um, I found it by the puffer fish exhibit," I say. "I can leave it with the security guard if you'd like."

"Yes, please. You're such a lifesaver. Wait. Would you mind giving me your name in case they give me a problem at the desk?"

"Ainsley," I say. "I'll let them know I spoke with you. It's awful to lose your phone. No problem at all."

"I was hoping it was you, *Ainsley*." The tone of the caller changes.

The hell? I freeze.

"I need a favor from you, Ms. Clarke."

CHAPTER 16

"Who is this?" I demand, knowing who it might be, but hoping like hell it isn't. UTG said they'd be in touch, but how could they get a phone inside Maskers, or know for sure I'd randomly stumble over it?

Am I being watched?

I glance over my shoulder to see if anyone has followed me. Then survey the exhibit for surveillance cameras.

"You know I can't tell you that, Ainsley."

"It is you," I seethe. "I agreed to find you a story, but I didn't give you permission to *stalk* me. Besides, the party has barely started. I need more time. And"—I pause, gathering my courage—"if you repost Violet's story, the whole deal's off. Got it?"

While I'm scared shitless, it won't help if *they* know that. Better they believe they're dealing with a formidable opponent.

"Only if you get me a photo of something naughty. I'll give you twenty minutes to send it. Think you can do that? If I don't have what I need in that amount of time, your little deal is off. *You* got that?"

They hang up.

Checking the time, I click on the contact list, but there are no saved numbers. Just a blank phone which, at present, is my only ticket out. "I can do this." I tuck it into my strapless top while I track down a bathroom.

Drugs. Please have drugs.

Running my finger along the countertop for traces of powder, I find nothing.

I kick open a few stalls, scanning the innocuous bathroom, but again—nothing. Guess I'll have to sneak into the men's bathroom. When I turn to leave, I nearly collide with a girl entering. "Sorry." I take a step back, but this is no deb. She's wearing a pale blue gown with a gold crest pinned to her chest.

It's a den mother. "Hi," I say, nervously.

"Ms. Clarke, right?"

"Um, yes. And you're Sara, right?" I know she's the one who helped at my luncheon, but not only do I suck at remembering names, the two younger blondes—Sara and Sloane—look nearly identical.

She nods.

"Am I in trouble or something?" I ask, my heart galloping out of my chest.

She waves her hand. "I hardly think you're in trouble if you've landed yourself *here.* Must be an exemplary deb. Not to mention . . . stunning dress." She adjusts a slipped strap on her own gown. "Better hurry back or you truly might be in trouble. The presentation is moving at a fast clip."

"I'm last," I admit, "but thanks. I needed a bit more lipstick for my pictures." Turning back to the mirror, I fiddle through my purse, trying to kill time, hoping she won't offer to escort me back into the ball.

Her look-alike blasts in, babbling about a seating problem, and Sara bids me goodbye.

Thank you, universe.

I have fourteen minutes left.

What did Cooper say? *Swim with the great whites?*

It's the place I used to make a beeline to as a kid—the shark exhibit. Maybe his comment was meaningless, but it certainly could serve as a metaphor for cocaine.

It's worth a shot.

Once again, I blast through the hallways, but they're empty. And dark. Since Maskers rented the entire aquarium, it appears they've closed off the exhibits they're not using.

Freaking eerie.

The only light that's on is soft and blueish, illuminating from the tanks. Which means I can barely see, and my mask is making things way more difficult. I untie it, and keep walking until I hear a thud.

"*Shh.* C'mon. We need to get back." A girl's voice slaps around the exhibit.

Using the wall as a guide, I follow the sound until I reach a corner.

I have no choice but to stop.

"The peacock chick is on deck. We have plenty of time," a guy says, like he doesn't give a shit about the presentation. Though I can barely make out his form, he appears to be leaning over, and I hear sniffing. "That's what I'm talking about!" he roars. "Legit shit."

My eyes start to adjust to the light: *One girl. Two boys.*

"At least *she* got a bird. I got a freaking horse," the girl complains.

The guys laugh.

"Couldn't be because your dad owns the top racehorses, hmm? How is that a bad thing? You practically live at the racetrack," the dude in a jester mask scolds.

"Just because I *ride* them doesn't mean I want to embody one." She holds back her long hair, dipping down to take a snort.

Racehorses? Holy shit—it's Rachel Levinson. Though she went to a different high school, we used to run in the same circles. Plus, I follow her on social media. She's on the equestrian team for her college. And those guys aren't wrong. Last year, her dad's horse won the Triple Crown.

But now, thanks to me, she'll be featured on Under the Gown doing drugs.

I make sure the phone is silenced and open the camera app, placing one hand over the other to steady my shaking.

I don't want to do this.

One photo. For Violet. The drugs are there. It's obvious what they're doing. I snap, and a photo fills my screen. That's it. I can go—

"C'mon. It's getting late," the taller guy pleads.

"No way, bruh. I'm not wasting three lines."

"We can come back. We'll get shitcanned if she's late for her presentation."

Their footsteps clod past and I shrink into the shadows. Holding my breath, I wait a few seconds longer, then step out. I need to go, but what if the photo is blurry?

I should take one more for absolute proof.

Inching closer, I zoom in on the white lines, shaking my head at the offending substance *and* my offensive behavior. I never thought I'd feel this way, but—*I'm ready for deb season to end.*

I snap, but the picture is shadowy. I need to use the flash —fantastic.

I snap again, and a clicking sound echoes around the room.

The hell?

I flip the phone on and off vibrate. I'm not sure that's the problem, but what else could explain the noise?

The phone rings.

Ducking behind the back of the exhibit, I hover my finger over the green button. I need to get this over fast. Cooper will kill me if I don't hurry back. I press the button. "I have it."

"I'll text the number to send the photo to. It's a burner phone. Don't get any wise ideas."

"Whatever." At this point, I'm way angrier than scared. Typing in the number, I hit *send.* "That's it, right? I'm done with this shitty deal."

"Not exactly. I have a photo for you in return. My, my, don't you look foxy."

Pulling the phone from my face, an image appears, and I gasp. It's a close-up of my face, inches from the lines of cocaine.

Someone must have followed me and took this photo.

The voice continues. "Here's your deal. Offer one—the photo of *you* gets posted, but I don't think that bodes well for your future. Not only will you be labeled as a coke baby, your face is clear as day at an event which prides itself on anonymity. A grave social grenade, wouldn't you agree?"

"Option two?" I ask, the muscles in my jaw tightening.

"Offer two means the photo you took will be posted and everyone will bear responsibility. What will Rachel do when her family learns of her rehab failure again?"

"Why are you doing this? What do you get out of fucking up everyone's lives?"

"I think you've got that wrong. Tonight, it's *you* fucking up three lives, Ms. Clarke."

"I did this so you'd stop tormenting Violet." I lower my voice. "Can't you please drop this? What is petty drama worth at the end of the day?"

"It's worth everything to me. One of you needs to feel the consequences for your evil deeds." They pause. "Look at what Rachel did with her freedom. She went to rehab because she got in a car wreck after driving high and nearly killing someone. How many lives do you stupid debutantes have to fuck up before people stop bowing to the next batch of pretty faces?"

"Okay, maybe Rachel made some poor decisions, but I didn't do anything. Nor did Violet."

"That's where you're wrong. You made a deal with a known devil. How innocent can you be?"

"Violet's medical records were leaked. If you had taken the time to investigate, you'd realize she isn't the villain you think she is."

"Doesn't matter. Even if there *is* a valid excuse for her violent display of anger, she's guilty of three deadly sins. Pride, greed, and gluttony. Flaunting her mountain of Anderson money at that obnoxious party. Not exactly an admirable character trait."

If this is the person behind Under the Gown, they're more than psycho, and I'm done. "Last time I checked, everyone is guilty of something," I say. "Climbing on your UTG soapbox to become their holy messenger doesn't give you immunity. In case you haven't heard, karma's a bitch."

"I'm growing weary. Of this. And you. Pick an option. Who's to be held responsible? *You* or *them?*"

"Wait—"

"If you don't decide, I'll post both."

"I-I didn't do any drugs. I did what you asked."

I can't go down for this.

"Use the first photo," I fume, while my gloves tighten around my balled fists.

"Told you! Whoever thought debutantes should dress in white was out of their minds. None of you are pure." They laugh.

"I did my part, so no more games. Deal?"

"Ainsley!" It's Cooper. And he sounds close.

"Drop the phone in the trash. If someone finds it, or you speak a word to anyone, I'll post both photos." The psycho on the phone talks fast. "Have a wonderful presentation, Ainsley. Don't forget to smile."

"There you are!" Cooper grabs my hand as I tuck the phone behind my back. "Where the hell have you been?"

"I'm sorry, Coop." I turn on the charm. He's obviously pissed, and I don't need him asking questions. "I, um . . . well, I kinda got lost. Turns out, downing several glasses of champagne and taking your mom's Xanax before a nerve-wracking ball can lead to a lack of directional skills." To fake being tipsy, I wobble dramatically.

He steadies me. "Whoa. No wonder you didn't want any more additives to your present mixture. Should've just said so." His face softens. "It's almost our turn. Put your mask on, and we'll silently announce you to the people who matter. Like I promised, I've lined up several heavy hitters for you to meet. Does Rob Larkins ring a bell?"

"Obviously," I say. Rob Larkins is co-owner of our football team, and a few weeks ago, I would've sold my spleen to get a one-on-one with him. "Wow, can't wait."

Trashing the phone, I babble mindlessly on the way back to the main room, only—*I'm not drunk*. At this point, I don't have any nerves left to medicate. What I am is angry, exhausted, and heavily besieged with guilt. I no longer care about the spotlight, these people clapping, meeting Rob Larkins, or any of Cooper's heavy hitters. What I care about is the fact that whoever is behind UTG is obviously insane, and I have no guarantee they won't repost Violet's information or my photo.

But what's even worse than that—I'm keeping secrets from the people I care most about—Piper, Eli, and Violet.

Bravo, Clarke.

Now, even if I attempt to tell the truth, I'll have to admit that I lied. And if we're unearthing all my lies, I'd have to explain to Eli how this past summer, I slept with his brother to get an invite to this stupid ball.

I curtsy at the small *X* marks and promenade around the room.

Good thing I have a mask on.

Turns out, I still can pull off the debutante smile while crying.

CHAPTER 17

THE NEXT MORNING
JANUARY 7

New Orleans is a small city. So small, you might skip the two closest grocery stores because not only do you know the schedules of certain friends, parents, and relatives, you also know when they show to poach the newest batch of Ponchatoula strawberries. It's a place where if someone asks where you went to school, they mean high school. Regardless of your age—eighteen or eighty—they'll cross reference that fact to gauge your social status. Then happily regale you with tales and names of former students and teachers if they happen to have attended, or know someone who did.

Their small talk is masking tape. A way to attach to your face and name whatever label they decide to write and stick on your forehead. In this city, where you go to high school matters more than your college, your profession, or any other screaming accolade you may accomplish along the way.

High school sticks.

So does drama.

The point is, whenever you want to hide from the world, you pick a grocery store far away to ensure no one will know you. For me, that's the West Bank. Forty minutes out of the way and exactly the reason I offer to run errands for my family.

As I search for the correct brand of crab boil—Zatarain's—my phone buzzes.

Piper must've found a way to outmaneuver my *Do Not Disturb* feature because this is her tenth text, and I know why she's text-bombing me. She keeps notifications on for UTG, which means, she saw their latest story:

Who Needs White Lies When White Lines Are So Much Sweeter?

I don't bet on horses, but I'd bet that the owner's daughter of the last Triple Crown horse is going back to rehab.

Rachel, I'd say I had higher hopes for you, but I hate to lie. Speaking of things I hate, how is it that two gentlemen put on suspension by their fraternity for not knowing what NO means are partying it up like they shouldn't already be behind bars? Karma almost took care of one of them. Guess your brakes don't know when to stop either. Right, Gus?

I don't need to see the photo. I'm the one who took it. I'm so guilty, even my skin feels like it wants to crawl off my tainted body because it's itching so terribly, no matter how much I scratch, it just won't stop.

Neither will these headlines. Or the fallout that's sure to follow. *First Cooper. Now this.*

Sliding to the ground, I rest my head between my knees,

blinking away the images from last night and the buried flashbacks from that numb-induced, passionless night with Cooper this past summer.

I don't care who sees me at this point. My legs won't stand even if I willed them to do so. Which I don't.

I deserve to be on the ground. Maybe lower.

What am I supposed to tell people? That I allowed one of my closest friend's brother to charm himself into my pants? And I did it as the "convincing" part he'd hinted at wanting, but never fully asked me for. Or explain that when it was over, I wanted to rub sanitizer over my entire body so I could forget about the person who touched it. Only to have the never-ending thought of—*you wanted this*—fly back in my face.

The saddest part is, I did it willingly. All in the name of opening up some hypothetical golden door. One I'll probably never get to see the other side of because I'm too busy choking on the guilt of ruining another person's life.

My phone buzzes. "Piper, did you not get the hint after I didn't answer your first thirty-three calls?" I huff, wobbling upright and dusting off my jeans.

"Bitch, I'm tenacious. That's why you love me so much. Besides, you have a shit-ton of explaining to do," she rattles. "I spent half the night with Eli and Blair as designated driver to the world's most love-sick couple, all because of your dirty little secret. Then . . . *Rachel?* Tell me that wasn't you."

"I'm both sorry and grateful to tell you it was." I rap myself on the forehead. "Please, please, don't repeat that. Like ever. I feel so awful. And Pipes, this Under the Gown shit . . . it's worse than we thought. They called me and gave me no choice. If I didn't narc on Rachel, they were going to post one of me instead."

"One of you doing what?" Her voice raises.

"Drugs. Or that's what anyone would've thought had they posted their photo. See, at one point I had to take a close-up of the lines. Someone followed me because they took one of *me,* bending over the drugs. It was a set-up. If I didn't send in my photo, they said I'd be deemed Coke Queen of the Deb World."

"Fuck, Ainsley. You didn't recognize anyone at the ball? Or have a hint who could've been on that phone? Not many people know about that ball. Or have the ability to infiltrate it. It had to be an inside job. Maybe your escort followed you?"

My mind flashes to Cooper. "I didn't recognize anyone," I lie. "And my escort came looking for me because I was almost late for the presentation. I doubt he had time to pull it off."

"What about Gus's livestream? You saw that shit, right? Über-creepy. Like, I'm-not-sure-it-was-an-accident level of creepy."

Yes, the icing on the current shit cake. Gus—one of the guys in the photo—who, for whatever reason, decided to livestream his drunk-driving karaoke session of a bad rendition of a Drake song. It was filmed right after the ball with the other dude, Thomas. Only minutes later, their nightmarish song turned into an actual night-mare when Gus yelled, "Bruh, my brakes! I can't slow—"

Then it ended.

Thank God they're both alive, but it was beyond awful. Of course, UTG didn't mind calling it out as karma. "Yes, Conn—I mean, Conn-*ie* texted it to me after I got home. Pretty scary, right?"

"Who's *Connie?*"

"A deb. From last night." My stomach twists. I hate lying to Piper. And each lie is getting bigger and stickier. If I don't find a way to stop soon, it will land me in that web I'd been spinning with no hope for salvation or redemption.

"Scary, yes, but want the real scoop?"

"*Sure?*" I squeak.

"Apparently those two douches convinced a freshman at their frat party to drink *way* too much. And the rest is a headline everyone should see published, but never will on the Daily News," she bites out.

I understand why. Sexual abuse is so common at college, everyone lives in constant fear of falling into that trap because there's never an easy way out. Nor is justice usually served. She continues, "Yeah, one of those infamous he said/she said things. Except in this case, it's two guys' testimonies against one girl. Naturally, it got swept under the good old boys' college rug."

"Naturally," I say. "How do you know this? Is she local? Is she a deb?"

"I Googled it after the post. Not much to read. One local school paper reported it in Charleston. I don't know who she is because she probably chose to remain anonymous." Piper lowers her voice. "This may sound awful, but, like, maybe those two assholes deserve it?"

"If they're guilty, yes, but I'm hardly the person to judge another's character these days."

While I had hoped my post would do nothing more than a bit of reputation smearing, which is bad enough, it did far worse. Choking up, I try to clear my throat. "If the brake thing is true, I don't know what to think."

But I do know what to think.

I'm the one who sent the photos. So if there's any chance this wasn't accidental—*I'm an unwitting accomplice.*

"Dude, I'm not suggesting you cut their brakes. But maybe steer clear of any more deals. No matter how noble your motives were, someone could've been hurt way worse than what happened. This shit is getting serious."

"It is." I pause. "Pipes, speaking of deals, you know how UTG made that post about inviting girls to their VIP party?"

"Do I even want to hear this?" She groans. "What did you do now, Ainsley?"

"I didn't do anything. Well, nothing new," I admit. "But after I got home last night, UTG sent a DM thanking me for the photo.

They said it earned me a spot at their party, and details would follow."

"Yeah—okay. That's not weird. They ask for scoop from a party, and when you give it to them, they invite you to theirs. I guess congratulations are in order for making their cut. Maybe they think you're good for more likes, or something like that."

She sounds annoyed. Not that I can blame her.

"The whole thing was super sus," I say. "When they messaged me, they sounded surprised I even sent the photo in. Like we didn't have a whole conversation on that creepy burner phone. It freaked me out. Wait—hold on." I move the phone away from my ear. "Okay, maybe I'm losing my mind or hallucinating, but I swear I just saw Hunter Boyd in this grocery store."

"Where are you?"

I zoom my cart around a young couple. "The West Bank. At Boyd's Mart." I laugh as realization hits. "Of course it's him. His parents own the store—duh. Which means I'm not hallucinating but could be experiencing early-onset memory problems."

"More like brain fog from stress," Piper says. "But isn't he supposed to be at some love shack with Laney? Since you're there, and he's there, march up and ask about her. Maybe they just got back. Fate set you on this path. Hopefully this one right can cancel out last night's wrong."

I wish it were that simple, but it's not. "Okay, I'll interrogate him. But stay close. And watch for my texts."

Careening through the store, I search for Hunter. He'll be easy to recognize because of his fleur-de-lis tattoo, which, after less than a year of dating, he added Laney's name in crappy script underneath. At least, that's what I've been told.

When I spot him, I speed my cart toward him, close my eyes, and collide into his stack of boxes. "Oh my gosh! I'm so sorry!" Scooping up some cereal boxes, I flash an apologetic smile. "Wait . . . *Hunter?*"

He looks me over while kicking the boxes with his worn Converse. "Who are you?"

"Ainsley. Laney and I went to St. Claire's together. I've seen you around at some games and stuff, senior year."

His eyes narrow. "Maybe? I heard her mention you a few times." He stops and scratches his crotch. *Gross.* I can't fathom what Laney sees in this guy.

I wait for him to stop tending to his personal problems, and he finally continues. "I'd say thanks for stopping by, but you kinda fucked up my chances of finishing on time for my raid."

"Let me help." I start placing boxes on the shelves. "How is Laney these days? We were surprised she skipped Crescent's presentation."

"You know Laney. She gets busy with stuff and the blinders go on."

I want to say *busy paying attention to her boyfriend who's angry she might put more energy into deb season than him?* But I don't. Because technically, it's gossip, and I have no way of knowing if it's true. While I don't need any more hexes cast my way, I do need to gain clarity.

"She was too busy for her presentation?" I ask, raising my eyebrows. "Laney's been planning for this since freshman year. She was fruit loops for this stuff."

He absentmindedly rubs her tattooed name, and I cringe. "I'm sure you'll smack into her in one of those fancy white dresses soon enough. Actually, she's out buying one today."

"A new dress? Really? She's back in town? Ooh, is she going to Le Orleanians Cotillion?" I cross my arms, bracing for what I'm about to throw his way because I've decided, hell on it, time to test his reaction. "Um, word is . . . you don't want her in any presentations."

His hand pauses on a box. "Where'd ya hear that?"

"Riley." I try to maintain eye contact, but he looks away. "She said you and Laney had been fighting over the fact that she was too obsessed with deb season."

"That little bitch. She eavesdrops on one argument, and she thinks she can judge me? Did you know I lost my dad? Hmm?" Hunter draws closer, his voice shaky. "He had cancer. So yep. Why should I be happy about my girlfriend planning a fucking party while I'm arranging a funeral? Screw Riley—I was mad for one day. I forgave Laney. Just like I always do."

"I didn't know any of that. I'm really sorry." I draw in a breath when he steps away. "I didn't come to start shit. I'm just trying to get in touch with Laney to ask about some work stuff. We're in the same major." I hesitate, trying to decide how much I should tell him about my party. "I don't know if you heard, but I got this creepy post that said *Laney sends her regards* at my luncheon. That, coupled with her not showing for, well, anything, has a few of us concerned."

Hunter starts restacking boxes. "Like I said, she's out buying a dress. Whatever you want to talk about, maybe do it at your next presentation. Can I get back to work, please?"

"Sure, sorry about the collision and your dad."

I text Riley.

A

> Any updates on Laney?

While I wait, I check for other texts.

VIOLET

> Hope you had a nice time at the rush party. Blair showed me photos of Eli. She said she never ran into you.

> You're probably hungover. Or sleeping. But are we going to this? I kinda want to go, but if my girlfriend is unavailable, guess I can take Blair.

Under the text, there's a photo of the invitation to Jane Marconi's murder mystery party.

Damn.

It's tomorrow night and I'd totally forgotten about it. With everything going on, I hadn't paid attention to the very calendar I'd chastised my family over. Or the one on my phone.

A

> Had to bail on toga party. Yes to Jane's party. Come hang later, please? I want to watch a movie with my cute girlfriend.

VIOLET

> Charming. Text a time. <3

I head for an aisle with popcorn and snacks because maybe I can still manage to make something positive out of these last twenty-four hours. Which means I need to buy enough junk food to fix the problem.

My phone buzzes.

I try to think of a witty reply to send Violet, but it's not her:

RILEY

> She texted yesterday. She and Hunter are having too much fun in Georgia to come home. Sounds like the vacay is working.
> :)

My mouth falls open.

If I'd been anywhere else but in East Jesus, looking at the very boy who is supposed to be in a different state with a girl he claims is out buying a new debutante dress, this would be the world's most reassuring news.

If Laney is not with Hunter, where the hell is she? And why is he lying?

CHAPTER 18

JANE MARCONI'S MURDER MYSTERY PARTY
JANUARY 8

When she's not sprawled across my bed, Piper can be found in her next favorite spot—my closet. "It's weird, right?" she says.

"Which part? The part that Hunter is lying, or that UTG hasn't posted a slanderous post in"—I scroll through their posts—"a full twenty-four hours." Pushing my foot into the carpet, my hanging chair is set into motion while Piper sifts through my outfits.

"Yes, that, but also because of this *murder* mystery party during the sketchiest season of debutante history, like, ever." Piper frowns. "Or the freaking theme. A twenties mafia party by the girl whose family *is* the actual mafia?"

"I'm pretty sure they're no longer active. Besides, at least *you* get to wear a dress," I complain. "I'd rather be a mistress than a detective."

Jane Marconi had hired a high-profile screenwriter to craft the script for her party. She included a list of assigned roles and lines for each guest in their invitation. But since plus-ones are never static, it stated they'd be assigned minor roles at the door. Which means Eli, Blair, and Jamie get to have fun, while Piper, Violet, and I will be roped into one colossal acting disaster waiting to happen.

There's a reason I never joined Drama Club.

"Don't forget. I'm Scarlett. Your mistress, idiot." Piper throws a shoe that I dodge. "Apparently, your long nights at the precinct and frequent visits to French Quarter dives have left you stumbling along with me, an up-and-coming female entrepreneur."

"More like the madame I'm supposed to bust, but instead, fall under your magical spell. Not even remotely cliché." I grimace. "But hey, you're welcome to whisk me away from my wife at any time, considering Jane thinks it's hilarious to assign Leslie to that role."

"I didn't know that." She winces. "Have you spoken to her since Violet's party?"

I shake my head. "I have zero to say after what she did. But I'm pretty sure Violet is still supremely pissed. She's been acting weird lately."

"Nothing in our lives is normal right now. Please, define *weird*?"

"Well, like last night, she seemed really distant." I give my chair another push. Though there have been no actual fights, a subtle tension has left me overthinking every weird glance or tight smile Violet makes.

"Didn't you say she's doing a double major?"

I nod.

"I know we're on break, but she did mention getting a jump on spring classes. Plus, she's doing that environmental study thingy, remember? Half of that girl's workload makes you and me look like total slackers." Piper grins. "Perhaps you're overanalyzing, Ainsley?"

"Okay, I'll chill, but did you know her role is the don's wife? She sent a picture of the fake wedding ring Jane mailed her. All I got was some stupid plastic badge."

"And all I got was exactly nothing," Piper exclaims. "Can I just kill Jane at the party? Or find her fancy scriptwriter and tell him we need a revision."

Putting my palms together, I pretend to read a book. "Jane, the widowed wife of the late Mr. Howard has graciously invited us into her home to commemorate his unfortunate demise and potentially seek justice." I recite the line from our invitation.

"How and *why* did you remember that shit?"

"Because I want to win, dearest Scarlett." I bow. "Do you think Jamie will lend me his jacket? Luke's and Eli's are too big. I need to rock my inner detective tonight."

Leaning against a telephone pole, I wait for Violet to get out of her car. "Excuse me, ma'am. Don't you know it's dangerous to walk alone in the French Quarter?"

"I'm sure my husband will be around shortly to help." She shifts into her assigned role for the party, then takes my hand, giving me a once-over. "My, don't you look dashing."

"As do you. I *love* that dress." She's wearing a light-pink sequined dress with a fringed hem and matching headband that vibes perfectly with her dramatic eyeliner.

"Oh, this silly thing? It has nothing on your suspender and tie combo." She slips a finger under my strap, and lets it snap. "Oops, sorry, *Dick*."

I laugh while she adjusts my fedora. "Detective *Richard* Conley is here to win, so hold on to your stockings, dollface."

"I wouldn't expect anything less. But Eliza Gambino would never rat out her husband, you cad." She winks. "Or maybe I will. Another mystery for you to solve, eh?"

Dropping the act, I wrap her in a hug. "Before we walk in, can I say how much I miss you, Ms. Anderson? Though you'll be fake married to a mafia don in a few minutes, I've won just by being with you."

A ghost of a smile appears before she flattens her expression. *That. She's doing it again.*

She grabs my chin and tilts it down. "Kiss me." Hanging onto my tie, we melt into a kiss, and the panic I'd been feeling about our relationship starts to fade. She nibbles my bottom lip, then presses her fingers into my stomach to keep me at a distance. "I hope that's a good enough reason to keep *me* on your mind, instead of some silly prize," she says, breathlessly.

"Prize?" I adjust my tie. "Do you think being paired with Leslie will have me running back to crazy land?"

"I wish she was my only problem." She grabs my hand. "C'mon, we'll be late."

I don't know what problem she's talking about, but I let the comment drop while we duck into a narrow French Quarter shop entrance. Inside, *I Love NOLA* shirts hang on the wall and alligator snow globes litter the shelves. A typical souvenir shop.

Violet glances around. "Think we're in the right place?"

"Ever seen a cashier wearing a Tag Heuer watch?" I point at the sliver of platinum peeking from the disheveled guy's sleeve.

"Good mouth and eye. Nice job, Dick." She squeezes my arm, then struts over to the register. "Excuse me. May I have a root beer float? My husband *Tony* said yours are the best in the city."

"Ah, Mrs. Gambino! Your husband is waiting in the parlor. Please let me escort you in." He shrugs off his jacket, glances over his shoulder, then kicks the wall behind him.

A door cracks open.

My mouth drops. "Was that in your briefing?" I glance between the two of them.

"Why, wanna swap roles?" Violet laughs, seemingly thrilled she's more informed than me at this juncture.

Holding hands, we follow the man down dimly lit stairs and through a winding, brick-walled hallway. "Mrs. Howard was gracious enough to host us tonight, but given the circumstances, she's asked everyone to remain discreet. Speakeasies were quite popular during prohibition with families like yours, Mrs. Gambino."

Violet nods and he opens the door. Music floods in. "Enjoy yourselves, but be careful. No need to add another ghost to this haunted town."

Stepping inside, it's like we've arrived at the movie set for *The Great Gatsby.* A big band graces the stage while people bustle about, decked in replica twenties costumes. "Can you two please sign in?" A den mother holds out a clipboard.

When she looks up, I notice it's Sara. The last time I'd seen her was at Maskers.

She shoots a shy smile, and I do the same.

Before we finish, another den mother shows, whispering something about a *situation.* Sara grabs her phone and prepares to head out. She probably needs to remove a drunk guest like they did at Collins Charbonnet's bash, or handle any number of problems that *can* and *will* go wrong at large gatherings like this. The debutante clubs stressed we should exhibit "a certain level of decorum at our parties," and though Piper and I initially thought the concept lame, the den mothers have come in handy on more than one occasion.

Too bad none of them stopped Leslie.

Sara calls out, "Have fun, girls. If you need anything, I'll be floating around. Look for the pin." She taps a gold stenciled brooch with the letters *CC,* for Crescent Club, pinned to her dress.

We make it three steps before Piper's arms encircle me. "Dearest Richie. I've been searching for you everywhere. Sorry we couldn't meet earlier, but you know how busy I get with my *girls.*"

"Scarlett, please. We're in public." I shush Piper, aka Scarlett. While it's fun seeing everyone in their outfits, I'm more than bummed that Violet has left for her own assignment. And I'm still upset Jane paired me with Leslie instead of Violet. Maybe it's harmless role-playing, but considering how tense the situation has been, it won't be easy keeping my emotions in check.

For me. Or Violet.

I go off-character. "Seriously, Pipes, how'd you figure out that door? Also, did Violet seem off to you? She's still acting weird."

"Yes, the door. Cool, right? When Jamie tried to buy candy and was rejected for a fourth time, the dude showed us in. Since Eli and Blair were being totally obnoxious, I think he wanted to get rid of us."

She turns to face me. "And can you please stop the romantic woes for a millisecond? The vibes here are insane. Flappers. Swing music. Sexy twenties to the max. Maybe the Marconis are still active, after all?"

I shrug. "Considering they have access to a hidden speakeasy and money to pull it off, guess it's a possibility. And yes, I'll try. Where's the gang?"

She points across the room to where Jamie is donned in a tuxedo, complete with a white shirt and bowtie. We wave and he shoots back a nervous smile. "Blair was assigned as one of my *girls*, so I sent her to mingle. And Eli, well, he's Tony Gambino, mafia don and Violet's hubby for the night."

"*Eli*? Seriously? Like *how*? Major roles are for debs. Not their guests."

"The role was assigned to *Laney.*" She gives me a look. "Since she didn't show *again*, Jane wrangled him into playing the part. Naturally, he didn't protest."

Of course Laney's not here, which further proves Hunter was lying. "Considering everything that comes out of Hunter's mouth is BS, who knows where she is. But whatever she's texting Riley seems to be enough to keep her police-chief father satisfied. So, I guess there's that."

"Yes. More reason to enjoy the party." Piper hoists up her garter belt. "You can go back to playing real PI tomorrow. I promise to keep an ear out for any relevant gossip." She pauses. "Which I'll be pursuing from afar. See ya!"

"Wait, Piper—"

I whirl into Leslie, which explains why Piper ran off. "Oh, Mrs. Conley! My beloved wife. I was just inquiring about your where-abouts." I grit out my lines.

She flutters her glittery, fake wedding ring. "Yes, here I am. What's a wife to do without her husband?" Leslie replies in full character mode, but at least the role-playing will be easier than having to actually *talk* to her.

"I'm sure you find ways to occupy yourself, darling," I answer coolly. "Be a gem and introduce me around, yes? There are some unaccounted-for alibis on the day of Mr. Howard's drowning. I'd like to get them checked off my list."

As detective, I've been tasked with investigating Mr. Howard's drowning upon the request of his widow (aka Jane), who's convinced someone killed her husband and staged the accident. Since most of tonight's guests were reported as attendees of the gala with the deceased, anyone is fair game.

She motions for me to follow, and we interrogate several witnesses, neither of us deviating from the script. We approach our final one. "I find it curious you were out sailing, considering the only thing you've been reported to *swim* in is whiskey and gin," I say.

The line is cheesy, but the boy's face pales, and Leslie and I laugh. While I'm still upset with her, our roles are fun, and it makes me even more pumped to solve this pretend murder because, if nothing else, being here is turning out to be a useful distraction from my own stressful life.

"Can everyone gather in the ballroom?" a voice booms, so we crowd into an expansive marble-tiled room with glittering chande-liers and arched windows dressed in blue silk.

"Hello, darlings! Thank you all for coming!" Jane drawls from atop the stair landing, stunning in a pale-yellow satin gown. "Though we're meeting under somber circumstances, my husband was one for celebrating life. So pick a partner and let's have a dance in his honor!"

People start to pair up. "Wait. Before you hurry off, I'd like to remind everyone to stay in character. If you don't, there could be consequences." She laughs and the music cranks up.

Leslie tugs me to the dance floor, and we waltz in silence. When Eli glides past with Violet, Leslie's face reddens. "I don't know who I dislike more. You, your *girlfriend*, or Jane for pairing us at this torture fest!"

I start to craft a snarky comeback, but I stop. "Can we both admit that while we agreed to be friends, we never actually figured out how to do that? You know, move forward with zero strings." I pause. "But I'd like to." Her eyes meet mine. "Move forward. As your friend. I'm sorry things got so twisted."

I never intended to apologize to Leslie, but tonight, I'm feeling extra guilty over the secrets I've been hiding about Cooper and UTG, and I'd really like to finish out deb season on a positive note, if possible.

"About that"—she bows her head—"I shouldn't have leaked her records. I'm also sorry." She offers a weak smile. "When I overheard those people talking about Violet at Crescent saying she had a shady past, I figured whatever it was, it might be enough to stop you from seeing her."

"Would you mind telling me—"

The lights flicker and the room blackens. I don't know if this is part of Jane's skit, but people start screaming, so I pull Leslie closer.

A couple slams into us, then bounces off.

"Relax." Leslie laughs. "I tampered with the lighting, but I can't say anymore. You'll have to figure out the rest on you own."

When the lights turn back on, everyone chatters excitedly, and

Leslie's mouth falls open. "Well, shit. Maybe I shouldn't have followed the script?"

She points to the stairs where Jane—Mrs. Howard—is collapsed with a knife handle shining from the middle of her back.

CHAPTER 19

"Step back!" I flash my badge, hoping this is part of the act because it's not in my script, and the sooner I solve this, the faster I'll get to hang with Violet.

"Jane?" I crouch to avoid the pool of hopefully fake blood. "Tell me you're not *dead-dead.*" She unfurls her hand, revealing a piece of paper. "Got it. Nice acting."

Meet me at the stairs. To make sure no one notices, create a distraction by announcing a dance. If not, you'll have secrets spilled on top of the blood.

A black fingerprint is smudged in the corner of the note. "There's been a murder!" I yell. "Mrs. Howard's been stabbed! Lock the doors!" I wing my lines, but, thankfully, bingeing true crime shows is paying off.

"Detective, I'm Officer Hale." Madison K appears, wearing a suit so saggy, it partially hides the police badge clipped to her belt. "How may I assist you?"

Her outfit is worse than mine, I think, trying to hold back a laugh. "Secure the weapon and make sure nobody goes upstairs," I say, spying a trail of bloody shoe prints leading up the staircase. "If I'm not back in ten minutes, come find my body."

Following the prints, the hallway splits. *Left or right?*

Using my phone's flashlight, I continue until I find an open door. "Um, hello? Detective coming in!" Though this is pretend, it's still creepy as hell.

Inside the bedroom, a window is open, but not wide enough for a person to pass through. I search for a light switch, but a shadowy figure beats me to it. "Detective. It's me. Tony Gambino."

"Well, if it isn't the don himself. How did you get past Madison, Eli?"

Eli thumbs his chest, like he's trying to warn me people are within earshot.

"Oh, yes, what I meant to say is, *Mr. Gambino*, how did you get past the *officer* on the stairs?"

"I paid her off." He pauses. "May I be blunt? My businesses are not always on the up-and-up, so if a spotlight is shined on this, people may start to suspect me. I simply can't have that."

"Mrs. Howard was murdered," I say. "I can't make them *unsee* that."

"If that's your final answer, I may be forced to reveal who's been seeing Scarlett these days." He raises an eyebrow. "Clearly, it benefits us both to close this case swiftly. Find the killer; you'll get a nice kickback, eh?"

Eli doesn't miss a beat or break the fourth wall once, and I must admit, I'm impressed. Before I can tell him so, a loud thud shakes the wall.

I grab his arm. "Did you hear that?"

"How could I not?" He drops the mafia machismo. "Like for *real*, Ainsley. Do you think that guy was messing around about this place being haunted?"

"He told y'all that too?" I laugh. "I think it's part of his script, but there's no such thing as an unhaunted house in New Orleans.

I'm more concerned about hidden doors. Quick, help me look around."

Tracing the seams in the wallpaper, we feel for cracks.

Nothing.

Eli lifts the mattress and pulls out a leather journal. "Someone went through the trouble to hide this. Guess we're supposed to read it."

I eye him suspiciously. "Maybe. After you go downstairs. You're still a suspect. I have no way of knowing if you plan to kill me next. Give me that journal."

Eli leaves and I settle in a chair. There's one entry, dated two weeks from the date of the alleged crime. It states that they were meeting Mr. Howard at the fountain, where they first confessed their love, which means Mr. Howard had a lover. These clues are cake. If Mrs. Howard discovered the affair, she had motive to drown him.

I compare the note with the handwriting in the journal.

Same.

If I can find Mr. Howard's lover—game over. Too bad things in my own life aren't this simple to solve.

As I exit the room, there's another thud. This time, fainter.

Weird.

In the next room, there's an open dumbwaiter with a pair of bloody shoes stuffed in the corner under a paint tarp. There's also a black thumbprint on the button of the dumbwaiter. Exactly like the one on the note.

My phone buzzes. Another post.

A murder within the Marconi family? Who would've guessed? Kidding. Poor Jane has to play dead while everyone plays their part. Hope they find out who did it

**before someone pulls a Britney, and "Oops . . . they did it
again."**

Downstairs, Madison K is still holding the knife with two
fingers, trying not to touch the blood. "Care to share your findings?" I ask.

"One stab wound. She bled out." She smirks.

While Madison would *never* miss a party, especially a deb party,
this is one she'd probably never repeat. At least, not if assigned her
present role and outfit.

"I've cleared most of the guests. The ones I haven't are in the
parlor." She smacks a wad of gum. "Oh, and some staff said they
saw Scarlett acting suspiciously during the dance. Here." She picks
up the note. "You dropped this."

"Thanks." I clap Madison on the back, laughing when her tie
swings in the air and whacks her on the nose.

On the way to find Piper, my stomach grumbles. I'm starving,
and at this point, I'd much rather eat, drink, and hang with Violet
than win this game.

When I find Piper, she's still in full-blown Scarlett mode.
Though I'm ready to call it quits, she seems to be having a blast,
and it's not fair for me to spoil her fun. "Scarlett, someone said *you*
were acting suspicious. I hope I've cheated on my wife for a good
reason, and *not* for a murderer."

"Just what are you insinuating, Dick? The only illegal thing I do
is offer fair, equitable work." Piper nearly flubs her line, trying *not*
to laugh.

"Get on with it," I say.

"My, aren't you rude! And, yes, one of my girls didn't get paid,
so I may have convinced a few people their secrets were better off
with me than their wives. Everyone is willing to pay when their
reputation is at stake."

How well I know that.

"May I ask who refused to pay?"

"Madison J . . . I mean, Holly Graves. She's a farmer with some weird sexual habits if you catch my drift." Piper giggles. "But we did run into Mrs. Gambino leaving the kitchen when the lights came on. And dude, I thought I saw a *ghost.* There was a blur of white by the window, then poof—*gone.* Oh, and someone is fucking the staff!" Piper makes a face.

"Are you acting, Piper? Or is this for *real?*"

"I did see a ghost, Ainsley." She drops her façade. "Plus an actual man sprinted from the kitchen in his boxers, then bolted out of the front door. Whether that's part of the script, I have no clue."

I turn to Violet. "May I have a word?" Whisking her to the kitchen, I'm happy to finally have an excuse for us to talk.

Once inside, Violet peruses the center island, plucking an appetizer from a platter. "What am I being accused of *now?*"

"A lot, if you don't give me those cookies." We both laugh but fall back into our roles when a guest passes. "Scarlett said you were in the kitchen when the lights went out. What were you doing?" I snatch a second cookie before she can take a bite.

"Eating these"—she points at the cookies—"and drinking." She nods at the liquor cabinet. "I needed something strong. It's been hard maintaining the relationships I have."

In real life, or is she pretending?

"Does this have anything to do with a naked man seen running for the hills?"

"Are you asking as a detective or a *girlfriend?*" She arches an eyebrow.

"I hope I don't have to ask as the latter." I catch her eye. "Why? Do I?"

"It's a joke, silly." She swivels on the bar stool. "But I did see a man in here. Staff. Doing his job. Nothing else."

I survey the kitchen, noting the open dumbwaiter. "Did this ever move?"

She shrugs. "I got the hell out the second the lights went out. I had no intention of playing corpse the rest of the night."

After fishing through trash in the dumbwaiter, I find a spotted dress with black stains, and an open ink pen rolls across the marble tile. "Someone switched roles," I tell Violet. "But everyone has secrets here. Not sure who to believe."

"What about you? Anything to confess?" Violet gives me a look.

"What's up with you, Violet? Like seriously—"

"There you are!" Madison N shuffles in, clad in an all-blue cop uniform. "I've been searching for you all night."

"Who are *you* supposed to be?"

"Officer Hale." She points at her outfit. "Do you think I wore this hideous thing for *fun*? Jane said something about a badge, but I couldn't find it."

I pause. Officer Hale is on the stairs, watching the body. Only that Madison's suit doesn't fit properly, so it can only mean one thing. For confirmation, I pull out Jane's note. A new black thumbprint is smudged on the back, which matches the original one on the note and elevator button.

Case solved.

Before I can brag to Violet about my genius deduction, a post flashes:

If you didn't find them by now, hope you realize . . . there's more to come.

Blasting through the parlor, I push guests aside. "You're under arrest for the murder of Mrs. Howard!" I say to Madison K.

"She killed him!" she yells, pointing at pretend-dead Jane. "He was going to leave her. She couldn't accept it. What did you expect me to do?"

"The note you gave Jane saying she spilled blood. Did you mean Mr. Howard's blood?"

She nods. "Yes, and maybe not just *his*. Didn't you see R—" She pauses. "The um, body?" she whispers as Madison N returns with Violet. "In the room with the journal."

Jeez. How many murders did Jane plan? At this point, I no longer care if Piper wants to stay. This is the last clue I'm investigating, then I'm dragging Violet to get beignets.

"Wait up." Violet follows me up the stairs.

"Eli and I already checked in here, but"—we enter the room—"Madison said something about a body." I approach the window. "This was open before, but wait—we never saw this."

There's a piece of white fabric clinging to the window crank. When the wind whips, there's a *thud*. Like we heard earlier. "I think something, or someone, is hanging onto that crank. Like for real!"

Violet clutches my hand, and I take a peek.

Holy shit—*it's a girl.*

Her eyes are bulging, face blue, with a makeshift noose, rocking her in the wind. A stronger blast of wind hits, and the body thuds against the side of the house, arm bent at an unnatural angle. This is no dummy or mannequin.

It's Riley Coyne.

The police chief's daughter. My former classmate. The girl I texted yesterday.

This cannot be real.

I wrap my arms around Violet, pulling us away from the window. "Don't look, okay? We need to call the police! Please, don't look." I close my eyes and bury them in her shoulder as I repeat the sentence over and over.

UTG was right.

There is another body, but it's not part of Jane's game.

I never planned this one. Not really.

Sure, I'd imagined worse fates for these airheads, but to actually execute my strategy, I have to say was quite frightening, yet, at the same time, oddly satisfying. The power I felt taking her down gave me such a high. Such a feeling of impotence, which scares me, because what does that say about me?

Does it mean I'm more like them than I care to admit?

I wasn't born a violent person. My anger has festered. Grown so large and encompassing, I can hardly separate it from who I am or who I used to be. But none of that matters because, in all honestly, I no longer exist. Not really.

Which brings me right back here.
To this.
To what I must do.

Once your hand is bloody, there's no turning back. A bloody hand leaves prints. Better to cut the whole thing off than implicate yourself for one silly misdeed. I must burn these societal leeches down, and if that means losing the rest of myself—the tiny, small fragments that are left—so be it.

I'm in it for the win. No room for losing or losers.
Victory goes to the last one breathing.
Me.

CHAPTER 20

TWO MORNINGS LATER
JANUARY 10

The sun shoots through the cracks in my blinds. I reach out to shut off my alarm before Violet can stir. Her black hair is fanned out on the pillow we shared, though last night, she ended up using *me* as the pillow.

"Do I have to get up?" She cracks an eye open.

"You asked me to set it. I don't wanna poach anymore of your time. I know you've been slammed." I sweep a section of hair from her eye, then kiss her full lips. "Thanks for staying the night though. It really helps."

First, it was the nightmares of Alexandra's bloody smile after her collapse at the ball. Then slashed tires. A lopped-off finger. A missing Laney, who may or may not be alive. Now this—*Riley*. Who was murdered and found by a very unlucky me. Which was neither accident nor prank.

Technically, Madison K found her first, but according to her, she thought Riley was part of the script—*as corpse*. Plus, she said

183

she saw her slumped by the window. Not hanging outside. Either way, it left a large enough gap of time for the killer to pose her and make his or her get away. As it turns out, the curtain she was hung by wasn't just for show, it was hiding a slit throat. And every time I think of her violent death, my own throat feels like it's been severed.

Violet pokes me. "You sure you're, okay?"

I nod, but honestly, how can I be? Seeing a murdered friend isn't something you just file away in your memory bank. And now, in addition to the nightmares, I'm having more frequent full-blown panic attacks.

"I may not have a magnolia coin for you to flip, but since yours promises to take me far away, mine would be to keep you close. And safe," Violet says, snuggling closer.

While I appreciate her support, I can't help wondering how she can be this calm. I mean, she was there. Maybe she didn't know Riley, but it's a murdered girl at a party we not only attended, but were the ones who discovered her dead body.

There's a scuffle in the hall, and Violet jerks.

"It's Luke. Don't worry."

"I'm still shocked your parents are letting me stay. Though not complaining. At all."

"After the party, my mom tried to stay up with me, but she kept nodding off, only to be awoken by me yelling in my sleep. So, know those pancakes she said she's making?" Violet nods. "They're probably thank-you pancakes. You're doing *her* a favor."

Once we were interviewed by the cops the night of the murder, we were all on edge, and Violet showed up the next morning with a giant stack of textbooks, making her own little nest to nerd out in.

"Being here reminds me families *can* be normal," she says, rolling out of bed in my baggy tee and boxers. She heads to the bathroom. "Speaking of being busy, my wetlands internship has wrapped. Since I've finished early readings for next semester, and

Blair is preoccupied with Eli, I can help you stalk Under the Gown. Guess I should've told you that before you woke me earlier than necessary."

"Perfect. I need the help, and no way are they *not* involved. They've posted about every accident that's happened and hinted another 'body' could be found at Jane's party. It can't be an accident, right?" I sprawl in my bed with the added space. "But the big question is *why?*"

"Why what?" Violet mumbles around her toothbrush.

"Why Riley? You'd think the police chief's daughter would be off-limits. Unless you want to get caught."

She turns off the sink. "Maybe someone went after her *because* of her father, and the party just became a convenient place to do it." She crosses the room, eyeballing a pair of sweatpants in my drawer, slipping them on before I can protest.

"There's nothing convenient about debutante season," I say, bracing for the protest that will surely follow.

"Here we go again," she mutters. "The infallible *debutantes.*"

"I'm serious. You're the one who thinks even the utilitarian master list is biased. As for Jane's party, we got in through a hidden door in a fake tourist shop." I sigh. "If this is some personal vendetta against Riley's dad, why pick such a difficult location to penetrate? Unless it *is* Under the Gown. Not only did they post details from the party, like Jane playing dead, they hinted at things no person attending knew." I sit up. "Quick. Text the gang for a brainstorming session. Six heads are better than one."

She shoots off a group text, and Eli replies first. He suggests we meet at his house, but I can't chance running into Cooper. Not with Violet around. She may detect my negative reaction, or he could accidentally mouth off.

I can't risk either scenario.

My thumbs freeze as I mull over my next words. "I'm assuming Leslie is a *no* for the think tank?" I glance at Violet.

She flashes me a look. One that means: *I don't want to talk about this, but you should know my answer.*

I nod, humming a tune which lets her know *I'm not sure about that*, but I'll compromise.

"She apologized to *you*," she says. "It's not your medical history on display for the world to see." She crosses over, settling on the bed. "I'm not trying to be a bitch; I just don't want extra drama on top of what's already happened. Besides, we don't even know who is behind Under the Gown. Best we play this one close to our chests."

"You're not insinuating Leslie is part of Under the Gown, are you?" I blanch. "She may be acting crazy, but I've known her a long time. No way could she do something so heinous as slashing Riley's throat."

"Yet she stole medical information, and who knows, maybe Riley's dad found out? She could've made up that whole spiel about being tipped off by someone else to shift the blame." She shrugs. "I'm probably way off base, but can you leave her out of it for now? Until there are things we actually know."

I had slipped Leslie a text to make sure she was okay after Jane's party, but that's all. It wasn't exactly the right time to ask who she overheard talking about Violet, so I didn't. And maybe she did act solo tampering with Violet's medical files. She certainly had been acting jealous enough lately.

"Okay. But for the record, I don't think she would hurt a flea— I mean, physically. I realize she hurt you, but she passed out in science lab during frog dissections because it was too gory. Just saying." I cross the room, looking for something to wear.

"Ainsley?" My dad's voice seeps through the door. "May I speak to you?"

I kiss Violet, then follow him to his office. I don't go in his office much, but when I do, the smell of his leather books and furniture calms me.

"How are you doing? Are the nightmares going away?" he asks.

Not in his doctor's voice, but in a caring, fatherly tone. "I spoke to Dr. Reed at the hospital. She specializes in PTSD. She thinks it may be helpful for you to try therapy."

"I'm feeling better," I say, hopefully convincingly enough. "Seeing Riley was rough, Dad, to say the least, but I don't want to sit around and talk about it. It's too fresh. Besides, being around my friends helps get my mind off what I saw more than any therapist could."

None of it is true, but I can't exactly tell him: *I plan to find out who killed her.* He'd have a coronary. "If I have any issues, I'll do so after this semester. Promise."

"We could visit your aunt in Boston. No reason to stay here with all this happening."

"Hasn't it already *happened?*" I ask, picking up on the weirdness that has crept into his voice.

"Well, yes. Your acquaintance was, um . . . murdered. And Chief Coyne has now listed Laney Wilson as *officially* missing, but" —he pauses—"I'm afraid I have further bad news. Alexandra Williams's family requested a more thorough autopsy. It seems the ruling of a heart attack is being disputed." He pulls off his glasses, rubbing the bridge of his nose. It's the first time I notice that two small wrinkles have formed between his eyebrows.

"How do you know?" I slide closer on the couch.

"Doctors talk, Ainsley. And I think something sinister is going on. I do not believe in untimely heart attacks in girls your age, unless there was an undiagnosed congenital heart condition, like I mentioned earlier. Nor do I think a murdered girl at a debutante party is, by any stretch of the imagination, a mere coincidence." He stares at his slippers. "Chief Coyne asked me to evaluate the head trauma inflicted on Riley. It appears someone knocked her out before slitting her throat."

He fills me in on the rest, and I sit, listening and nodding, while my mind reels.

"The poor man thinks someone he arrested may be targeting his family. I'm very worried." He looks up. "Whoever put Riley's cell phone down her throat is more than a grave cause of concern. I don't want you near any of this."

"What? A cell phone down her throat?" I clutch my throat protectively. "What kind of monster does such a thing?"

"Geez, I'm sorry, honey. I didn't mean for that to slip. I certainly don't want to add to your trauma. There is a remote possibility this *is* a warning message for the chief."

"Jesus, Dad. Do you think it's wise to hide that some insane murderer is going around my friends' parties, slitting girls' throats and stuffing things down them? Not just some in-the-heat-of-the-moment random act, which is awful enough."

If my dad's right, and whoever did this to Riley wanted to send a message, the looming question remains: Why?

Is it because she ratted someone out?

The drive to the park where I suggested we meet is quick. Barely a few Spotify songs are fought over before Violet and I reach the hedged letters that spell out *AUDUBON PARK*.

Pulling into the lot, I zip into a parking space under a moss-laden oak.

Eli waves us over to a blanketed spot on the grass where he's sitting with Blair, Jamie, and Piper, who've also beaten us here.

"You had to pick somewhere outside, didn't you?" Piper swears, swatting at a bug. "January is supposed to be cold, yet the mosquitos don't seem to have gotten that memo."

"It's seventy-two. That *is* cold by Louisiana standards," Jamie says, pushing up the sleeves of his blue hoodie.

"Can we worry less about mosquitos and more about said person spilling blood?" I snap, catching their attention. "It's Under the Gown. It has to be. None of this shit happened before deb season, and I'm fairly certain there's no record of things happening before our year. Or like ever."

Piper starts to object, but I cut her off. "Those were rumors, Piper. And some girl freaking out over a huge case of nerves. Nothing more."

"I thought you were joking when you said your season was cursed, but I'm starting to think you're right. What happened to Riley was beyond wicked," Eli says. "I drove by that place the day after the party. Cops were zipping down the street, knocking on doors, taking photos, and measuring shit." He pulls up a clover and tucks it behind Blair's ear.

"Considering it's a speakeasy, they probably have zero cameras," Piper adds. "Jane bragged how it was the perfect hideout, totally authentic to her script. Unless there's an actual miracle on the tech side, I doubt the police will find anything."

"Maybe they'll find something on her SIM card," I mumble, and they look my way. Violet appears the most surprised. "Um, yeah. My dad kind of let it slip"—I pause—"I'd tell you, but it's really gory."

"Say it," Piper demands. "We're adults. We can handle it. At least, I hope we can."

I fill them in on the grisly details about the cell phone, letting them know I'd just learned about it before leaving the house, and they sit in silence, digesting the information.

Violet mouths: *You okay?*

I nod. Only I know she's probably wondering why I didn't tell her on the drive over.

Jamie whistles. "Morbidly ironic the girl who put a gag order on Laney's BOLO gets a phone shoved down her throat. C'mon. This shit is obvious."

"He's right." Blair shakes her head. "Without Riley's daddy intervention, Laney's report would've gone public. Riley made her dad stay quiet, but no one knew that. She only told you, right Ainsley?"

"I don't know. She was half drunk. She could've told any number of people. Just like I told you guys." I wring my hands, on the verge of another panic attack. "In high school, Riley was the first to throw parties with alcohol. She believed that either her dad wouldn't suspect her of wrongdoing, or if he did, she could talk her way out of it. Back then, he was just a sergeant. Now, he's chief. Apparently, her bravado increased after his promotion. Basically, she thought she was invincible, until she wasn't."

"What if Under the Gown knows Laney is missing?" Violet suggests. "Riley thought she knew where Laney was, but Hunter told a completely different story. Either way, she hasn't been seen in weeks."

"So if Under the Gown knows where Laney is, they'd know Riley was lying since she's apparently *not* with Hunter." I mull over Violet's theory.

"Or *was*." Eli grimaces. "Hate to say that, but if Laney crossed paths with whoever did this to Riley, how great are her odds?"

"Remember what the post said before you were served that finger? *Laney sends her regards.*" Piper quotes the message I'm unlikely to ever forget. "They must've known she wasn't around to rebuke the post. Otherwise, why risk it?"

The thought of another person being dead, especially another classmate, especially Laney, makes me ill. While she isn't my best friend, we'd known each other most of our lives. At school, we were either paired together or pitted against each other when it came to sporting events, but I'd always admired her skills and thought of her more as a worthy opponent than a competitor.

"Or they know where she is, and it's somewhere that doesn't have internet," I counter, trying to hold on to hope by presenting a less evil scenario. "Laney had been texting Riley, right? So, if we go with the theory that she's been kidnapped, then said kidnapper would need to keep her alive to continue the texts. But now that Riley is dead, it means we need to find her fast. Especially since no one seems to be looking."

"Why not just contact the police and stay out of it?" Blair says, wrapping the remains of her half-eaten sandwich into wax paper, placing it back into a paper bag. "I don't think we're equipped to handle this. At least, I'm not. It's not exactly how I envisioned my semester break."

I reach for her hand. "I told the police about UTG. When I mentioned the account, they acted like it was some teen meme or something. If they won't investigate, we need to."

I pause for a second, summoning my courage. "Remember the incentive they dangled to get an invite to their party?" They nod. "Most girls will send in God-knows-what scoop to get an invite. How about we send in our own? Rumors that they'll have to confirm. We can trap them at their own game."

"Trap a murderer? Fairly certain that won't end well," Piper deadpans.

"It's not the *worst* idea. At least we'll have a chance of finding out who's behind the account. Then we can go to the police and be taken seriously," Violet says. "Besides, if all of us are in, it's six against one. Pretty awesome odds."

"I'm confident in my brawling skills." Eli throws a few air punches.

"How do you get an invite again?" Jamie asks. "Do we even know when or where this bad-idea party is?"

"It's this weekend. The location is yet to be announced, but I'm sure it will be in town. I got an invite," I admit, rolling my eyes.

Violet laughs. "So did I," she says, and my mouth drops. "Hey, *I* didn't ask for anything. They said I make good press."

"Me too," Piper says, and I look at her, surprised she never told me. Then again, I hadn't told them either. "They literally called me your sidekick. I was trying to think of something less depressing to tell you, but these *are* desperate times."

"Ainsley is right. If we dangle irresistible scoop, they'll have to come out of their shadows. And I doubt anyone would suspect we're working together. Or that we think they're the killer," Eli says, cracking his knuckles. A habit he does when he's nervous or psyched, which I'm assuming he's both. "Hopefully it will blindside them, and we'll be able to get intel on Laney. Then we call the police." He pokes Blair.

"Why does this sound so much easier than it will be?" Violet takes the last sip of her root beer and stretches out on the blanket. Propping her head in my lap, she reaches for my hand.

"Because we're trying to play a game on their board and by their rules," I say, aggravated it took me this long to figure out. If I hadn't been so focused on being the perfect deb, maybe I would've recognized the monsters through the masquerade. "Which means we need to present the world's best hand or ironclad bluff to the UTG game master. Otherwise, we lose to a murderer."

CHAPTER 21

UTG ROCK AROUND THE CLOCK PARTY
JANUARY 13

Time is tick, tick, ticking. I bet you debs are holding your breath in anticipation for Rock Around the Clock tonight. We're stoked to be hosting the debutantes who exemplify the spirit of this season. If you've sent in scoop throughout the month, you have details on the when and where.

At UTG, snitches don't get stitches. They get invites.

"I don't see any events on your handy-dandy calendar, so why is there a dress on your bed and what's with all the makeup?" Luke asks, peering into my room, gym bag slung over his shoulder.

"It's not on the calendar." I curse, skipping back several minutes on the smoky-eye makeup tutorial I'm watching. "Do you have to be this nosy?"

"Let's see. Why, yes, considering you've driven me crazy listening to this crap for years, and Dad has put a can of pepper spray in each room. I think that earns my curiosity." He leans against the door, smile fading. "Do Mom and Dad know about this event?"

"Can you *not* make this into a thing? I don't have the time or energy to play sibling games, begging you not to tell. Please be a decent human for once."

"Ever think I might be worried?" He shrugs. "I didn't put up with you this long for you to get axed."

"Yet you've prioritized every event of yours over mine since we were children. If I were younger, and allowed to be the petty one, I'd promise to haunt you if I ever get axed." I shake my head. "But I won't. I fully intend on staying alive to annoy you further. Besides, it's just a party."

He sighs. "Okay, but where are you going, just in case?"

"The skating rink where you used to play hockey." I frown at my crooked eyeliner, but for once, I don't give a damn whether or not I'll fit into their dress code. "Eli is picking me up in a few minutes. We're meeting the gang there, so you can text them if you decide to be a real nuisance."

"Too much work for me." He heads down the hallway. "See you later. Make good decisions, Ass-ley!"

Nothing about tonight sounds like a good decision. The only *good* thing I can do will get me blown up in the crossfire, but what choice do I have? Piper and Violet have already tried baiting Under the Gown with their own phony stories. They didn't bite. At all. Which leaves me with one final strike to knock something out of the park.

Going through my contacts, I pause on his name. It's the only way I can clear my conscience of the shitty decisions I've been making lately. The last time I put someone else on Under the Gown's podium, they got their brakes cut.

"Hey, you." Cooper's voice is raspy. "I was starting to think you didn't like me so much after Maskers. I feel quite . . . used." He laughs.

Asshole.

"I think that's my line." I rub my face as pain shoots from my jaw.

"Aww, c'mon. I'm just teasing, *Ainsley*." He draws out my name. "Surely, you're not calling out of some moral objection to a past encounter."

"I need the picture," I blurt. "I know you didn't delete it. I want a copy."

"What picture?"

"C'mon Cooper. Stop being an asshole. The only picture you and I have together."

"You mean *our* picture?" His voice changes. "It took a lot of convincing to get you to take it, so what gives?"

"I made a deal with someone. Let's just say they can open a lot of doors for me if I have something of interest to trade. Not like it will harm you if people see it," I counter. Which is true. It will only up his street cred.

"Your ambition is really hot. You know that, right?"

Is that supposed to be a compliment? If he was in front of me, there'd be nothing to keep me from punching him in the face.

"Honestly, it's one of the things I respect about you," he says. "You know exactly what you want and will go to hell and back to get it."

Yes. I've already done that.

He is hell and back.

But none of that matters because it seems all my ambition is about to blow up in my face. "Cooper, please. Just send the photo."

"Under one condition," he says. "That we meet up afterward. New year. New deal. Besides, if a certain person sees that, doubt you'll be welcome in my house by Eli for a very long time. So, consider it an offer of friendship. My brand of friendship, Ainsley."

No way will I sleep with this asshole—again.

I feel like throwing up just thinking about it. "Deal," I lie. "Send it, now."

The phone buzzes, and I check the text, hanging up before he can say another tainted word.

It's Cooper. Bare-chested and grinning. Kissing me between my shoulder blades. My head is turned toward the camera, hair mussed. I'm topless, smiling, and barely covered by the bed sheets.

A disgrace.

Cooper likes trophies. His room brims with shiny medals and large golden cups he's won from various sports and leadership positions he's held throughout his life. So, that night, when he mentioned he liked to take photos of the girls he slept with, it wasn't surprising, no matter how much it disgusts me now. And rationalizing how I ended up in that photo, that I was drunk, or curious, or simply wanted an invitation to Maskers, no longer matters. In that moment, I'd already forced myself to *be* with him. I certainly wasn't going to go through all of that and lose out on our deal for refusing to take one photo.

I look at it again, and my stomach twists.

This photo may be the single thing I need to beat the game master, to bring down a killer. But no matter how great my hand is —*I've already lost.*

"Ready to go?" Eli hangs my garment bag in his truck. "Gonna head to Piper's. You can get dressed there, so your dad won't flip."

"Sure." I climb into his truck, musing what a loyal friend he is and how crushed he'll be when he learns I deceived him by not being honest about his brother.

"You good?" He looks away from the road to analyze me. "Because you're a lot of things, but quiet is never one of them."

"I'm just nervous, considering everything that's going wrong. Pretty sure that's normal." I shake my shoulders out, trying not to appear as stressed as I feel.

"We've got your back. All you need to do is lure in the big fish. We'll be your net, swooping in to rescue you." He shifts gears on his truck. "Are you sure your ammo is enough?" He taps on the steering wheel in sync with the song that's blasting.

"I hope. If it means we'll find Laney, or stop this psycho, guess it will be worth it."

"Amen to that." He pulls through Piper's wrought-iron gates and parks on her flagstone drive. Violet's car is here, which means Blair is too. "Tell the girls to hurry their asses." He gets out to retrieve my bag. "I'm going to pick up Jamie. Meet us at the rink."

I nod.

There is no time to back out or rethink my way around this. I have to commit.

Pulling off the highway, Piper parks in front of the squat building, a peeling Coca-Cola logo across its entire length.

"If this doesn't ruin roller skating for me, I don't know what will," Piper says, unmoved by the lively disco music as we tromp through the lobby and into the dank skating rink.

There are people scattered about, lacing up skates or leaning over the low cement wall. They're cheering on their friends' valiant efforts, because even if you *can* skate, you take your life in your hands when you do so at this beat-to-shit rink.

Under the Gown sure has a following, I muse, as my heels stick to the maroon soda-stained carpet, which appears unchanged since the time we hosted parties here in grade school. Almost every kid at school had one or more birthday parties here.

On some weird level, it feels nostalgic to be back.

"Instead of the attire saying short dresses, it should've said a suit of armor, or at a minimum, knee pads and a helmet." Blair points at the rack. "Gonna eat shit trying to skate on those things."

I eyeball the skates, trying to spot a pair with the least number of chips in the wheels. "These things haven't been repaired or replaced in decades," I say. "I used to wear Luke's old hockey skates when I was younger, so I didn't break my ankles. That was like ten years ago."

"Do we have to skate?" Violet squints at the rack. "Not like we're here to have fun."

"We'll stick out way less if we participate," Jamie pipes up from the bench where he's lacing up his skates. "Might as well play along."

"What's wrong? Oil Princess doesn't know how to skate?" I nudge Violet's shoulder.

"I took figure skating for nine years; I think I can manage," she sniffs as I balk at her admission. Of course she did. What über-rich girl doesn't take dancing, gymnastics, swimming, piano, and yeah, I suppose, ice-skating, as well.

Eli wobbles up on a pair of janky skates. "Let's split up. We can skate around, check out anyone here who does *not* look like a narc." He tries to roll across the carpet, but fails. Steadying himself on a nearby table, he motions to Blair. "C'mon. Time's a-wasting."

"Yay, I get Yamaguchi." I nod at Violet, and she smirks. "Piper, obviously you're with Jamie. I'll text when I hear back from them."

"*If* you hear back. But you better." Piper holds out her hand for Jamie, who is doing remarkably better than Eli. "C'mon hot stuff."

"This would make a perfect meet-cute scene, if it wasn't potentially murderous," Violet says, flipping her hair, trying to walk gracefully in the clunky skates. "At least it's a party. Not a presentation where we'd have to curtsy. I'd really fall on my ass." She makes it to the rink, catching onto the railing after a few feet.

"My theory is right," I say after joining Violet in the rink. "Figure skating has nothing to do with the skill needed to survive in this rickety-ass rink."

"What is this shit made of? Plastic?" She blasts a string of curse words.

"Your guess is as good as mine, but"—I skate ahead, looping once around to show off—"whatever it is, *young* me mastered it a while ago. Even in these crap skates."

"When are you not Ms. Confident?" She grabs the back of my sweater. "Please come back. It's your duty as my girlfriend to not let me bust my ass."

"Is it? Well, I'm kind of fond of your ass. You should've said something earlier." I place her in front of me, positioning a hand on each hip to guide her. "Alright, I'll kick us off. Try not to wobble, and I'll keep you straight."

"Your job is to keep me *straight*? Guess I'll be falling sooner than I thought." She yelps as I pretend-bite her shoulder. "Stop. I'm kidding! I'm kidding."

Eli passes us, swinging Blair along. He sticks out his tongue.

"Testing, testing. Hello, can everyone hear me?" a referee with an orange megaphone booms, making his way to the middle of the rink. "Listen up. The illustrious host of our party has a message for all you debs and plus-ones. But first, as the only responsible person here"—he pretend coughs—"I must caution; do not drink while skating."

He points at a boy with a red Solo cup, who sheepishly sets it atop the wall. "Wise choice, young man. Now, let's get this party started. Here's a little welcome greeting from your host."

He clears his throat, preparing to read the note he's holding. "'Nostalgia brings out the best of us. Or, in this case, the most sacred secrets. I hope this setting will inspire you to be your best self this year. Quick question. Does anyone know another term for *rocking around the clock?*'"

He scans the crowd, but no one says a word.

"'Dancing around a time bomb, of course.'"

Violet and I exchange confused looks. "It's time to let you in on a little surprise. Tonight isn't about showcasing debutantes. It's about revealing your secrets. And I'll be doing exactly that as you scramble to figure out what wires not to cut to avoid getting blown up in the process. For those of you whose wishes I've granted, DM me. I'll let you know where to look. Once again, thanks for the shrapnel. Under the Gown would be nothing without you!'"

He skates off.

Phones buzz and alerts light up everyone's screen.

I believe in balance. For every secret you've shared to gain a spot here, I'll spill someone else's secret. Here goes— Did you know Henry Boudreaux is about to be a father? And the mother is skating around this very rink! Dresses are great for hiding baby bumps.

"Are you kidding? This is another high-key shit-show," Violet fumes.

I nod, though I'm not surprised. I'd already experienced their corruption firsthand, and really, it makes perfect sense. UTG feeds off chaos. The more people that get pissed about their secrets being exposed, the more tips they'll send out of spite or to defend those allegations.

I look at Violet. "Everyone will be so focused on saving their own asses, they won't pay attention to anything else going down. A perfect setting for another catastrophe."

My phone buzzes again. It's a DM.

UTG

There's a redhead at the snack bar. Her father is head physio for your favorite NFL team. She's promised you that internship. Say "you're welcome"!

My dream internship? All I need to do is walk over and talk to this girl, and it's mine?

I glance at the concession stand, and sure enough, a girl with long strawberry-blond hair is sitting on one of the retro bar stools, noshing on nachos.

"You're not going, are you?" Violet fumes, having read my message. "Jesus, Ainsley. There are more important things at stake than a *job* offer. If it's even true."

"Did I say I'm going? I may have wanted to be a debutante for the connections I could make because, unlike you, I'll need a stellar resume and impressive referrals to get into grad school. Let alone secure a job down the road. But everything's poisoned. It's no longer worth the cost."

It's easy to say the words I know I need to say. The words Violet wants to hear. But the reality that I'm about to lose an edge which could help me succeed in life hits hard. "To be completely honest, it's heartbreaking," I add. "I feel like I'm dropping out right before the finish line."

"Not everyone gets to be in your kind of race, Ainsley. Kind of rigged from the get-go." She squeezes my hand. "You don't have to play by these archaic broken rules. You can get everything you need or want on your own merit. You're a much smarter and kinder person than you give yourself credit for."

She sounds just like my dad.

But I haven't been. Not by a longshot.

I grab her hand. "Look at me. I need to tell you something that is very important. I'm about to send my message to these idiots, but before I do, I want you to know I'm really working on being that person. The one you think I am. Even if this next revelation doesn't reflect that."

It takes every bit of courage to keep holding her hand, knowing what I'm about to do could hurt her. Knowing how she'll probably react when she learns the truth. "You're not going to be the only one mad. I hope you'll be able to see past it."

I open the app and message UTG:

A

Since you adore pictures so much, what if I have one to go with a very nasty admission of guilt?

A chat bubble appears.

UTG

Don't be a tease, Clarke. What do you want for the story?

A

I want to meet you. In person. At this party.

UTG

Absolutely not. No story is worth that.

A

You'll be worth nothing after this season if you don't live up to your hype. I can give you a story to cement that. Plus, I can see if my hunch is right.

UTG

You'll never be able to tell anyone who I am.

What's the story? How delicious is it?

A

> A member of The Mystic Maskers traded an invite to escort one of the debs for sex.

UTG

> Okay, I'm interested. Who? Do you have proof?

A

> I can bring a witness along with photo proof.

Violet's eyes widen. "How did you get someone to agree to *that*?" She lowers her voice. "Whoever it is will get destroyed. Not only for agreeing, but outing the organization for existing."

UTG

> Meet at the arcade in five minutes. The Pac-Man machine in the back has enough room to wiggle through. We'll meet you and your witness there. If you drag anyone else along, I'll disappear and run the story with your name tagged on it. Don't double-cross me.

"Tell everyone what's going down," I say to Violet. "Wait five minutes. Make sure no one is watching." I start to skate off, but she pulls me back, crushing her lips against mine.

"Please be safe. Don't do anything stupid. If you think you're in danger, stall, and know we're coming to get you. The second you know who's behind UTG, we'll call the police, and this shit will finally be over. Promise me you'll be careful."

"I promise." I scatter kisses across her face. "Whoever this is will not stop me from coming back to you."

If she wants me back.

Skating past my friends, I give a thumbs-up and hop off the rink. I take one last look at the girl by the snack counter, knowing that any chance I had for that internship is now sunk. Surprisingly, failure doesn't feel as bad as I thought.

At least, not yet.

I'm probably as familiar with the arcade machines as the staff, since Piper and I hid between them as kids whenever we grew bored at birthday parties or Luke's long hockey practices. Jammed next to each other in the shape of an oval, they create a perfect, empty middle ground to hide between.

And it's *dark*.

Sliding through, I hold my breath as a flurry of dust swirls. The only light keeping the space visible is from the cracks between the machines. It makes navigating the jungle of cables in my skates even more difficult. "Um, hello?"

Switching on my phone's flashlight, panic surges. I should put my back to the machines, so the only place they can come at me is from the front.

"Where's your witness, Ainsley?" A voice hisses through the machines.

I whip my light to the spot. No one. "Where are you?" I trip over more cables.

"Tell me where your witness is, or this is over." The voice shifts. It's higher in pitch. More menacing.

"Not wise to play games when you're out of your league."

It sounds like two different people.

Shit.

They're the ones playing games. "It's me," I say. "*I'm* the witness." I try to speak louder than my heart is beating. "I have the photo to prove it. Come see."

"Should've guessed it was *you*." They laugh. "Always so desperate to be better than everyone else." A figure emerges from behind a machine.

I stare at my red-faced former classmate. "Madison?"

"You call us Cerberus for a reason, right? You think it's funny, but we think you're stupid. Anyone with half a brain knows three heads are always better than one. Welcome to *our* debutante party, Ainsley. Didn't you think it was odd we didn't have one listed on the calendar? Well, here it is. Surprise, surprise."

She laughs as the other two appear—effectively sealing off my exits.

CHAPTER 22

The Madisons were always messengers—or gravediggers, at best—exhuming drama to make their social value go up in high school. But it never crossed my mind they could be the ones responsible for burying an actual body. It's just as impossible as believing they have the ability to keep a secret like orchestrating Under the Gown.

My mouth drops open. "Of all people . . . what would possess you to do this?"

"You're in no position to ask questions," Madison K says.

I shine my light her way, and something glints. Arms crossed, the tip of a knife she's holding nearly pokes her forearm. A chill runs up my spine.

Maybe I don't have an advantage in way of a weapon, but I do have my fury. Coming face to face with the people that have been wrecking lives like it's a game makes my throat burn to scream their names.

And the fact that it's the Madisons—it only adds to the insult.

"You realize you've been destroying a tradition and the organizations you three are part of? On top of the individual lives your stories have torn apart," I spit. "And for what . . . *recognition?*"

"You're one to talk." Madison J huffs. "The only difference between us and you is we never got the spotlight you've always taken for granted. We've put in just as much work, if not more, yet we were always cast aside."

"But see, people like you, you need an Under the Gown," Madison N chimes in. "Not like we're the nicest group of girls in the first place, so all we did was offer you and your clones an appropriate battleground to fight on. Don't blame us, you all picked up a weapon to fight. Debutantes are just social soldiers. Their chosen suit of armor and battleground, a gown and a ballroom."

"Go fuck yourself, Madisons," I snap, in spite of the angry glint smoldering in their eyes. "You couldn't cut it in any real social games, so you made your own?" I shake my head. "Can you honestly say it's worth it?"

"Oh, please! Stop playing martyr. *You* sent the photo of Rachel doing drugs." Madison K points her knife my way. "You had to know she would get sent back to rehab. Her dad pulled her out of school like that." She snaps her fingers.

Crap. When I didn't see her at other events, I'd hoped she was laying low until the bad press died down. Maybe these three had put the metaphorical nail in her coffin, but they're right. I purchased it and dug the hole.

I can't think about that. I need to stay focused.

I have to find a way to make them admit their wrongdoing. "What about the boys who were with her? How could you cut their brakes? You could've killed them. Or maybe that was your intention all along?" I accuse. "I had no choice but to report Rachel. If your selective memories can work for a second, perhaps you recall your psycho phone call?"

Madison K and N trade looks, then stare back with puzzled expressions.

Is it possible one had gone behind the others' backs to call me?

"We never hurt anyone," Madison N says. I eyeball Madison

K's knife, and she follows my gaze. "That's different. It's for *our* protection. We're not stupid. Though it sounds like your memory is the one with issues."

They won't confess to anything—great. I need to try harder. "What about Laney?" I ask, holding my ground as they inch closer.

"No. Tell us your story before *I* lose my patience." Madison J shoves me, whipping my head into the back of a machine.

Crying out, I catch a flash of green through a crack.

Violet—they're here.

"I will. When you tell me where Laney is." I force a smile, trying to ignore the floaters dancing in my vision from the blow. "She's been missing this whole season. I know that, and so did Riley. I think you three did too. You all gave different stories when I asked about her at Leslie's party. Back then, I chalked it up to early mimosas, but y'all are always on the same page. What's the real story?"

"Used up all your skills deducing that, huh, Miss Detective? No wonder you were too late to help Riley," Madison K says sarcastically. "Show us yours. We'll show you ours. You said a member of Maskers traded a hookup to get some pathetic girl in. That you had a photo of the girl and a witness. Something tells me you're both. Am I correct?"

Every piece of my pride begs to be elsewhere. To dash off to where my friends have settled, all probably leaning into the machines to listen to what's happening. Or to motion them in before this gets worse, but I can't.

Which means—*they'll hear everything.*

"I am," I admit, watching their faces light up as shame courses through me.

"Ooh, show us the picture. This I'm dying to see!" Madison K's hands are outstretched, like a kid waiting for candy. "I'll even answer part of your question. Yes, we knew Laney wasn't participating in deb season. But I won't tell you why until after that." She points at my phone.

Madison J tips the screen toward her clones. "Just to make sure you don't try to text anyone," she says. "Go on."

I swipe into photos, take a deep breath, and tap on the picture of Cooper and me.

"No way!" Madison N shrieks. "Oh my gosh. I should've seen that one. You're a shittier friend than I thought!"

"Have to say, Cooper *is* a hottie. Guess if you had to whore yourself out to someone, at least you have decent taste." Madison J laughs. "Can't believe you took this photo, or after, didn't burn it to the ground."

"He has the copy." I ignore their giggles, slapping their hands when they try to zoom in further. "He promised to get me an invite to Maskers. This is why."

"Piper didn't get one, right? Or did she whore herself out too?" Madison K grins as she reads my face. "So you screwed one brother for the price of two friends. Yet, you're on your soapbox, preaching how we're messing with people's lives?"

The last thing I need is for these three hyenas to point out my sins when I'm already wallowing in the watering hole, waiting for my lion friends to eat me whole. "I didn't hurt anyone," I seethe. *Except myself.* "I'm not saying it was a good decision, but there is a difference."

"Sure, sure. Whatever helps you sleep at night." Madison N laughs.

"You have what you want. It's your turn. Tell me about Laney. How did you know she wasn't going to participate? And what did that fucked-up post at my luncheon mean? Or the finger? Where did it come from?"

I feel like I'm about to break, but I need to hold on. I need to ignore their comments until they tell me where she is. I've sacrificed too much not to help Laney now.

"Can I tell you a secret?" Madison J pauses, and I nod. "Laney doesn't like you. Like, at all. Never has, if we're being perfectly honest. You two were forever competing for the same role on teams or homecoming court, but you always won. That burned her fiercely. So, when you started texting, asking how she was doing with her internship, she knew what you were after. Ainsley Clarke trying to get ahead. She wanted to sabotage your party, so we agreed to help. And since Hunter happens to have a cousin who's a waiter that gigs at the Monteleone, it wasn't hard to ruin things."

While Madison is still physically holding the knife, she just metaphorically plunged it into my heart. I can't let this sink me. Whether Laney is a true friend or not, I still need to help her. "That doesn't explain where she is now." I need to keep my emotions stable. Get them to make a mistake. "Hunter said she was home, shopping for a dress. Riley said she was in Georgia. Which is it?"

"Riley's phone ended up stuffed in her throat. I think she was fed more than just bad information, don't you?" Madison K quips.

How do they know about the phone? The police chief told my father, but as far as I know, it's not public record. Unless—

They're the murderers.

"Where is she? What did you do to her?" Raising my voice, I hope my friends take the hint. *Please save me.*

I don't want to die by way of the fucking Madisons.

I will never live this down. Even in death.

Madison J faces me. "We planned to have her come out, after being a no-show for Crescent, and in the meantime, we'd run a few stories. Especially the one about your party. We knew it would blow up the site. But you two are cut from the same cloth, because she ghosted us. Guess she decided to do her own thing." Her eyes harden. "That's why we had to kill her and her little plot arc from our site. This isn't high school. We don't have to bow down to girls like you or Laney anymore."

"I'm sure the girls in prison will be much kinder," I say.

"Help!" Madison K screams as Eli and Jamie blast past the Pac-Man machine and head straight for her, knocking the knife from her hands.

Blair and Piper block the other two, while Violet zips around with her phone on record. "For people manipulating the narrative, you'd think you would've planned better alibis. But no. Can't get any more incriminating than that!" She aims her phone at each of their faces. "Three on one, waving a knife at a girl. It looked bad enough without the audio. Too bad I have both."

Madison K tries to wrangle out of Jamie's grip. "We were thinking of unmasking ourselves at the end of the season, anyway. You're just giving us a more dramatic way to finish. Take your hands off me!"

"I doubt the police will be watching with popcorn, you crazies," Jamie says, tightening his hold on her. "This shit was nuts in the first place, but for you three to amp it up to this notch, you're truly insane. Whoever heard of killing for social media *Likes*?"

"Kill? We didn't *kill* anyone!" Madison N yells. "We fucked with people, yes. But we didn't murder anyone."

"I spoke to you. One of you"—I point between them—"on the phone the night of Maskers. The night those guys' brakes were cut. That wasn't an accident. You posted about it."

"FYI, we got that video and scoop from one of Gus's friends, and I don't know how hard you hit your head, but I didn't fucking call you, Ainsley. Considering how apprehensive we were to meet today; you should know better. We weren't invited to Maskers. Which is why we asked for a story from it in exchange for taking Violet's down," Madison J explains.

"In exchange for *what*?" Violet's eyes widen. "Ainsley—"

"None of that matters." I cut her off. "They're not admitting anything. Call the cops so they can search them. Maybe link some DNA or something."

"Go ahead," Madison K says. "If you call them, I'll use my one call to send that story out about you and Cooper."

Eli's pained expression nearly takes my breath away.

I mouth: *Sorry.*

"Later," he says, brows knitted.

"Go ahead—run the fucking story." I get face-to-face with Madison K. "You three are finished either way. Who cares about my reputation if it saves a person's life, sickos."

"No, wait," Madison J falters. "Give us a day. We won't run the story. Violet has everything on video. If we do anything, or go anywhere, you can call the police."

"Why should we give you a day?" Piper asks.

"Because if I'm getting arrested on some BS charges, I'd like to see my family one last time. Or get a freaking lawyer." Madison J counters. "What will it hurt? You caught us, right? No more Under the Gown posts. No more mayhem."

"Why should I care about *your* family, Madison?" I ask. "Did you care about Chief Coyne or the rest of Riley's family when you murdered her? How about Laney's family, hmm?"

"Are you dense? We didn't *kill* anyone. Jeez." Her face turns red, like she might cry. "If you give us a day, I'll prove it. Plus, maybe figure out who's actually doing this." She stares at Violet. "For someone who's been accused of something she didn't do, I'd hope you might be the one to grant leniency. Considering how often your family is accused of various offenses."

"I'm not my family," Violet shoots back. "Besides, none of you cared to learn the truth before you released my story."

"Then be better than your family. And us," she says. "Think of it as good karma. What does another day hurt?"

"Why are you being charmed by liars?" Eli growls. "This one had a *knife*." He kicks the offending weapon away from her foot.

"It's for protection. And yes, maybe a bit of intimidation. We didn't want someone snitching on us." Madison K's voice quivers.

"We didn't plan to hurt anyone. Riley is our friend. *Was* our friend. We're not evil."

Jamie slides next to me and Piper. "What if she's telling the truth? Would one day hurt?"

"Why negotiate with terrorists?" I say. "That's what they want. More time to do God knows what. Look what they did with that website. Do you want them to have time to kill another person?" I pace. "C'mon. Guys don't give in."

Piper looks at me with disgust. "Obviously, you have more blind spots than you think, Ainsley. I think it's fine." She turns to Violet. "It's up to you."

She hates me. She will never forgive what I did.

"I can send the video to everyone here," Violet explains. "If any of them are unaccounted for tomorrow, it goes to the police. And if you three don't check in with us every hour, then it goes to the police." They nod. "Stay your asses home. No contacting each other. No posts. Nothing," Violet cautions. Again, each snake nods. "If you attempt to screw with any of us, I'll cause a greater hell than the one you've put everyone through. Understood?"

They bobble their heads, and Madison N wipes tears from her blotchy face. "And end this fucking party! I'm sick of this stupid season," Violet says, slipping between the machines without another word.

"I'll take this." Eli points to the knife. "It has your fingerprints on it, so your murder weapon stays with me." He wraps his coat around his hand and grabs the handle, exiting from the arcade circle.

Holding hands, Jamie and Piper also file out.

They're obviously done with this night. And me.

"Wait up," I yell, lungs burning as I try to catch them in the parking lot. "You have no idea how sorry I am. Eli, I wanted to tell you so many times, but I couldn't."

"I can't do this." He books it to his truck with Blair following behind.

Piper whips around. "You and Cooper? *Really*? If you wanted the spot to Maskers that bad, you could've told me. My God, you didn't have to do that," she shouts. "You lied to me, Ainsley. I'm your best friend. At least, I thought I was. But you took every shortcut to beat me to a finish line I didn't even care to compete in. I know this shit is important to you, but deb season doesn't define your whole goddamn life like you think it does."

"I wasn't trying to beat you," I sob.

"Then what? What were you chasing?"

"Me! I was chasing *me*, Piper." My voice catches and I suddenly feel weak. "My entire life, I've tried to fit in. Tried to find a way to feel like I belong in this city. Its culture. Every time I thought I'd succeeded, the goalpost moved, and I was back in last place. When I finally got asked to be a debutante, I figured it was my one shot to make my mark. And the only way I knew how to do that was to make sure I networked with anyone who was anything. Because if not, what chance would I have later?"

"Ainsley," Piper hugs her sweater to her chest. "I love you, and I'm happy we have a trio of psychopaths detained. That we no longer have to worry about *this* anymore. But today is not the day for me to praise you for realizing what everyone already knows."

Biting back tears, I nod.

Violet starts to say something, but I shake my head. "Go. I'll get a ride. You can chew me out later. I can't leave knowing you all hate me at the same time."

"Ainsley!" Violet yells as I walk back to the entrance, but she doesn't chase me.

Not that I blame her. I deserve this and so much more.

. . .

Luke answers on the fourth ring. "I said I was worried, but I'm kinda at a party."

"Pick me up. Please," I sob.

"Hold on." His phone rustles. "Okay. Now I can hear you. Are you still at that janky rink? I didn't know you were upset. Are you hurt? Please don't cry, Ainsley. You're making me nervous! I'll be right there."

Keys jangle and his car starts.

"I should be happy because we stopped everything. But I'm not, Luke," I choke out. "Everyone is so angry at me. And I don't know how to fix it."

"You're not making sense. Stop crying," Luke pleads.

But I can't stop crying.

I cry so much, by the time he picks me up from the rink, I've almost lost my voice. While I know what I did was right, it certainly doesn't feel that way. Not after all the people I hurt in the process.

Or the fact that there's a nagging voice in my brain, whispering:

What if we're wrong?

What if the Madisons are telling the truth?

CHAPTER 23

THE NEXT MORNING
JANUARY 14

Catching a killer or killers should warrant the brightest morning afterglow, but I'm tucked under my blankets, hiding from the consequences it took to get there. Maybe I'm not the biggest villain of this story, but tell that to my friends, because if this hadn't been life or death, I probably would've kept on lying.

They know that. Exactly why they're angry.

"Ainsley?" My mom knocks. "I made breakfast. When I said it was chocolate-chip pancakes and you refused, I knew something was wrong. Like to share?"

"Dad's down there, and . . . I-I just can't," I mumble through the covers. Last night, when we got home and my dad was sitting in the living room, I ran upstairs without saying a word.

"Your father is concerned. As am I." She settles next to me. "You understand why we're worried, right?"

"Yes, Mother. I'm intimately aware of the situation." I poke my head out. "I know what Chief Coyne told him about Riley. And that Alexandra's family thinks she may not have died of a—"

"Alexandra was poisoned," she blurts, wringing her hands. "He didn't want to scare you further, but it wasn't an accident."

"*What?*" My mind reels back to her bloody smile. "Oh, God. I-I could've sworn her mouth was bleeding before she hit the ground, Mom. I thought I remembered wrong, out of shock or something, but it was real, wasn't it?"

"I'm no expert, but it's likely the poison was taking effect. From what we've heard, a substance has been isolated, but they're still running tests. Whoever is doing this is playing a very wicked game."

The Madisons were at Crescent. Since they weren't in the presentation, they certainly had the time and opportunity to dose Alexandra, or anything she might have come in contact with. Since Under the Gown blew up after her death, especially after the vigil, they didn't just profit from her death—they caused it.

"Sweetie, are you okay?"

No—I'm not. "I'm sorry. What were you saying?"

"I said whatever happened with your friends, I'm sure you can fix it."

"That's the problem." I stick my head out further. "I keep thinking I can fix everything, but I've failed on an epic level. Grandma Gertrude told me there's nothing you can't fix except death and Scrabble. But I don't know how to fix this."

My mother shakes her head. "She cheats at every game. Her first husband was arrested trying to *fix* a minor league baseball game. Your grandmother may be wise in many ways, but never take her literally."

"What am I supposed to do?" I sit up, groaning as the sun blasts my eyes. "Lose?"

"If you're playing a game, you've already lost." She removes the section of hair I pulled over my eyes to block the sun. "You need to stop hiding. Figure out what you can control and let the other variables go. Just like hurricane season. We watch the news. Fasten the storm shutters, and hell, can even drive eighteen hours in traffic, but that storm is gonna hit somewhere, no matter what we do. And we have to deal with the aftermath, right?"

"You're saying my best option is to stall, run, or blindly create a storm shelter to cry in?" I flop back onto my pillow. "How does that work for people?"

"As in anyone, or just that girlfriend of yours?"

"Both. They all mutually dislike me enough to stop a storm right now," I respond weakly. "I kinda deserve it."

"Then sometimes you need to get rained on." My mom laughs at my wounded expression. "If you need me to be your umbrella, ask. In the meantime, please come downstairs and eat."

"I can't—"

"Luke's been staring at your food. He said if you don't come down in five minutes, he should be allowed a free pass."

I jump out of bed before she can stand, yelling at Luke and his black hole of a stomach because suddenly—I'm starving.

When Eli calls, I nearly spit out my orange juice. I want to throw my phone in the oven and hide from whatever verbal ass kicking I'm about to get, but I don't. "Um, hello?"

"Hey . . . yeah, this is awkward. Can we meet? Pontiff Playground?"

That's all it takes to get me moving.

I don't know how, but Eli looks sadder than me. Leaning against the gazebo by the tennis courts, his beanie is tugged low around his messy hair, his hoodie stretched tightly over his muscled body.

"I'm sorry—"

"I'm sorry."

We say it in unison.

"You don't have to apologize to me. You should be mad. I went behind your back with your *brother*."

His mouth twists. "Do you remember when we were kids and Piper had a momentary crush on Cooper?" He motions for us to sit on a rusty picnic bench. "I was so jealous I asked you to pretend-marry me, so we could get back at them."

"I remember," I say. "You made me a ring out of weeds, and I wouldn't put it on because the little flowers clashed with my dress." A tear slips down my face, thinking of that memory, which further reinforces how awful of a friend I've been.

"You told me you thought boys were gross, except for me. You said you had a crush on Laura Wilkinson and didn't want to mess up your chances." He finishes the story, laughing. "Honestly, I loved how much you *didn't* love Cooper. You saw through his bullshit and would rather play with me, no matter what."

The tears keep coming, despite me trying to whisk them away. The last thing I need is for Eli to feel sorry for me. *This is my fault.* "You're just giving me more reasons to apologize." I sniff. "I didn't mean to betray you. You've always been an amazing friend."

"Ainsley, do you like Cooper? Like at all? Romantically, physically, hell, even platonically?" he asks, baby blues boring into my soul.

"No," I answer without hesitation. If there's one thing I'm sure of—and there's not much these days—it's that. "I just wanted an invite. I asked him if he could get me one. It wasn't until later I figured out it came with strings. It was the only way he'd ask me."

"And the picture?"

"It seemed to be part of the deal." I shrug.

"Then I'm the one who should apologize because my brother is a manipulative asshole who used something he knew you wanted to get something for himself." He kicks a rock in the grass. "Sure, I'm upset you didn't tell me. But even more, I feel like the biggest idiot for not stopping him. I failed you, Ainsley, because I didn't protect you."

"W-what?" My throat constricts.

"This past summer, whenever you came over, you seemed extra jumpy. If you heard the front door, you'd zoom upstairs to my room. I figured you were stressed over this deb thing. That you didn't want to deal with everyone's antics. But the second I heard you telling the Madisons last night, it clicked. Cooper's lucky he wasn't at that party last night. I tore through the house looking for him when I got home."

"Don't feel bad for me." I clutch my arms. "Not like he forced it. There are people who deserve actual sympathy. I used Cooper to get ahead. That's on me."

"What if Cooper used *you*?" Eli moves to my side of the table. Looping his arm over my shoulder, he gives me a big hug.

"Then I'm the idiot who got played," I croak, snuggling into his hoodie, crying even harder.

"It's okay. You can't always be two steps ahead of everything. Sometimes, it's not worth it. Even if you make another mistake, I'll be here to knock some sense into you, or anyone who thinks they can mess with my friend." He's doing his best to soothe me. "You were ready to give that picture to Under the Gown and ruin your reputation. Hell, maybe even your future, to stop someone else from getting hurt. I think you're brave as hell."

"Stop being so nice." I groan, my head bouncing on his chest as it rises and falls from laughter. "I had this whole plan on how you'd be so angry, and I'd know what to say. I never expected—"

"You haven't been doing well with your plans recently." He uses his sleeve to wipe my face. "Please . . . stop crying. I feel like the bad guy. Sure, I was mad, but I back-talked everyone in the car after we left. I gave Piper an earful for chewing you out. She started bawling about being a horrible friend, and Jamie became a human napkin."

"I need to call her." I grab my phone. Eli puts his hand over it and points at his truck, where I see Piper hovering in the passenger seat. "Thanks. I owe you one."

"You owe me more than one. How about just letting me win at Clue next time?" He grins. "I also may have told Violet to show in fifteen minutes. That will give you and Piper time to put your best-friend Band-Aids on, or whatever it is you girls do. When you're done, I have snacks. Figured we could celebrate the end of this rotten season, given our victory."

I dash to his truck, nearly colliding with Piper as she jumps out, flinging her arms around my neck. "I'm sorry." She wails. "I was so angry you hid something from me, instead of thinking about how you might feel."

"Thinking about myself is what got me into this mess. I've been a debutante-zilla. We could've just had fun. Enjoyed the parties. But I decided to stake my whole life on this shit." I drop my head. "My only salvation is that I got to trade in one of my shittiest days ever to catch those psycho clones."

"Oh, about that . . . they've stayed put. We've been taking turns stalking their houses, in between hourly texts. Violet makes her driver pass every hour to amp the intimidation." Piper pulls back from the hug, adjusting my rumpled hair. "Your girlfriend can be very intimidating, you know."

"I know." I groan, and we both laugh. "But she's on our side, so it's cool. Plus, she's really hot." Piper whacks my arm. "Eli said she's on her way. Is Jamie coming too?"

"Yep. He and Blair had last patrol. They should be here shortly. Plus, they're bringing beignets and coffee."

As we talk, I text Violet:

A

Sorry how messy things got. Heard you've been doing overtime with the girls. Thanks for helping out.

VIOLET

I should've gone with you. I'm sorry. I didn't know what to do or say, so I poured energy into turning the outside of the Madisons' homes into an episode of S.W.A.T.

A

I have silver dollars and you have a small militia. Maybe we should've just gotten each other flowers.

VIOLET

You're too weird for something that normal.

A

Gee, thanks babe : -(

VIOLET

You're my fave because you aren't normal. Save the seat next to you for a groveling girlfriend. Be there soon.

A

<3

Placing my phone in my pocket, my excitement builds over seeing Violet.

Piper nods toward the sidewalk. "Speak of the devil, here they are."

Blair waves her white bag in the air like a flag as she rushes to Eli. "Figures she went to him first. Sucker." Piper rolls her eyes. "I know Jamie's got coffee, but look at him. Slow as a sea slug."

"That's your boy." I watch as he bobbles the drink carrier, grinning.

"Yes, he is." Piper's voice is full of pride. She's finally in a positive relationship, and I couldn't be happier. She points across the field. "Get a look at that retro jumpsuit that jogger has on. Remember when our moms wore those velour tracksuits?"

"Yes. The ones with bedazzled statements on the ass. Hate to break it to ya, but they're back in style. Minus the logos, thank goodness."

"Never going on this ass." She slaps her butt, then points at the jogger again. "Wait, what's that on his face?"

I cup my hands to block the sun. "A *mask*? Weird, right?"

"What kind of freak jogs with a Mardi Gras mask?" Piper grabs my hand, rushing us toward Jamie. "Jamie! Turn around!"

He turns and his eyes widen. "Hey!" he yells. When he does, a crack of lightning rips the sky, and a murder of crows rise from the fence, cawing their grievances as they're spooked from their spot.

Except it's not raining. The sun is out. And it's not lightning.

I've shot enough skeet to know what a gunshot sounds like. Even if I hadn't, it doesn't take more than a second to realize it's what I've heard when the drink carrier slips from Jamie's hands.

He collapses on the sidewalk.

"Jamie!" Piper runs faster. "Eli, help!"

"Call the police!" Eli screams, streaking after the jogger who is now halfway down the block.

"They have a gun, Eli! Don't go!" I yell, watching his figure fade, then I sprint over to Piper, who is on her knees, cradling the upper half of Jamie's body.

"I think I spilled the coffee . . . sorry. Must've w-walked too fast." Jamie tries to joke, pulling a hand from his chest, blood covering his palm. "Fell pretty hard, huh?"

"You'll be okay. Just keep talking," I say, watching Piper pressing her hands over his wound. "He needs a hospital. Now!"

"Blair is calling 911," Piper says, never taking her eyes off him. "Baby, hang on! We have that movie marathon this week. You're gonna explain those Marvel movies to me."

"C-can't wait. You'll love Spider-Man. He has these webs . . ." He trails off, waking again when Piper yells more questions.

"Tell me about his webs!" she sobs, tears running down her face.

All around, blood pools on the white cement, filling in the joints of the sidewalk, leaking into the grass. This is not good—*he's losing way too much blood.*

"He uses webs to fight the bad guys," Jamie sputters. "I don't think we caught the bad guys, Pipes."

"We did. We came here to celebrate. Remember?" She sobs louder. "Call 911 again! Help, Ainsley, please!"

I rush to find out if Blair has reached anyone. Her phone is glued to her ear, and she mouths that she's been calling nonstop. That every dispatcher says the same thing.

Five minutes.

He may not have five minutes.

I scan the playground, looking for anyone to help, but it's empty. "Should we drive him ourselves?" I ask Blair while she talks to another dispatcher.

She shakes her head, so I dial 911. The lady says we could do more harm than good if we move him. That as long as the wound's compressed, it's best to keep him still until help arrives. She offers to remain on the phone, but Blair's already holding on.

I hang up.

Blood colors my fingertips and stains my phone.

I'm drowning in Jamie's blood.

My phone buzzes. "Yes, hello? Are you on your way?"

"Clarke? It's Leslie."

"I can't talk—"

"It's important, I swear," she rushes. "You asked how I knew to look into Violet's files. I wanted you to know I overheard Alexandra telling a den mother there were some weird flowers in her bouquet. She said she thought Violet messed with them."

"Leslie, I can't. Jamie's been shot! I have to go."

"Wait, what—"

I hang up. I can't think about anything but Jamie.

Sirens blare in the distance, but Piper is wailing louder. "No, no, no!" she yells.

Blair and I run back to Piper and Eli does too, panting from running. "I couldn't catch them. How is he?" he asks. It's like he's suddenly afraid to look at Jamie or touch him. He glances at me, then Piper.

"Eli, help him!" Piper screams, answering his question. "I can't stop his bleeding! Why aren't y'all doing anything?"

She's frantic, and I don't know what to do. Jamie has been shot in the stomach. There's no way to tie it off, or whatever they do when someone's bleeding from a limb.

Two ambulances blaze into the parking lot and EMTs swarm.

My eyes flick back to Jamie. He's staring at the sun and his face is losing color.

Please, don't let him die!

"Piper. You need to let go." I grab her shoulders gently. "Let them do their job. They'll take care of him."

I manage to pull her away and they start chest compressions. Moments later, we watch them load him onto a stretcher. Piper's hands hover in the air where Jamie was, rocking back and forth on her knees, staring at the ambulance as red lights flash. They drive away with Jamie. "He didn't have a pulse, Ainsley. They can fix him, right?"

She sobs, and I wrap my arms around her.

She's broken and I don't know how to help her. Or Jamie.

Remember, Ainsley, my grandma's voice echoes. *The only thing you can't fix is death.*

CHAPTER 24

THREE DAYS LATER
JANUARY 17

Jamie's murder makes headline news.

Day three and three mourners sit in a bedroom, wondering where our fourth player of Clue went, how we could've fingered the wrong suspect, the wrong weapon, and didn't even predict the right location. It seems the entire city has something to say, except for me and Piper, who refuses to go home because there are way too many Polaroid photos of them pinned to her walls, which she can't bear to look at or take down. Or Eli, who hasn't left Piper's side, talking mainly to himself, repeating what he should've done, but didn't.

"Pipes," I say softly, since anything louder may startle her. She stops pacing and settles in the window seat of my bedroom. "Do you need something to eat or drink? Can I do anything?"

"I thought we did enough." She stares out the window. "But we didn't. And no—nothing matters anymore."

"There's still a killer out there. One that ran past a bunch of houses, which means he's bound to be seen on someone's Ring or security camera. The outfit was pretty unique." I cross my room and sit on an ottoman across from her. "Whoever did this to Jamie deserves to rot in jail. We need justice. For *him*."

"You can slip out of a tracksuit, pull off a mask, and *bam*—you're a new person," Eli says from where he's seated next to the door, a hockey stick leaning against him. "If the police had footage of the person, pretty sure they would've shared it with the public. My guess is no one knows shit."

"Jamie never heard of debutante season before us." Piper frowns, the flat line of her lips growing wobbly. "We dragged him into this. Yet, he's the one paying for it. How is that fair? Stupid us . . . we thought it was the Madisons."

"Blair should've told us," Eli curses. "We assumed they were guilty because they knew about Riley's cell phone. Without that, we wouldn't have been as confident."

Though Eli is upset, in actuality, Blair wasn't trying to betray us. She later admitted she'd tipped Under the Gown off about the details regarding Riley's death before the party in a last-ditch attempt to have them meet her. The Madisons used her information to try to scare me off.

"I'll be back." I tap Piper's knee, but she barely notices.

With Luke at wrestling practice, I've started hiding in his room during the day whenever I feel a panic attack coming on. I can't let Piper see me like that. It could derail her further.

Sitting on his bed, I close my eyes and do my breathwork.

After several minutes, my heart slows, and I dial Madison N. "Ainsley, I'm . . . we're so sorry about Jamie," she says. "I told you we didn't hurt anyone."

"This isn't the time for *I told you so*," I snap. While they may not have pulled the trigger or sunk a knife into a body, they certainly set the stage for someone else to do so. "You said you needed a day to figure things out. Your time is way up."

Papers rustle in the background. "About that. I printed the

timelines of where we were when tips came in to prove we couldn't have cut those boys' brakes. Or hurt Riley."

I remember Leslie's call. "Hang on. I'll call you right back."

She answers on the first ring. "Ainsley, I'm so, so sorry about Jamie. When you said he was shot, I never thought you meant *shot-shot*. By a gun. This is horrible."

"Pretty hard to believe. Piper is completely out of it."

"Do they have any leads?"

"Not yet." I let out another breath, hoping not to have another attack.

"I'm sure you're not ready to talk about it, but if there's anything I can do for you or Piper, please let me know."

"There *is* something you can do for me."

"Of course."

"Can you finish telling me what went down at the Crescent presentation? Like, with Alexandra and her flowers? So many bad things have happened. I keep thinking maybe they're connected in some weird way."

There's a brief silence on the other end.

"What I did with Violet's records is *not* connected. Just me being a bitch, but sure, anything to help. Like I said, Alexandra was freaked about her flowers. I heard her say she thought Violet had something to do with it."

"What was wrong with them? Did she say why she thought Violet did something?"

"She said Violet had a grudge over something that happened years ago. And basically, she was medically insane." She pauses again. "It's what gave me the idea to dig into her files. Partly, I was curious. Mainly because, well, I was jealous. I thought if she had more secrets than you thought, you may break up with her. Which I guess she does."

My mind reels—*Olly*. Violet said a girl had apologized for poisoning her dog.

"You didn't hear anything else?"

"No. And Ainsley . . . I'm sorry about Jamie and for posting Violet's records. If I had a do-over, obviously I would choose differently."

I call Madison back. "Sorry. I had to take a call from my mom," I lie. "This may seem like an odd question, but would you happen to have a photo of Alexandra from, um, the Crescent presentation?"

"That's dark." She sighs. "We would never post something like that."

"I didn't ask if you posted it. I asked if you have a photo. Please don't tell me everyone grew a conscience and didn't record it or pass it around."

She doesn't respond.

"This isn't another scare tactic. I don't even need to see *her*. I just want to see her bouquet."

"Sure, whatever. Check your phone."

I tap *speaker* as Madison's message loads. It's a photo of Alexandra on all fours, with her flowers scattered on the ground. She had dropped them right before she fainted. Pinching the screen, I zoom in on her bouquet.

Red and white petals litter the ground.

Our bouquets were red roses, nothing else. I know because I still have the thing with all its browning petals stuck into a pen caddy on the corner of my desk.

I zoom in tighter . . . holy shit.

Oleanders.

We used to have a bush in our backyard until my parents realized it was poisonous and chopped it down.

"Are you there?" Madison asks.

"Yes. Um, you wouldn't happen to know where Alexandra went to school?"

"St. Philomena's. Why?"

Violet never told me where she went to school, but I'm pretty sure she also went to St. Philomena's. It's not hard to confirm, and if she did go there, it means she failed to mention she and Alexandra were schoolmates.

"I don't understand what's happening. Or why," I mumble. "If you three aren't guilty, who then? Someone slashed our tires, so it means—"

"Um. . . ." She coughs. "That kinda was us," she blurts. "We were so pissed at you for giving us a dressing down in front of everyone at the memorial, Madison K decided we should teach you a lesson. You know, flatten something of yours, like you did our egos. She stuck a knife in your tire, but once she did, we got scared. We figured it would look too suspicious to have only yours slashed. We decided to spook everyone instead of just you."

"How very thoughtful," I fume. Even with everything she's admitted, the dots aren't connecting. If anything, they've become more like random facts on a widely variable, nonlinear equation:

The finger—Laney's idea.

The suspicion that the killer tipped Leslie off to Violet's files— no longer viable.

Even our slashed tires are being claimed by the Madisons.

We kept assuming the killer had been wholly responsible for the mayhem, but it looks like any number of people have contributed to the carnage with their own brand of cruelty. "What about the phone call at Maskers?" I ask.

"Like I said, we have no clue about that. Swear. We were shocked when we actually got your photos. Yes, technically we bribed you for proof, but we never thought you'd come through. But yours came the same night and nearly the same time as your girlfriend's. We got a twofer and could hardly believe our luck."

"Wait—what? Violet sent you photos from *Maskers*? How?" I grip the headboard of the bed. "She couldn't have. She didn't go to the ball."

"Tell that to Ms. Owl," Madison snips. "While your photo was amazing, Violet hit the motherlode. She messaged some from the ball, which not only proved it exists, but included photos of the members, though most were masked. She even sent a shot of the program with each girl's symbolic animal listed."

"If she was there, why didn't she tell me?" I pause. "If that's true, why didn't you expose Maskers with *her* photos?"

"Because we know better. We *do* live here, Ainsley. Despite what you think, we're not stupid. Your photo only implicated Rachel and those two guys. Not Maskers. But you keep playing with your aged-up Scooby Doo gang. I want no part. No way am I becoming the next Jamie do-over. No offense."

Madison clears her throat, like she's getting choked up, but it's a little late for remorse. "For the record, I think whatever sicko is behind this used Under the Gown to further their purpose. Or maybe they just wanted to frame us? Either way, I think they used the posts as leads for easy hunting grounds."

While I agree that UTG, in one way or another, is responsible for serving up a killer, one thing doesn't make sense. "Maybe, but aren't most of your followers debs or members of the clubs? That narrows it down quite a bit."

"It's still a giant list, Ainsley. It includes alumni, some parents. Not like we could vet everyone once we started getting such a huge following." She sighs. "Why, what's your angle?"

"What if someone used a fake profile? Can you check the names to see if they're all legit?"

"That will take forever. Why should we—"

"Because you three could still get in trouble for fucking up everyone's life with your shitty slanderous account and wild tire-slashing spree," I snap. "You're not innocent. Why don't you use this chance to turn your garbage attitude around? The least you could do is try to help catch whoever killed Jamie and Riley. Not to mention, Laney is still missing. In case you've forgotten."

"Harsh. Of course, we haven't forgotten. And fine, but that

means we'll have to do a post. We can do an OOTD, or some other boring shit. That way, El Psycho doesn't get suspicious, and we won't become his next targets."

I hang up, throwing my phone at Luke's pillow. I need to talk to Violet, who I'd been avoiding since Jamie's shooting because on that horrible day, of all days, Violet was a no-show, and the more I allow the idea of Violet being guilty to marinate in my brain, the worse I feel being around Piper.

If I let a snake into our group, I'm responsible for its bite.

"I'm going to meet Violet," I say, bursting back into my room.

Eli and Piper jerk their heads up.

"I don't know what she's done, or didn't do, but I need to talk to her. So keep an eye out if I don't call back soon."

"She *was* at every event. Knew exactly where we'd be and when," Eli says, cracking his knuckles. "But there's no way, right?"

"Be careful, Ains." Piper sniffs. "I can't lose anyone else; you understand?"

Magazine Street is packed with cars, shoppers, and enough buildings to duck into should it become necessary, so I'm no longer terrified about the thought of being in the open like I was an hour ago. Hopefully, we can just walk and talk on this very public, very busy street.

"Hey." Leaning against her car, Violet's black hair is pulled into a messy bun and she's wearing an oversized cardigan, leggings, and ballet flats. Low-key for sure, but just the sight of her makes me angry and my heart ache at the same time. "I've been calling. How's Piper?"

"Traumatized. Heartbroken," I say coldly. "It's been hard on all of us. You know, to see a friend get shot and *die*. Guess you wouldn't know since you never showed." I land my first dig.

"I was running late, Ainsley." Her face tightens. "I don't know why you're so angry I wasn't there. Not like I could've changed the outcome."

"Where were you?"

"On the phone with my parents. They want me back in Texas until things settle down. I had to fight with them to stay here. With *you*." She sighs. "I've been by your side through everything, and I'm trying—"

"*Trying*? Like at Maskers?" I unleash the elephant and let it stampede across the pavement. Her eyes widen. "Why didn't you tell me you were going?"

"Why didn't *you* tell *me*?" She fires back. "When I saw you, I tried to follow you, but you disappeared; then I had to haul ass back for the presentation."

"I'm sorry. I was too busy being blackmailed on a call from whom I assumed was UTG, but now have no clue who I talked to."

"You sent the photo of Rachel doing drugs, right?"

"I did. And you sent numerous others," I counter. "Tell me how that was possible? Tell me how you managed to keep your phone?"

"I brought two." Her face flames. "I'm not the first in my family to attend that ball, but I certainly hope to be the last." She pauses. "Guess UTG spilled the tea, huh? Did they mention they said *you* were using *me*? That my family was just another sports connection for you. They said you sent in the photo to implicate Rachel, and you weren't worried about finding Laney at all. They said all you wanted was to steal her job or use her to get your own."

"And you believed them?" I raise my eyebrows, but she doesn't respond. "You know how upset I've been about Laney. That as soon as Riley told me the cops weren't looking for her, I wanted to help. And obviously, still do."

She holds her hand out, but I shake my head. "I know you won't believe me, but I told them that. I defended you."

"UTG didn't give me a choice, Violet. I had to throw the person actually doing the coke under the bus, or fall under it for them," I snap. "In case you don't remember what the Madisons said at the rink, I only agreed to send in a photo to get your goddamn post pulled. I could've stayed away from all of this if it wasn't for you. So, the real question is: Why would *you* send Under the Gown photos to expose Maskers? Because I did it to help someone I cared about."

Her eyes spark. "I went because my family made me. I figured if I could get UTG to post about it, maybe it would lose appeal for the next go-around. Possibly spare someone else from this social circus. But those cowards didn't post one."

"Always the martyr." I laugh. "I forgot how much better you think you are than us. Turning the debutante scene into your own modern-day crusade."

"It's not a sin to try to tear down a building that should've already been condemned." Her voice raises. "Didn't you learn your lesson after Cooper? Look how much hurt you caused the people you care about over meaningless shit."

"You mean the way you hurt Alexandra?" I say it softly, because as mad as I am, this is a do-or-die moment. "Leslie overheard her telling a den mother you messed with her flowers. Oleanders, Violet?"

She looks away, and I hold my breath, waiting for an answer that could divide us forever, whether she's innocent or not.

"I didn't hurt her." She exhales. "I-I just wanted to scare her. I was so angry to be back in this city that when I ran into her, I felt like the kid they kept picking on all over again. Her apology only made things worse. It proved she had grown up. That she was trying to move on from a heinous middle school act. Yet, here I was . . . still bitter."

Seeing Violet this vulnerable punches a hole through my heart.

I want to believe her. I really do. But I've been wrong before, and I can't allow my emotions to sway me into making another mistake. This is no longer about Violet and me. There are lives at stake. "Why didn't you say something? Why couldn't you have given me a reason to believe you?"

"You were the only one who didn't judge me. Is it wrong to want to keep it that way?" She steps forward, looking pained when I step back. "Once everyone grew suspicious of the season, I was scared to say anything because what I did . . . it was wrong."

"You think? She died from *poison*, Violet." I level the accusation at her. "You were at the party with Riley. And you knew where to find us when Jamie got shot. But your excuse is simply that you've been trying to overthrow the whole fucking system as your motivation? What am I supposed to think?"

"That your girlfriend isn't a monster. That I'm incapable of doing something so horrible." She stares with watery green eyes. "That I would never accuse you of what you're accusing me of doing."

"Then give me a reason not to," I plead. "Give me a solid answer I can tell Piper, who is comatose in my bedroom. Or Eli, who thinks he's failed us all."

"I really cared for you." She wipes the tears pouring down her face. "You managed to worm past every wall I tried to keep up, and I let you. But this is how you repay me? You're looking at me the same way everyone does when they read my files. The way people look at my family. I'm just a big, bad Anderson. Guess I check off all the boxes to solve your mystery, right?"

"Violet." I reach out on instinct.

This time, she shakes her head. "There's nothing left to say. Go find the evidence you need to incriminate me, and I'll keep being exactly who I've been this whole time. Bye, Ainsley."

"Are you going back to Texas?" I ask, feeling like the shittiest person alive at the look she throws back. Because the unspoken translation of my words is—*I need to know where you are, in case you're the killer.*

"Don't worry. I'll be around. Andersons don't run away." Her frown morphs into a hardened smile. "Not all of us can hide behind photographs, Miss July. Maybe you can sleep with that dreamy officer, and he'll solve this for you."

I gasp, trying my best to keep standing. To keep breathing while my heart vacates my body. While she shakes her head and walks away.

Because really, what more could I say after a kill shot like that?

CHAPTER 25

JANUARY 18

"I don't want to lose Violet," I mumble into my bowl of cereal, exhaustion beckoning me back under my blankets. I hadn't slept. I kept trying to recreate scenarios where Violet *wasn't* guilty, replaying our last argument over and over. Thinking of the things I should've asked or said because despite my suspicions or the awful things she'd said to me, my heart still aches.

And once again, I don't know how to stop the bleeding.

"Ditto with Blair," Eli says, tilting the family-size box of cereal into his mouth, crunching more Cheerios.

"I've already lost Jamie." Piper pushes around the untouched food on her plate. "Do you really think it's her? Is it possible she was working with the Madisons?"

Once I came home and relayed what happened, Piper started to brush off the dust that had settled on her catatonic state and became motivated to solve the crime. "Negative to the Madisons. She'd never met them before the season started. What I think is she hid lots of things that make her look suspicious, but nothing

237

that merits an actual accusation," I say. "Jamie's case is still considered a potential robbery gone bad, so there's that. But I do think whoever came after him did it because we stopped Under the Gown."

"Who we thought was the killer," Eli says. "So when we took out their smokescreen, they retaliated?"

Piper jumps from the bed, becoming more animated. "Maybe, I mean, Violet is the only one in our group who wasn't there. But honestly, any of us could've told the killer where we were meeting, hypothetically speaking. What if Violet *not* being there is the perfect foil? They might want us to suspect her, instead of the *actual* culprit?"

"Alexandra was poisoned. Violet admitted she put oleanders in her bouquet for revenge." I say, shaking my head. "Not exactly great."

"It doesn't mean she murdered her. Besides, don't you have to actually eat them to be poisoned?" Eli asks, tapping away on his phone. "I may be put on a watchlist for searching this subject, but according to this, I'm right. She'd have to ingest it or breathe in its smoke."

"What now? Do we need to go back to where this started?" Piper asks, swiping Eli's Cheerios box, while Eli and I trade smiles.

She's eating. It's a great sign.

"You mean their first post?" Eli asks. "Wasn't it about some ass-wipe cheating?"

"It was," I say. "But if we assume UTG isn't pulling the fatalistic strings, Piper's correct. We need to go back further." Piper and Eli look confused. "What's been off-kilter since the beginning of deb season?" I ask.

Piper shrugs.

"Laney," I say. "I asked about her whereabouts at Leslie's party, and the Madisons lied. Each one gave a different reason. She must've already been off-grid. Otherwise, why act so sketchy?"

Eli shakes his head. "That was planned. You heard the clones. They were helping her get back at you."

"Yes, but they said she went rogue. That they never heard back from her," Piper says, crunching more cereal. "Several people thought they knew where Laney was, when in reality, no one did. The Madisons assumed she was planning a comeback. Riley said she was with Hunter—"

"Who lied about the dress shopping," I interrupt. "Hunter hasn't given us one honest answer." I stand up, shaking out my cramped leg. "We need to talk to him. Let's not forget he orchestrated putting a human finger in my food."

"I'm coming with you," Eli says, holding his phone to his ear. "Hello. Yes, can you tell me if Hunter Boyd is working today? He left his wallet at my house. I wanted to return it. Oh, he is? Great. Be there soon."

"That's settled." I smile. "What about Piper?"

"Um, hello. Stop talking like I'm not here. Or made out of glass." She frowns. "I needed a few days to hit rock bottom, and I did. But Jamie would want me to help find his killer. I *need* to help. For him and me."

Reluctantly, she agrees to stay put. We ask her to check in with the Madisons to see how their "profiling of their profiles" is coming along while Eli and I gather our keys and phones to head out.

Hunter's a weird guy. The last thing Piper needs is to be present while we confront some freak who could be involved with the murder of her boyfriend. As we head out, we pass Luke in the hallway. "Hello, beloved brother. Do you think you can keep an eye on Piper? She wants to go home for a bit," I say quietly, trying not to alert her. "Could you take her? Maybe get her something to eat."

"Wha—yeah, fine." He concedes, knowing enough about the circumstances to not argue. "Piper! I'm taking you home, but I'm starving. We're going to Cane's first," he yells. "Also, you're going to wrestling practice with me. I can't be late!"

The last thing we hear is Piper screaming, "Ainsley!"

Love you too, Pipes.

My phone buzzes, but when Cooper's name appears, I silence it. He hasn't stopped calling since he sent me the photo.

Eli frowns. "You sure you don't want me to say something? I can ask him to delete it. Or punch him in the face."

"I'd prefer he not know you saw it. He'll find a way to make it worse." I grab an empty grocery cart, waiting for the doors to slide open. "I'll figure something out with him soon," I say, hoping to pacify Eli, but in actuality, I have no idea what to do about Cooper.

I don't want to see him again. Like ever.

"One word. That's all I need. Keep me in the loop." Eli grabs random snacks as we peruse the aisles. "Where did you find Hunter last time?"

"Produce aisle." I aim the rickety cart in that direction. "I ran into the boxes he was stacking to start a conversation."

"And now?" Leaning on the cart, he nods at Hunter, whose back is turned.

"I can run into him again." Pressing my weight into the cart, I haul ass.

"What the actual fuck!" Hunter pulls his foot from underneath the wheel, his hip pinned by the corner of my cart. "What the hell is wrong with you, psycho?"

"You had someone put a finger in my king cake, yet you have the nerve to ask what's wrong with *me*?" I press into the cart, forcefully. "I've had a few bad days, just warning you. My tolerance for BS is extremely low."

"Where were you January fourteenth?" Eli blurts.

"How in the fuck should I know? Why?"

"Because my friend got shot on that day, asshole. And we plan to find out who did it."

"I heard about that. Fucking awful. Sorry, man. And I do know where I was. I remember hearing about it the night I had lunch with my mother. She posted a pic of us eating at Camellia Grill on Facebook. Look it up."

"If you're lying again, I'll joyfully beat the crap out of you," Eli warns.

"Check it out," I say, turning back to Hunter. "I heard that a family member actually did your awful deed, but why would Laney want to do it in the first place? I don't understand."

He shrugs. "Dunno. Something about wanting to win. She said it had to send a message no one could top. It was kinda funny, no? A middle finger. Get it?" He laughs. "In addition to my cousin who temps as a waiter, bet you didn't know his dad—my uncle—is a mortician? That's how she hatched her crazy-ass plan. You'd be surprised what they can do with closed caskets."

"Not funny. At all. It's warped!" I seethe. "If Laney wanted to make such a macabre gesture, where is she now? Hmm? And don't give us that crap about her buying a dress because you lied."

Eli waves his phone, displaying a date-stamped post of Hunter with his mom. While his story may check out, he remains guilty in my book.

Hunter's face mottles. "I don't know because she broke up with me. I think she was planning to do it for a while. Way I see it, she used me to mess with your party first."

"Got that tattoo a little early, huh?" Eli mocks, ignoring the glare Hunter throws his way. "So, you're saying you have no clue where she is?"

"We didn't end on the best terms. Basically, she blackmailed me. She said she'd tell the police it was me who messed with the cakes if I said a word about her. When her parents called, I told them we broke up, and that I hadn't heard from her. Since Laney was constantly fighting with them, I figured she went off-grid until things cooled down. Or maybe to get away from them. And me."

Though he's lied about everything else, this feels like it could be the truth.

He continues, "I've had to field calls from her family and Riley, for fuck's sake, all because that bitch decided to lie to everyone. Including me."

"Riley's dead," I deadpan. "Didn't that tip you off something was wrong?"

I release the cart so he can breathe, and he rubs the spot where he'd been pinned. "I told her sister Ashley that, but she brushed it off. Laney's family doesn't like me. And after the way she dumped me, figured I did more than my part."

"Laney has a sister?" Eli looks at me for confirmation.

I nod. "How do you *not* know that? I'm sure Cooper knows her. They're pretty close in age, and she was a deb." I think back to our conversations in school. "Laney always talked about her sister's parties and the dresses she got to wear. She idolized Ashley."

"In case you forgot, I *don't* idolize my sibling. Plus, Cooper and I never hung out socially. So, no, I don't know Ashley."

Hunter cracks his neck, left, then right. "Maybe I'm the one who should be calling the police? That crazy bitch might have more involvement in this debutante take-down than messing with you. One thing about Laney, she loves to play games. What better stage to win on than New Orleans's fucked-up social scene?"

While I can't wrap my head around the fact that Laney doesn't like me—like, at all, according to the Madisons and now Hunter—something feels off. Because the Laney they keep describing is not the funny, ambitious, deb-struck one I knew and *liked* in high school.

I wonder what changed?

Hunter is still talking. ". . . once your party was a bust, I figured she'd come home to gloat, so don't be surprised if she does just that. Never wise to count Laney out. Then you can pin her down with a shopping cart to get your answers."

"It's no longer that important, considering everything that's happened." I hold my phone out. "Would you mind giving me

Laney's home number? I only have her cell. I think it's time I try to call her."

He pulls his phone out and shares his contact. "Good luck with that."

Leaving Eli with Hunter, I step away. After a second ring, a girl answers. "Hi," I say. "Is this Ashley?"

"Yes. Who's this?"

"Ainsley Clarke. I went to school with Laney—"

"I know who you are, Ainsley. You've been to my house like twenty times."

"I'm sorry. I didn't know if you remembered me, but um, me and a couple of the debs have been talking about Laney not being around, and with everything going on, I thought it would be nice if we reached out to her family, and, um, to you. Or," I hesitate. "Maybe even talk to the police if you think that might help."

"That's kind, but we've already spoken to them multiple times. We filed a missing report weeks ago." Her desperation oozes over the phone.

I want to press further, but she sounds broken. Maybe if I approach it from a different angle, I can get the answers we need without upsetting her. "Is there anything we can do to help? Like maybe distribute flyers? Or has anyone suggested a neighborhood search? I hope I'm not being rude, but if my brother went missing, I'd have the whole city out with megaphones—"

"The police told us to stay quiet. We figured they have their reasons. I did get a text."

"From *Laney*?" I freeze, waiting for her response.

"Fuck it. I'm tired of not saying anything. Someone texted, but it wasn't Laney. Someone has her phone." She pauses. "They said she'll be safe as long as we keep our mouths shut. They're black-mailing us, on top of holding my sister hostage. If you're really her friend, you won't go blabbing this around. It could cost Laney her life."

"I understand. Someone did something similar to me," I say, thinking about the phone call at Maskers. "I don't want to scare you, but we're afraid whoever has Laney may be the same person who killed our friends."

She pauses. "The guy who got shot?" Her voice cracks.

"Yes. And Riley."

"I heard about Riley. It was horrible, but I don't think there's a connection between my sister and your friend. The guy Jamie, he wasn't a local, right?"

"No—Michigan," I answer, wondering why that's relevant. "He goes . . . I mean, he *went* to LSU," I correct myself, stirring up a new wave of anxiety. Every time someone mentions his name, I realize Jamie is actually *gone,* and I feel sick all over again.

Her voice drops. "I shouldn't be telling you this, but I think whoever did this is trying to hurt *me.* Not my sister."

This is the last thing I expected to hear. "*You*? Why—"

"There's an old video. It would've gone viral on that Under the Gown shit site if it were circulating now. And . . . well, I'm in it. Along with some others. It's not pretty. We were bitches back then. It was a prank that went way too far." She sniffles. "Now, I don't care if someone posts it. Not if it helps find Laney."

"Do you have the video?" I'm practically hyperventilating at this point. "I can see if anything looks similar to what's been happening at our events."

"I don't. They only sent a screenshot from the video to prove it still exists." Her voice turns venomous. "I'm sorry. I really can't say anymore. Ask Cooper Kane."

"*Cooper*?" I whisper, hoping Eli doesn't hear.

"If anyone is holding a vendetta against us, it's him."

CHAPTER 26

JANUARY 20
8:00 A.M.

Getting Cooper to agree to meet isn't hard, considering he'd been hounding me ever since turning over the photo. It's just a matter of prep work.

All three of us had been digging into Ashley Wilson's deb year for the last two days, trying to find more about the video she'd mentioned, or who could be involved. I scratch another girl off my list, cursing at the gigantic row of unchecked names that remain. By splitting the debs into groups, we figured we could search faster, but the process is tedious.

I'm tired.

"Have you heard from Violet?" Piper asks, popping her head up from her laptop, a pen tucked behind her ear. "I'm still waiting for the Madisons to call back."

"She's sent a few geo-tagged snaps, so I'd know she's still in town. Basically the photographic form of giving someone who accused you of *murder* the middle finger. After that . . . radio silence."

"Blair hasn't spoken to me either, if that makes you feel better." Eli peels a pink Post-it note off his arm. "Burned my ear off about your fight with Violet, then nada."

It doesn't make me feel better. I want to call Violet just to hear her voice, even if all she does is yell, but once that seed of doubt was planted—after we accused the wrong person of being a killer the first go-around—the knowledge that our oversight had cost Jamie his life has amplified everything.

I can't let my emotions cloud the facts.

And the only fact I know is Violet *may* be involved. Maybe not in everything, but enough not to ignore. "If it isn't her, hopefully she'll forgive me in several decades." I sigh. "If not, I'll have to settle for a prison wife."

Piper smiles, which is rare these days. I don't know how to help my best friend other than pouring myself into unraveling what happened to get justice for Jamie. For as much as I care about Violet, if an inch of Piper thinks she's guilty, I have to stand by her side until we know otherwise.

"Did y'all find anything on an Ophelia Larson?" I ask, staring at the nearly blank search results. "There's not much on her. Like, at all."

"She's not on my list, but her name sounds familiar," Eli muses. "Have a photo?"

I shake my head.

"Nothing on my end either," Piper adds. "Was she a deb?"

"There's a newspaper article about her being presented at Crescent Club. That's it. No photos from the night. Or social media." I flip the laptop around for them to see.

But Eli doesn't look at my computer. He jumps up and grabs his keys. "Catch y'all later," he says, sprinting out of the room before we can ask where he's going.

I look at Piper and she looks at me. We shrug.

"There are not a ton of photos from that year, but her name isn't on the list of girls presented," I tell Piper, and she frowns. "She's in one write-up from a summer mixer, then she *didn't* go to the ball? Does that make sense? I mean, sure, lots of girls drop out for different reasons. But the only girl we know who missed her presentation is allegedly being held hostage by a killer. Ashley was presented by Crescent that year, so whatever video she's talking about, it's probably from that night." Then it hits me. "Wait—what about that girl who tripped?"

Piper's mouth falls open. "Dude, that's probably her. You said her name started with an *O*. Call Ashley back. Now," Piper says. "Or send me her number."

Maybe Piper can whittle out more information than I received, so I share her contact. "Feel free to try, but she's pretty wrecked, understandably. She told me she couldn't say anymore. Oh, and to ask Cooper."

Piper looks up. "Cooper? Why *him*?"

"Something about the video. And who, by the way, just texted." I flash my screen, trying to bite back the irritation I feel just seeing his name. While what happened wasn't completely his fault—I had as much, if not more, of a responsibility for what I let happen— ever since the ball, I can barely think of him without feeling guilty. Knowing how close I'd come to losing everyone I cared about over my own ambition. "He wants me to meet him at his house. He said Eli is at *school* and won't be there to interrupt."

"Gross." Piper makes a face, and I nod in agreement.

Cooper's ignorant bravado is beyond comprehension. When we were kids, he and Eli weren't close, but I shrugged it off due to their nearly four-year age gap. It seemed natural. But now they're adults, and he still doesn't seem to care what Eli is up to. Obviously, Eli is not away at school because, hello, it's still semester break.

What makes it sadder is the fact that their mother died almost five years ago. While Luke is a royal pain, if something ever happened to either of our parents, I know we'd be there for each other.

"Are you sure you want to meet him?" Piper shuts the laptop, her attention focused on me. "We could get Eli to ask him."

"No way. Eli's fuse is short enough these days with his matchstick of a brother. Even if he managed to talk to him without punching him, Cooper would probably be suspicious of Eli pumping him for information from four years ago. If Cooper thinks something's off, he won't talk to any of us." I sigh. "*I* seem to be the only shot we have."

"Please be careful," she says. "In every meaning of that word. I'll text Eli that you're going to his house. And you text updates. Actually, call me before you get inside. I'll put my mic on mute, so he can't hear anything. That way, I can keep tabs on you."

"Good idea." I throw on the jean jacket I'd been using as a pillow. "When you find out where Eli went, let me know. Love you."

"Love you too. Be safe!" she shouts. "Luke! I don't wanna be alone. Come sit in here!"

I smack into Luke leaving his room. His hair is ruffled, and he looks slightly, but not overly peeved. "If I don't get into heaven for this, I'll be pissed." He stomps down the hall, then turns. "Don't say I never did anything for you, Ass-ley."

Going through my inner checklist, I think: *Piper's listening. Eli will know where I am. Everything will be okay.*

I have to stay cool. Then I need to ask about the video and get the hell out.

My phone buzzes before I ring the doorbell.

PIPER

Ophelia Larson died her deb year.
Whatever reason they're blackmailing
Ashley is BIG. : (

A

How do you know?

PIPER

Eli texted. He said Cooper jogs through the cemetery every morning, and one time when he tagged along, Cooper pointed out a tombstone as a girl he dated who died in a "freak accident." Eli drove to the cemetery to confirm the name. It was Ophelia's tombstone.

Which means the guy you're about to meet with runs past the grave of a dead girl who happens to be the central figure in our season being cursed.

A

Fantastic!

"Fuck!" I poke the doorbell. As if Cooper couldn't get any creepier.

In a red tank and Nike running shorts, he opens the door. "At long last, you made time to come see little old me." Cooper flashes a wide smile—dimples popping—and beckons me in. With his muscled arms spread, I have to brush against him to get past, which is probably his whole intent. "Living at home during law school has financial benefits, but trying to plan a day where the Kane fam isn't around—more than tedious."

"I'm sure it doesn't stop you," I drawl.

"And you'd be right." He laughs and I eye the staircase I've run up and down hundreds of times over the years, knowing the left side creaks due to Eli's failed attempt to slide down in a sleeping bag that ended with him crashing into the railing and breaking his nose.

Except now, I'm not going upstairs to play a video game with Eli. I'm heading to Cooper's room, where the door gapes open, ready to suck me in and swallow me whole.

"Sorry it took so long to get back to you." I wander around his room, taking two steps for each one Cooper takes toward me.

"I was worried you weren't going to honor your side of the deal after I did you such a *huge* favor." He trails behind me, like a dog tracking a bone.

"There was a bit of a setback." I pause. "See, my friend . . . he got *murdered*." I turn to face him, and he ceases his pursuit. "Besides, I'm sure you never erased the photo off your phone. It was one click worth of work."

"I heard about your friend, Clarke. Eli hasn't been around to explain the details, but a real bummer. My brother seemed to be in a good mood that morning, trekking off to Pontiff. And to have it end that way, it more than sucks." He offers a sympathetic smile, but I'm not sure if he's being genuine or not.

"The cops say it was a robbery gone bad, but personally, I think our deb season is cursed." I lean in like I'm sharing a secret. "Too much trouble, you know?"

"When are you girls *not* trouble?" He laughs. "There's always a group of you using your heels like stakes to drive into some poor guy's heart. I've seen those antics, year after year. Most of it is harmless fun."

"Until it's not." I stop in front of his dresser, taking in the multitude of framed photos perched on top. His top drawer is ajar, like a corner of cloth got stuck, and he never bothered to close it.

"If you want my clothes off, they're over here." His hand covers mine while I try to press the drawer in, but he spins me into him.

"Wait." I push against him, prying his mouth away from my chin. He lets out an exasperated sigh. "I need to talk to you first."

"I didn't invite you over to *talk*, Ainsley." He paws at my buttons. "Can't we do that *after*?"

"I'd need to get this off my chest. That way, I can focus more on *you*." I force a smile, trying to stuff down the immense loathing I feel for him at this moment. "Please?"

"Since you asked so nicely, sure." He positions me near his bed while leaning against the dresser. "What's up?"

"I ran into Ashley Wilson a few days ago," I say, and a sour expression settles on his face.

"Go on." He motions for me to hurry.

"I don't know if you're aware, but she's been out of sorts with her sister *unofficially* missing. It seems bottomless mimosas at brunch are a terrible mix with a guilty conscience. She kept babbling about feeling bad over something that happened during her deb year."

"I heard about Laney. I'm sure Ashley has a lot on her mind." He shrugs. "Or maybe she's just fretting over wearing the wrong color dress to a presentation." He laughs. "I wouldn't put too much merit into her champagne-addled rant."

"Were you a member of Crescent Club Ashley's year?"

"Maybe?" He crosses his arms. "Been to so many events, it's hard to tell one from another, besides the few landmark parties, you know."

How convenient. Distancing himself from the event before I can even ask. "It wasn't that long ago, and well, she remembers you." I cock my head. "I may not have believed her, had she not sent me a photo. Apparently, it's part of some video she feels awful about."

Based on what Ashley said, there's a high probability Cooper's in that video, otherwise, I'm about to torpedo this whole conversation.

His posture stiffens. "Why are you nosing around in past affairs? What do you hope to gain?"

"Nothing. I mean, I'm sorry her sister is missing, but I'm really trying to figure out which asshole fucked up *my* party," I say. "There's a rumor Laney's behind it. And after Ashley did all that drunk babbling, I figured maybe the two were connected. Like,

Laney might be trying to mimic what her sister did at *her* presentation."

I serve him up a lie. Hopefully, it's one he can get behind.

Not that the thought didn't cross my mind after Ashley admitted her deed. Laney looked up to her sister. It wouldn't be that far of a stretch for Laney to want to mastermind her own prank. If that's the case, her statement to Hunter about winning, about doing something no one could top, may have more to do with her sister than me. Either way, she managed to cover both bases with one grisly finger.

Cooper waves his hand in my face. "Hello?"

"Sorry. As I was saying, when she mentioned a video, I couldn't help but think of you. A guy with a penchant for photographing girls who has a photographic memory. I figured you'd remember the night, even if you never saw a moment of that video."

"You think I have a photographic memory?" He grins. "I mean, yeah, maybe."

Flattery will get you everywhere. Especially with someone like Cooper.

A moment passes, and he stares at the wall, like he's deep in thought. Then he opens his top drawer. "Close, Clarke, but no cigar. Blaming the wrong sister." He pulls out a phone from the drawer, taps the screen, and throws it my way. "Have a look at what Miss Wilson feels sorry about."

The video is grainy, but it's clearly from Crescent Club. The music in the background is the same song they use every year to present the girls. Whoever is holding the camera is running down the hall while a group of ball-gown-clad girls wave, and Ashley is one of the girls. "It's about to be her turn!" Ashley calls out, giggling, as others hover near the entrance. "Did you help her get dressed? Are you sure it will work?"

"Course it will," another replies. The video goes quiet, and the applause stops.

"Miss Ophelia Julia Larson." The master of ceremonies says, and clapping resumes.

"Let me through." Ashley's hiding behind the stage, apparently trying to get a closer look at Ophelia as she's escorted by Cooper. "Pull it at the first *X*, okay?"

The camera zooms in on a small white wire or string, clinging to Ophelia's dress like a spiderweb.

This isn't going to end well.

When Ophelia curtsies, the string is tugged.

I hold my breath, not wanting to watch, but nothing happens.

Then a piece from the bottom of her dress falls off. Her shoes are on display as more of the dress unravels. When she realizes what's happening, she tries to cover herself. Cooper looks shocked. He yanks off his tuxedo jacket, but the string unravels her shoulder straps. In less than a minute, the whole dress is eaten off the girl like termites feasting on a rotten branch.

The crowd gasps.

The girls in the video giggle.

Ophelia runs from the stage in her underwear and bra, with Cooper trailing behind. He catches sight of the camera at the last second, and the screen goes black.

I'm so shocked, I don't know what to say or think, except now I know why Ashley believes someone wants revenge.

Cooper takes the phone. "Too bad I wasn't the only one with the video or Ophelia wouldn't have had to see it posted all over social media that night and the next day. Those girls ruined her life for fun. Someone told me they picked straws for who they'd play the prank on. So, really, just randomized cruelty."

That part doesn't seem true, considering a prank like that would take intricate planning. It would take access to her dress beforehand, and even then, I don't know how they did it. "I-I've never seen anything like this," I say, wondering why something so combustible, so blatantly mean, wasn't whispered about in the hallways at school or resurfaced on the internet. Sure, Laney told us about an incident, but her account was a watered-down lie. This girl didn't trip and run away. She was sabotaged by Laney's sister and her friends.

The real question is—did Laney know the truth and was protecting her sister? Or did Ashley lie to cover up her own wicked web?

"How did that not go viral?" I ask.

"It would be defamatory if this was the first thing that popped up when someone searches for our club, no?" He points at the phone. "Ophelia overdosed the next day. No one knows if it was intentional or accidental, but she was super upset, and those bitches were scared they'd be held liable for posting it. So they wiped their phones. Since Ophelia didn't officially finish her presentation, it made it easy for the club to erase her from their records."

"That's awful," I say, trying to remain calm while my mind reels over the multiple repercussions this one malicious act set off.

"Here, since you like pictures so much." He tosses a framed photo from the dresser. Cooper's in a tux posed next to Ophelia, while another girl, a pretty redhead, smiles beside them. "It's the last photo I have of my girlfriend. It may've been the worst day of her life, but it's the last time I saw her alive. I'll keep it forever."

I stare at it a second longer, setting it down gently on the bed, like to do otherwise might cause something in Cooper to break. I don't like him very much right now, but I feel terrible about what happened to Ophelia. She didn't just *die*—she apparently lost her life because of a pack of selfish girls. When Ashley told me about a video, I figured Cooper must've played an integral part. I never imagined he'd be an innocent bystander—*a victim*. Standing on that dance floor, as helpless as his girlfriend was embarrassed.

"I'm really sorry. I don't know how anyone could do something so awful." I pause. "Does Eli know?" I ask gently, but I know that answer. If he knew, he would've told us about it. What I don't know is *why* or *how* Cooper was able to keep the cause of her death quiet.

"Eli doesn't know." He toes the floor with his Adidas. "I never got a chance to introduce her to the fam. We didn't date that long, but I really cared about her. The whole thing . . . one big mind fuck, and then"—he puts a finger gun to his temple—"*bam*! When they found her, she was basically brain dead, but her family didn't have the guts to pull the plug. Months later, when they did, they kept her burial private. No obituaries. Or cause of death. It's the way they wanted it. I certainly wasn't going to be the one to change that narrative or defile her further."

He looks up. "Under the Gown ran smear campaigns this whole season, yet you're shocked anyone would act this way? Really?" He snorts. "All you girls tag yourselves in posts even when you don't send in something damaging. Perfectly fine to be spectators in the Colosseum, as if that makes you any less guilty watching other people get torn to pieces."

I hate to admit—*Cooper is right.*

We accepted Under the Gown so easily, and in return, played their game by their rules. "Do you think whoever saw this video is going after Laney because of what Ashley did?" I ask. "You can't be the only one who thinks this is wrong."

"I'm not. But why hurt someone's *sister* for revenge? Go after the guilty party is my motto." He rubs his face, looking far less handsome and way more exhausted. "Are we done with the inquisition? I wanted to do something enjoyable today. Not have a bucket of crap dumped on me."

"No more questions." I hold up my hands in fake surrender and he approaches me. He places his large hands on my shoulders where I sit on the bed and peels off my shirt.

"Be a good distraction. Kiss me." Leaning down, he lifts my chin to claim my lips while I swallow down bile.

I jerk my head away from his mouth, the heat of his hand burning my chest. "Do you, uh . . . have condoms?"

I have to get out of here, and I need an excuse. An escape route. Anything.

"They're in the bathroom. Be right back." Leaving more bruising kisses on my lips, he whistles as he hurries to the bathroom.

I snatch my shirt from the dresser, listening as drawers are opened and closed.

When I pop my shirt back on, a blur of purple, green, and gold peeks from the top drawer. The same one he pulled his phone from.

Easing it open further, I freeze.

I tap in the password on my phone. On the third try, my shaky hands open the camera app and I snap. Sending the photo to our group chat, I whisper, "Piper, if you're there, call the police. Now." I pray she's listening. "He shot Jamie. He has the mask."

The puzzle pieces start snapping together. Cooper mentioned Eli heading off to Pontiff. He knew where we were, just as much as Violet, but he has the mask.

I pull my phone back and hit 9-1—

A puff of warm air hits the back of my neck.

"Ahh, Ainsley. This could've gone so much better."

CHAPTER 27

11:00 A.M.

A sharp pain rips through my back as he pins me against the dresser. Struggling to peel his hands off, I wheeze, "S-stop" while I kick at his legs. "Police. They know. My phone," I gurgle, and his force lessens.

Digging through my front pocket, he glares at the active call banner on my phone.

It's now or never, Clarke.

Locking my hands into one fist, I swing over my head and crash down on his arm. I suck in another breath and shove him toward the bed. He falls back, stunned.

I run.

Something hard cracks the back of my head, but I keep running. Two steps at a time, I head down the stairway toward the front door, and somehow, it opens—

Eli.

He stares with wide eyes while I launch into the air.

"Shit. Ainsley!" he says, catching me. "You're bleeding!" Pulling his hand back from my head, it comes away crimson. "What did that asshole do?"

"Your brother," I pant. "He has the mask. The one the jogger wore. H-he shot Jamie."

Eli surges forward, but I use all of my might to yank him back. "No! I don't want you to get hurt."

"Why did you fucking do it?" Eli yells at Cooper, his voice breaking. "Jamie was my friend. Why did you hurt him, y-you, monster!"

Sirens blare.

Thank you, Piper.

"Shut up! It was supposed to be a warning shot," Cooper yells from the balcony. "Your idiot friend turned my way at the last second. I was trying to stop you fools from snooping around. He recognized my mask, recognized me from Jane's party."

I gasp. "Did you hurt Riley too?" I scream, as police jump out of their cars and swarm the house. "Why, Cooper?"

This is Eli's brother. I'd practically grown up with him. How could his psychosis be hiding in plain sight?

Poor Eli and Mr. Kane.

"Oh, Ainsley. You're missing so much," Cooper sneers. "I thought you were way smarter. It's quite disappointing." He raises his hands above his head as officers surround him. "Too bad about that girlfriend of yours, though."

"*Girlfriend?*"

I sprint toward him, as the police snap on handcuffs. "Did you do something to Violet? Tell me!" I scream, but this time, Eli holds me back.

"The better question is where is she?" he says as he's dropped to his knees.

"Tell me!" I demand again, but it's too late. The police drag him away.

I dial Violet. "Pick up, please!" One, two, three missed calls, all leading to her voicemail.

"Shit!" I call Blair.

"What do *you* want?" she snaps.

"Tell me Violet is okay. Cooper shot Jamie. And he made a creepy comment about Violet. I need to know if she's with you."

"*Cooper*? As in Eli's brother?" Blair's voice cracks, but why wouldn't it? No one could've seen this coming. "Violet was *way* off target. She was sure it was someone else. She's been on this manhunt the last few days, trying to prove you wrong."

"When did you talk to her last? Are you back in Dallas?" I riddle her with questions.

"I talked to her yesterday. And no, I'm in Lafayette, visiting family. Violet is still in New Orleans. She kept rambling about knowing where to look." She hesitates. "I texted her earlier, but she hasn't answered. Oh God, I should've stayed with her."

"Text her again. I'm going to check her house." I wave at Eli while he talks to the police, pointing at my car, and he nods.

I can't imagine the hell he's going through, but I can't stay to console him. Not now—

Violet's life's in danger.

"Find her!" Blair pleads.

Zipping down St. Charles Avenue, I arrive at her doorstep and bang on the door. I hadn't been to her house since her party, and it looks way different without the *Dynasty* decorations.

A man with black buzzed hair and green eyes opens it.

"Hi. I'm Ainsley. Is Violet home?" I wedge my Converse in the door in case he tries to shut me out.

"Oh, the *girlfriend*. My sister's kept you hidden away, or more likely, she's keeping us hidden from you." He smiles, and it seems genuine. "She's out, but you're welcome to wait."

"When did she leave?" I step into the foyer. Portraits of her green-eyed family members that either I hadn't noticed or had been removed for her party stare down from the walls.

"This morning, but she usually checks in by dinner." He glances at his Patek Philippe watch. "She should be back soon."

When he starts toward the living room, I stay put. "Do you mind if I wait in her room? She, uh, borrowed a jacket. I think I left my license in it. I can't really drive without it. If you let me check, I'll be out of your hair."

"Upstairs and to the right. Second door." He points.

I know exactly where her room is, so I climb the stairs, once again stunned by the enormity of her home. "Violet?" I call out, hoping she'll answer.

She doesn't.

I inch into her room and stop in my tracks. Without Violet's dazzling presence, the room feels bland. Soulless. There are no pieces of modern art on the walls or shelves brimming with books. No wonder she prefers to stay elsewhere. While it doesn't reflect the Violet I know, at least it will make my search easier.

"There's nothing here," I say to Blair, balancing the phone on my shoulder while I continue to rummage. I don't know what I'm looking for, but I'm hoping to find anything that could offer a clue of her whereabouts.

"Check her desk drawer. Fourth down. She used to store liquor under its fake base."

Seconds pass, and Blair blurts, "Anything yet? She's not picking up my calls. I'm starting to freak out, Ainsley. Are you sure Cooper wasn't bluffing?"

Removing the fake bottom, I push a bottle of vodka to the side. "There's a journal. Is Violet a closeted writer?"

"No."

I open the book and a pang of guilt hits. "It's her, um, alibi."
She wrote this because of me.
This proves Violet had been trying to figure out who killed

Jamie to prove she didn't hurt anyone. At the top of the page, circled in red, it reads: *Outsider or Insider?*

Names of those involved in past crimes are listed with arrows pointing to each other. There's a star next to the Madisons with a call back scratched out as of last night. And another name—*Prince*—underlined with a crown doodled next to it. I have no idea what that means. "I'll call you back," I say, hanging up to call Madison N.

"*What?*" she answers bitchily. "I thought we settled this."

"Did Violet call today?"

"Yesterday. Why?"

"What did she want?" I ask.

"She wanted an update, so I told her everything we found on your wild goose chase. Did she not explain this to you?" She groans. "Obviously, you two have communication issues."

"Considering she may be missing, I guess we do," I snap. "Explain it to me again."

"Oh shit. I had no idea." She drops her sass. "We triple-checked the girls and guys involved in all the clubs that have access to our page. Everyone checked out."

"And?"

"I figured we were done. Then Piper called, asking me to investigate Ashley Wilson, and bingo. We found a ten-second video of her messing with a girl from their deb year."

"Ophelia Larson, I know. How did *you* find it? It's nowhere on the internet."

"Say what you want about UTG, but a few leading questions and a bit of mild blackmail makes most people talk." She gloats. "Anyway, story is Cooper dumped Ashley for Ophelia four months before deb season. Probably why she pulled the prank."

"Violet doesn't think it's Cooper." I recheck her notes. "His name is barely mentioned."

"If someone pulled that prank on Piper, who would be the first person to burn everyone to the ground?"

"Me, obviously. I'm her best friend." I think for a moment. There was another girl in Cooper's photo. A redhead. "Do you know who Ophelia's best friend was?"

"I do. Anna Sara Prince. As in the Prince family that owns Carnival Creations," she says. "Turns out, she was one of our first requests to be on Under the Gown."

"Why accept her? She's not a deb—"

She cuts me off. "Anna Sara Prince, who now goes by *Sara* is—"

This time, I cut her off. "A den mother."

CHAPTER 28

3:00 P.M.

On my drive home, I fill Officer Roy in on our findings. "S-a-r-a Prince—whose name is legally Anna Sara—has been in the background at almost every debutante event. She has authority, access, and a wealth of intelligence due to the accidental assistance of Under the Gown to guide her revenge quest. None of us could've expected it was her because Crescent Club wiped all evidence of Ophelia's prank-turned-wrong from the internet."

"It hasn't been twenty-four hours." He reminds me. "We can't officially report Ms. Anderson missing, but when the time elapses, her family will have to be the one to do so. That is, *if* Ms. Anderson fails to return."

I'm not getting through to him.

"We can't wait that long! The person who got arrested, Cooper, made a sketchy comment about Violet, and no one's seen her all day. Plus, she's not answering her best friend's texts. Or mine. Are you going to dismiss this after everything that's happened?" I snap, ignoring the honking of cars as I slip-slide between lanes.

"You said it yourself," he says. "The person accused of these crimes is in *custody*. Thanks to your bravery or stupidity, whatever you wish to call it." He laughs, sending my stress level higher. "As far as Ms. Prince, we can't accuse someone of a crime just because they made a bad decision in their past. If that were the case, nearly every high school or college kid would be behind bars."

I whip into my driveway. Piper is here. So is Blair's car. She must've blown past every speed trap to get from Lafayette this fast. The only missing variable in our equation is Eli, who must still be home. At least, I hope he is—I need to catch him before it's too late.

"Okay, but for the love of all that is holy, can you look her up?" I beg, resting my head on the steering wheel, the adrenaline of the day washing over me. "Please?"

I text Eli:

A

> There's a phone in your brother's top drawer. We need it.

ELI

The police are everywhere. I can't.

A

> You must. We need what's on that phone.

ELI

Fuck. I'll see what I can do. What are you looking for?

A

> A video of Ophelia's presentation.

"You hung up on me," Blair chastises as I enter my room. She's perched on my bed, Piper's in the corner on her laptop, and Luke's swiveling back and forth in my hanging chair.

"Violet wasn't home," I say, then turn to Luke. "Why are you here?"

"I'm the babysitter, in case you've forgotten—why are you bleeding?" Frowning, he heads to my bathroom.

"Cooper threw a trophy at me, that's why," I say when he returns and dabs my head with alcohol. "Before that, he was acting his ass off. I even started to feel sorry for him. Until I spotted the mask."

"I can't believe he shot Jamie." Piper tears up.

Blair and Luke are waiting for me to fill them in, so without going into every morbid detail, I give them a condensed version of my ordeal. ". . . so what was supposed to be a warning shot became"—I glance at Piper to make sure she's okay—"well, we know what it became."

"I guess Cooper didn't know we had fingered Under the Gown for the crimes. If he had, maybe he wouldn't have felt it necessary to scare us off his trail," Blair says, plucking a loose string off her sweater. "Do you think Violet, being a no-show, was just a lucky accident for him? Considering you guys accused *her*."

I feel nothing but shame as I evade her stare. "Maybe?" I toe the carpet with my shoe. "What I know is I seriously messed up. But during the same time span when Jamie was shot, not only did we realize we chose the wrong killers, we found out Violet had put olean-ders in Alexandra's bouquet after learning she died of *poisoning*, not some weird heart attack. Super bad timing for that secret to come out."

"It would be easier to forgive you if she wasn't missing due to her stupid attempt to prove you wrong." She stands up. "I don't have time to be angry. We need to find her."

My phone buzzes.

ELI

Here's the video. Wait for me to watch it.

"Eli's on his way. No more babysitting, Luke. Shoo." My brother gives me a wounded look. "Go ahead and tell Dad. There's no way I'm *not* looking for Violet. But I can't allow you to be in the middle of this mess and get hurt. Hopefully, one day you'll thank me for watching your back."

When Eli arrives, his hair is a mess, but how well can anyone look when their brother has just been arrested for potential murder?

After everyone hugs him, he pulls out his phone.

"This is awful," Piper and Blair moan, more than disturbed by the video.

"I'm confused," Blair says. "You think Cooper did all this to get back at these debs in the video?"

"I think *she* did." Pausing the video, I point at a once redheaded Sara in the back of the line. "Laney idolized her sister and vice versa. What better way to punish Ashley than to be the reason her sister is missing and possibly hurt? Plus, no one else involved in this video would willingly come forward. They'd be canceled in a heartbeat."

"Hold on." Piper rewinds the video, pointing at two guys. "Isn't that the dudes from Rachel's drug-fest? Damn, Ainsley, you're right. Maybe this isn't about implicating Rachel. It looks like they wanted revenge against them, hence the tampered brakes."

"She blackmailed me so I'd send their photos in to Under the Gown to get them in trouble for *drugs*?" I try unraveling the narrative as I speak. "Does that make sense?"

"Yes. For revenge and as a worthy distraction. Certainly not stupid. But how does Riley fit in, or my, um . . . brother?" Eli's voice cracks, and I feel so awful this is happening to him. To his family. Sure, he and Cooper aren't super close, but it is his brother.

Blood is blood.

"Maybe Sara was pretending to be Laney, texting Riley and Hunter, which means she has her phone and probably Laney. If

Riley grew suspicious after talking to us and started asking too many questions, it could explain the cell phone. . . .”

I trail off, not wanting to think about what was done to Riley. Or that, once again, our investigation could have indirectly caused someone’s death.

“Wait!” Piper jumps off her chair, startling us all. “Sara was at Jane’s murder mystery party. Remember, she checked us in, Ainsley?” she asks, and I nod. “And later, when I was in the kitchen, she came in and I asked her why she wanted to be a den mother. She said she’d been a debutante a few years back, and that it was the perfect way to relive the moment. She also mentioned that she’d signed up the minute she heard about it.” She pauses. “Think about it. The den mothers know every detail about the parties. Setup times, guest lists—”

“What if it’s both of them?” I blurt. “She and Cooper could’ve been working together. It makes total sense.” I know it’s the absolute last thing Eli wants to hear, but if Cooper and Sara were working in tandem to seek revenge for a dead friend and girlfriend, it would explain why we weren’t able to figure it out.

Our theory has been missing half of the equation from the start.

I continue. “Cooper was the first to mention Crescent was doing things differently to keep the girls under control. Using the stalker incident as his perfect foil, he could’ve sold the club on his whole twisted ‘den mother’ idea to give Sara access.”

I take a sip of water to soothe my tightened throat, then go on. “He was my escort at Maskers. With full run of the aquarium, he certainly could’ve staged the phone and let Sara know when to call. He also dropped the shark reference that tipped me off on where to look in the first place.” I shake my head. “I ran into Sara in the bathroom. She was probably following me the whole time. Which means Cooper took the blackmail photo while she did the calling. They both had motive and opportunity.”

Blair is chewing her lip, and I can only imagine what she’s

thinking. She's probably wishing she'd never gotten involved with any of *this* or *us*. "We're wasting time. We know what happened to Riley. We need to find Violet. Fast," she says.

"Give me that phone," I say, worried once Sara learns Cooper's been arrested, she'll know it's only a matter of time before he snitches on her. If she has Violet, this could be our last shot. "We need to piss her off enough that she'll have no choice but to confront us."

"You want to gamble with Violet's life?" Blair fumes.

"Do you have a better plan?" I frown. "The police can't do anything for twenty-four hours. Nor will Sara willingly unveil herself. Way I see it, it's the only way we can get Violet back. Or Laney . . . if she's alive."

There. I've said what I'd been fearing this whole time.

"You better be right about this." Blair appears on the verge of tears.

"Text the Madisons. Ask them to post this and tag Sara," I instruct Piper.

Moments later, an Under the Gown post appears with a photo of Ophelia's unraveling dress, frozen in time.

A beastly blast from the past! Do you know why you let sleeping dogs lie, Sara? They bite back. I wonder what people will pay more attention to—the message you hoped to send as vengeance for your friend, or a viral video of Ophelia's demise immortalized for this generation of debutantes to pass around and laugh at?

Curtsy gracefully, and give back the girl.

Or the only ghost we'll remember of Ophelia Larson is this video.

Unknown Caller lights up my screen.

"Who do you think you are making demands?" Sara's voice drips acid.

"Someone with a bartering chip," I say. "The police will put this together soon. Why waste everything on a girl you never factored into your revenge plan?"

"See, that's where you're wrong. Violet perfectly fits my profile. Another rich, nosy debutante, too smart for her own good. Did you know she's top of her class at Rhodes? We've had quite a bit of time to talk, but honestly, I'm bored."

"Don't touch her!" I swear. "If you hurt her . . . if something happens to her, I'll ruin your life."

She laughs. "My life was ruined years ago. I've been stuck in this sinking city, waiting to move on. Waiting to *stop* seeing Ophelia limp and unconscious in her bedroom. Or for illustrious karma to work its magic on everyone who kicked out that metaphorical chair from under her feet. But know what?" She pauses. "Nothing happened!"

"You could've gone to the police—"

"Had any luck with that, Ainsley? Let's not lie to each other. We both know no one would do a damn thing. They never do, until it's too late. When someone's reputation is on the line, they're more than happy to bury the body. Look what everyone did on Under the Gown. So ready to rip each other's throats out. You people never change."

Her voice has a hollow echo to it, but there are no other sounds. No cars or birds.

She's inside, but where?

"Violet hates being a debutante. She was forced in by her family. Let me take her spot. I fit your description exactly."

I mean every word. I'd swap places with her in a heartbeat. I don't care what Sara does with me. If I hadn't barged my way into

Violet's life, she would be happy back in Texas or at college, making fun of the insipid parties. Enjoying her life.

"Ainsley, stop," Piper says, and Eli shakes his head.

"Aw, look who wants to be a hero. Very noble of you, but—no! I like Violet better!" I hear a crashing sound and a groan. *Shit.* "Though I might be willing to make a deal, hmm?"

"I'll do anything."

"Bring me that video, and I might give you a shot at finding Violet. Mardi Gras may come a bit early this year. Good luck!"

"Wait no—fuck!" I throw the phone down. "I have no clue where that psycho is. How will we find her?"

"She could be anywhere." Eli frowns. "Did she say anything else?"

"Just some cryptic BS about Mardi Gras coming early."

"Mardi Gras?" Piper's forehead creases.

That's it! During my call with Madison N she had mentioned that Sara's family owns Carnival Creations. "The Princes own the second-largest Mardi Gras den in the city," I say, and Blair throws up her hands like I'm speaking another language. "It's where certain krewes store their floats between seasons," I explain. "Sara's voice had an echo. A warehouse could give that effect."

I wait for Piper to pull up the business on her phone. "If Violet was on her trail, and she had Sara's name in her notebook, she probably went there to confront her."

Piper flashes a satellite view of the location, and my heart seizes.

The warehouses span blocks. If it appears that big on my *phone*, it will take forever to find Violet and stop this psychopath.

There are no other options.

"Let's go!" I say.

CHAPTER 29

6:00 P.M.

We set out after dusk. If it were any other day, I may have commented on the beautiful winter sunset. This evening, I have great fear of the encroaching dark.

Fifteen minutes later, we veer into the Carnival Creations parking lot.

"That's Violet's car!" Blair pounds on the window of Eli's truck, pointing at a navy Audi in the visitor's section.

Eli pulls next to it, while I read the sign on the metal building. *Authorized Visitors Only. Cars will be towed after thirty minutes.*

"If that's true, why didn't they call a towing company?" Blair fumes. "No one's heard from her all day. She's obviously been here longer than thirty minutes."

Unfortunately, I know the answer to that question. Sara doesn't want anyone to find Violet's car without her in it.

She has to be here. *I need her to be here.*

"Lots of ground to cover." Eli squints at the fog-blanketed buildings and decades-old streetlamps, flickering like lightning bugs

271

in the evening air. "I hate to be that guy, but we need to split up. No way we can cover this one warehouse at a time."

I count the buildings.

Five.

"Eli, take the two on the right. You're the fastest, so haul ass. If Sara isn't there, I doubt Violet is either. I don't think she'd leave her unguarded."

I grab the paper grocery bag on the floorboard. "Blair, take the far left. Piper, the one next to that. I'll search the middle."

Luke's stint as a Boy Scout is about to pay off. Our parents had stockpiled enough flashlights to get us through years of camp outs, not to mention the multitude of hurricane-induced blackouts. I hand everyone a flashlight. "Let's do a group call," I say, as everyone holds out their phones, joining, then testing their mics. It saved me with Cooper; I'm praying it will do the same here. "I left a voice-mail for Officer Roy, so he'll know our location." I jump out of the truck, tucking my flashlight into my jeans. "And the police department, who hung up on me twice because they thought it was a prank."

While the jury is out on whether they'll show—considering response times are usually longer than two hours in the city—we can't wait around.

Violet's clock is ticking.

"Be safe. Let's end this fucking nightmare! This is for Violet and Jamie." I squeeze Piper's hand before we split up. When I reach my warehouse, my sneaker catapults an object into the air, and it *plinks* as it hits the ground. Scanning with my light, something reflects back.

It's a coin—the one I gave Violet.

I'd promised to take her away from the madness of the world, and tonight, I hope I can honor that promise. But the coin not only proves she's been here, it means she's close. I pocket it with the intention of handing it back to her myself.

Speaking into my phone, I say, "Check your spots, but I think she's here."

Eli answers first. "Anyone's door locked?"

"Nope," Piper replies.

"Mine either," Eli says.

There's no response from Blair.

I jiggle the lock, and the door swings open. "Same here."

Floats are big money. They take a copious amount of time, material, and artistry to construct and maintain, so it's more than odd that not only do they *not* have security, the doors were left wide open.

No way is this an accident.

"Holy shit," I whisper, after nearly being swallowed by the jaws of an enormous creature.

I look up. It's the Rougarou float, a local legendary cryptid and crowd favorite. Shining my flashlight across it, I see no evidence of anything *alive,* but I still shudder. Exploring a pitch-black warehouse filled with creepy floats like this colossal structure is more than a physical nightmare; it's like I'm moored in hell.

After checking the first level of the float, I have to climb a rickety wooden ladder to get to the next. It's exhausting, and there are hundreds more floats like this—

Violet could be anywhere.

Holding my breath, I climb onto the next float, but trip over a long felt bag.

Please, don't be a body.

I tap it with my toe, and foam balls spill out. I sigh and move on. Float after float. King Cobra certainly looks more terrifying in this warehouse than parading down the Avenue covered with beads on a Saturday night.

Eli's voice crackles. "I'm moving to the second warehouse. The floats here are massive, but there were only ten."

"Can't say I relate," Piper says, and I think—*me either.*

Row after row, I inspect floats, yet, I feel like I'm making little progress. There must be a better way. *Think, Ainsley.*

The next float has a number on its sign, just like in the parades. "Anyone know how many years ago Ophelia died?"

"Four," Eli answers. "Why?"

"What if that psycho stashed her somewhere with significance? Like the year she died? This whole debutante murder-sabotage has been about commemorating Ophelia. She very well could have picked a float with meaning."

"Mine went from the teens to twenties. Negative to all," Eli says, but his voice sounds worn. Defeated. I can't imagine how he's holding it together. Not only did his roommate die, he was murdered by his own brother. The guilt must be taking a toll.

"Same here," Piper says. "Do you want us to come to your warehouse when we're done, Ainsley? Oh, I found a crowbar. I'm now armed, but not very dangerous. Only she doesn't need to know that."

In spite of where we are, I bite back a smile. Through thick and thin, Piper's had my back. While I probably don't deserve any of it, I'm grateful for her support.

I go back to checking floats.

"I'm nearly finished my second warehouse," Eli responds ten minutes later. "I agree with Piper. If Violet's here, I'm betting she's in yours."

A familiar wave of panic pummels my heart. Of course she's in my warehouse. Which means—so is Sara. "My floats start in the fifties," I say. "I'm going to work backward, so come to the rear."

I hear a crinkling sound and pause. "Guys, I think she's here."

When I reach the twenties, I slow my pace.

Twenty-four, twenty-three, twenty-two . . . twenty-one.

It's a pirate ship with large swooping sails and unlit sea creatures projecting from its sides. The beam from my flashlight hits and the shimmery materials glisten. "Listen up. There's a pirate ship in the back. I'm about to check it," I whisper, grabbing the handle to hoist myself up.

Before I take a step, a force knocks into me. Pain explodes in my stomach.

Don't scream. Don't—

Groping for the pain, my hand hits a stubby handle sunk through my now wet shirt.

I've been stabbed—

"Watch where you're going," a girl's voice echoes in the eerie abyss. She gives me a shove and my weight shifts backward, tumbling me off the float. My head cracks on the cement below. Everything hurts so much . . . I can't breathe.

Don't panic.

Arching my back, I suck in a breath. "Help!"

"Ainsley! Where are you?" It's Piper, but her voice dies in the darkness.

Footsteps clomp, and I see a boot crushing my phone.

"Oops," the girl says. "Maybe I cheated, ambushing you like that, but you broke the rules. *You* brought friends." She flicks on a switch, and neon colors swirl.

It's Sara.

But she's no longer the pulled-together, refined girl we'd relied on during our events. Her eyes are wild, hair cut shorter and matted.

She pulls out a pistol from behind her flannel shirt and slides back its rack. "I used to come here as a kid. Me and Ophelia would play hide-and-seek. It was our secret headquarters."

"This won't bring her back," I bite out, trying to keep the scream that is welling up inside me from betraying my bravado. "Nor will it bring justice," I say, but my words are slowing, each syllable weighted with blood.

Sara's hair glints in the neon hues, along with her gun. "I don't want justice. I want her back!" she yells, her echo reverberating against the cold steel walls like the building has merged with her mood. "I'm not crazy. I know I can't get what I want. So my next best choice was to ruin what you heartless bitches wanted. The parties. The gowns. Gatekeeping in opera gloves. Deciding who's good enough to get invited to parties. Or who will provide the most entertainment if you screw with them. None of you deserve a season to celebrate yourselves."

"I get it," I say, crying out as her foot connects with my ribs.

"How would you know, Miss Sell-Her-Soul-and-Body-for-a-Coveted-Invite? Did you know Cooper loves to gossip about his newest conquests?" She laughs as I try to wriggle away in fear of another assault. "I think he wanted a reason to hurt people, ya know. If it weren't for me, he would've just found a less dramatic way to do it down the road. Like tormenting naïve interns once he became a partner, but I focused him on the rot in the debutante foundation."

"And you're so much better," I mutter, despite the rage it may provoke. Wiping my mouth, my hand comes back bloodied. "If you won't tell me where Violet is, what about Laney? Is she also in one of your floats?"

"I thought you'd never ask." She snatches my flashlight, aiming the beam at the front of the float, where it appears a mermaid was once mounted.

Only it's no longer a mermaid.

It's Laney.

Fear sweeps my body. "Dear God!"

I turn from the sight of her body. "She's been dead this whole time, hasn't she? This was all a farce. It was y-you texting Riley."

"Of course it was me. Had her idiotic friend cared an ounce about her, like I did for Ophelia, she would've realized that and told her little cop-daddy." She tilts her head. "But *you* . . . you started putting ideas in her vacuous head. So *poof*. I had to let her air out."

"*You* killed Riley?" My voice cracks.

"I hadn't planned on it, really. But once I did the deed, I forced Cooper to string her outside that shitty party until the coast was clear. Besides, even if Riley hadn't been suspicious, she was just a hop, skip, and a jump away from being a crooked cop, majoring in criminal science. So you're welcome."

My teeth chatter—*I'm so cold.*

I don't know if it's from blood loss or because I realize—*we may not make it out of here.*

Not me or Violet. Or Eli, Piper, and Blair.

The depth of Sara's insanity is mind-boggling, but I need to keep her talking. It's the only way to distract her. "Will you please tell me where Violet is?" Pressing a hand over my wound, I glance around, hoping for signs of life.

Fuck it.

"Violet!" I scream. Then get one knee up—

"Shut up, you idiot! She's alive. For now." She waves at the float. "Although it can get windy on those upper decks. I hope I tied the rope tight enough to keep her head up."

Wriggling myself upright, I stumble when a wave of dizziness hits.

My white shirt is crimson.

Too much blood.

"You asked for the video in exchange for Violet, but you stomped my phone." I point at its shattered remains on the cement floor. "I held up my end of the deal. Please, let her go."

I slide up an inch, hopefully undetected. "I never intended to post it in the first place."

"How do I know your friends won't?" She shakes her head. "I don't trust you."

I lock eyes with her, hoping to let her know, even with a knife in my stomach, I'm going to put up a hell of a fight. She may succeed in killing Violet, but she'll have to go through me. "I'm not here to mess with Ophelia's legacy. I'm not even here for you. I want Violet. Let me go to her. You can leave this behind. Start over. Isn't that what you want?"

I inch up again. A tiny bit more and I'll reach her.

"My outcome will be the same in any state. Same prison. Same lifelong hell." Tears drip down her face. "But what choice did I have? Stay quiet and watch another Wilson brat do the same thing to another innocent girl? The thing that caused Ophelia to *die*? I had to wait until Ashley's sister's debut to make sure that shit didn't happen again. Thanks to Cooper's brilliant den mother idea, having full access made it so much easier."

She pauses for a moment, her voice lowering. "I didn't plan to hurt her. I just wanted to cause a little mayhem. Teach a bit of humility. But when I realized she messed with you . . . I-I snapped. Turns out, Laney was just like her sister."

She sticks the gun into her pants. "Too bad for her it became her grand finale. Lucky for you, you fell victim to her prank. Or you might have been strung up right alongside her. Why do you think we took that photo of you at Maskers? We needed leverage in case you fell out of line."

"What about Alexandra? What did she do wrong?" If I'm going to die, I'd rather go out knowing the truth.

"*Alexandra?*" she scoffs. "*I* didn't touch her. Though she certainly served my purpose in the end. So many things were going wrong; no one knew where to look or who to suspect. Especially with Under the Gown spitting venom, twenty-four seven."

I don't know if she's telling the truth, but if she didn't poison Alexandra, who did? Either way, she killed Laney because of me, because of *my* party, which means more blood on my hands. "It was a shitty thing for Laney to do," I say, "But I didn't *die*." I'm growing weak, but I need to keep her talking. "I'm really sorry Ophelia did. What I saw on that video—it never should've happened."

I sneak up another inch.

Almost there.

"My best friend, Piper, means the world to me, but she'd never want me to destroy myself for her. No matter what happened. Would you want Ophelia to do that if the situation were reversed?"

Her expression blanks, and I freeze.

Does she realize how close I am?

"Of course not. I thought being debs together would be a way to kick-start our lives as adults, you know? I talked her into the whole thing." She puts her hands over her face. "I knew the girls were up to something. I just didn't know *who* or *what* . . . and I-I should've done more."

If this were any other situation where Violet's life didn't depend on Sara, I would console her. Tell her it wasn't her fault. I'd do whatever it took to make sure she got into the back of a police car, but today is not that day.

"I'm sorry," I say, "but it's my turn to do more."

Closing my eyes, I crash my forehead into her nose.

A second later, the room echoes with the pop of a bullet. Holding my side, adrenaline kicks in as I run to the pirate float. Shots embed into its sides and I trip over piles of slick Mardi Gras beads, but I manage to keep going. Dragging myself to the second level, I hurl bags of beads and stuffed animals over the side like bombs, hoping to keep Sara away.

That's when I see Violet.

A gag in her mouth and a noose around her neck, she's balancing tippy-toed on a wobbly chair propped underneath, but her eyes light up when she sees me.

I scream loud enough for my gang to hear. "Violet! I'm here! Don't move. I'll get you!"

Pulling on the rope, I pause when it tightens around her neck. I can't see where it's attached, but I know it's out of my reach.

She mumbles something, but I don't understand. I climb on top of an empty barrel and ease off her gag. "The rope." She coughs.

"It's tied to the sails. You'll never reach it." She's pale with a tear-streaked face. "Ainsley, your stomach. I—"

The chair beneath Violet's legs goes flying, and I try to stay balanced on the barrel, grasping for her flailing feet. As long as I keep her upright, she'll have the height to breathe.

Sara jabs the gun into my thigh. "Move! Now! You get to watch your girlfriend die for breaking my fucking nose." She yanks me by the shirt and drags me off the barrel.

I count the seconds.

I can't leave. She'll die.

"Please let me help her!" I beg, trying to slip out of my blood-soaked shirt, despite the gun in her hands.

"Too late," she spits. "You'll bleed out soon enough. Maybe you two can haunt my warehouse together and become the ghosts of Mardi Gras past." Her laugh echoes, hollow and sinister.

I have one last shot. Summoning every ounce of remaining strength, I elbow Sara and rush to Violet, expecting to hear the gun pop.

"You bitch!" Piper screams. Then there's a loud *thwap.*

Blair scrambles up and tries to help me hold Violet up. "I can't untie the rope!" she yells.

I reach for the knife embedded in my stomach.

"Ainsley, no!" Violet yells.

"Yes." Gritting my teeth, I scrape the knife out of my gut. It hurts, but not as bad as I thought. In fact, I barely feel a thing. With the knife in hand, I hack the rope to pieces, bit by bit. "I'm sorry, V!" I sob. "I shouldn't have accused you. You're gonna make it far away from here. I promise."

The room blurs, but the next person I see is Eli. He's pressing his hand over my wound. "Is she okay? Is everyone okay?" I ask, his face zooming in and out of focus.

"We will be. The police are here, Ainsley. Piper has Sara. Just hang on, okay?" he pleads.

Next it's Violet, hovering over me. "You absolute idiot! Why did you do that? Please, stay awake. Talk to me."

"I needed a good apology. I hope it was enough." I try to laugh, but it's hard to breathe. Or speak. The pain is back. This time, it hurts.

I blink and Violet disappears.

I blink and I think she's calling my name, but I can't be sure.

I blink and I'm no longer sure I'm alive—

CHAPTER 30

ONE WEEK LATER

Three fractured ribs, seventeen stitches in my abdomen, and thirty bruises later, I'm lying in a hospital bed with a newly developed vendetta against Jell-O. "Nurse Ratched hates me. She keeps giving me yellow on purpose." I stab at the jiggly mass with a white plastic spoon. "It's my last day. Can't I get a cookie for being a good patient?"

"Maybe if you stop calling her that she won't give you crap food." Luke shakes off his hoodie, squinting at the hospital lights. "I'm over vending machine dinners. You're getting wheeled out today, Ainsley, regardless of your health status."

My mom shoots him a look. "Your sister is a trooper. She only complains every half hour, instead of every five minutes. I call that progress."

She shoots me a smile. "Relax, honey. I'll stay with you for as long as you need."

"I'm fine. Dad makes rounds every hour. I thought I might be hallucinating or dead, seeing him around so much."

My last checkup is in fifteen minutes. If I pass that, I'm free. No more hospital food, IVs, or scheduled guest time, which has me desperate to see my friends. And Violet.

Especially Violet.

"It's your fault for turning into some gown-wearing vigilante." Luke points at the TV where a reporter stands in front of Carnival Creations. "They've been airing your case for a solid week."

"Any updates?" Rubbing my head, I wince when I hit a tender spot. "Last I heard, Cooper ratted out Sara."

"Those two are like see-saws," my mom says. "She blames him. He blames her. If they keep accusing each other, soon they'll share the same jail cell. I still don't understand who did what to whom. Only that they worked together and caused all of this." She waves her hands in a circular motion over me. "Are you sure you don't want to stay another day?" She bows her head. "I'm really sorry you missed your classmate's funeral."

"It's okay, Mom. I doubt I could've handled it, injured or not. Is that a terrible thing to say?"

"No, Ainsley. You've been through a horrific trauma. Laney would understand."

I hold my hand up. "Mom, please. I can't talk about that today. Is that okay? One day, I will, just not now. I want to go home. I want to take a shower. I want to see my friends. Piper texted that she made chocolate cupcakes."

"As long as your nurse gives the okay, we'll go."

"Speak of the devil, here she is." I scoot up in bed, trying to look as healthy as possible. "Have I mentioned how cute you look today? Cool necklace," I say, as she peruses my chart, ignoring my attempts to charm her.

"I adore this house," I say, hugging my couch as I stretch out in joggers and a tee. It's been over a week since I've gotten home and though my bandages are still visible underneath, I don't care how ghastly I look.

I'm home.

With the people I care about most.

"It smells like food. Real food. Not thawed in a body freezer." I sigh as my mom sautés onions, bell peppers, and celery—the holy trinity—in a cast-iron skillet. During one of my pain-induced rants, she promised to cook all of my favorite meals as long as I didn't go near a molecule of trouble again.

The doorbell rings. I try to get up, but it hurts too much.

Luke does the honors.

"You okay?" Piper wraps two healthy arms around me.

"Wait—*ouch*!"

"Did you injure yourself again?" she asks, while I bat her prodding hands away. "How is that even possible?"

"Because it's *Ainsley*. She's as disaster prone as she is a trouble magnet," Eli jokes, edging closer to the couch. "You look okay to me." He pokes at my bandaged ribcage.

If I had the strength, I'd punch him. But I don't.

"Be nice! She's a hero," Blair defends. "She found Violet. You helped, babe, but she deserves her moment."

"I'll give her as many moments as she needs," Violet says, gingerly kissing the bruises on my face.

While it's awesome to see them, I'm not sure I'm ready for the onslaught. "Wait." I address Violet. "I thought you had to get back to school?"

"Turns out, I can afford to take off a semester, since I'm ahead by like a year. Oh, here." She holds out an envelope. "Leslie caught me outside and asked me to give you this."

She passes me a pink envelope.

I pause, trying to gauge her reaction. "Read it dummy. You think after all that we went through, I'd hold a grudge against your ex? We're totally cool. I asked her to come in, but she said she'd stop by later."

I smile. "It would be nice if we could all be friends," I say, opening the card. When I'm done reading, Violet loops her arms underneath mine and lifts me from the couch. "What are you doing?"

She guides me to the door, letting me use her as a crutch.

"Momma Clarke said it's okay," Piper says before I can protest. And with both of their help, I'm led outside and boosted into Eli's truck. "I don't know if you'll love or hate me for bringing you here," Piper says, laughing. "Guess we'll see."

"Here *where?*" I eye Piper suspiciously.

"Patience, Ainsley," Eli says, driving extra slowly while bopping to a song, and I have to admit, it feels great being back in his truck. Pain and all. "If you don't let yourself heal, who knows how much your slapshot will suck for next year's winter games?"

"Piper! Straighten up. It's a *fastball*. No curve to adjust for!" I yell from the folding chair Eli had set up in the batting cage next to where Piper is presently striking out. I'm happy to be back in the batting cage, even though I feel as beat up as their ancient pitching machine.

I'm touched they thought to bring me here. So much, I had to wipe away a tear when we pulled up. *Familiarity. Normalcy.* It's the only way I'll be able to stop the flashbacks and nightmares. The only way I can get back to being myself.

This is certainly a great first step.

"Why does it go so *fast?*" Piper pulls back and the ball slams into the net.

"You're holding your bat wrong. Let me—" I try to stand, but I'm immediately tugged down by Violet.

"You have to stay put. We promised your mom. But one day,

you'll make a great coach," she says. "How about Pee Wee baseball in Texas? I could visit on lunch breaks."

"Ha, ha." I roll my eyes. "Maybe, after I have a Super Bowl or championship ring from whatever team I therapy my way to winning."

She nods. "Of course, but since I'll be hanging around your hometown for a bit, guess I can finally go to one of those football games you drone on about." She smiles. "The things I do for you."

Leaning her head against mine, she tries to shield me from the sight of Eli fouling out.

I shake my head. "Keep up. Baseball first. Football season is over. Either way, there will be plenty of *games* in your future." Shifting in the chair, I wince. "Though riveting hockey has been known to soothe all wounds. Even in *Texas*."

I'm partly kidding, partly serious. "I already took a knife for you. Won't hurt to expand my internship horizons for *love*."

Her eyes meet mine. "What did you say?" Her face is blank, which I can't tell if that's a good thing or bad.

"That I *love* you?" I cock my head. "Do you think I'd get stabbed for anyone?"

She kisses me until we both start laughing over the loud booing coming from the cage. "No PDA in batting cages!" Eli shouts. "Unless it's Blair and me."

"Guess I'll be third-wheeling it for a while." Piper points at me and Eli. "So make your plans accordingly." She seems to be in an upbeat mood, but I know this can't be easy for her.

I raise an eyebrow, which she knows means—*are you okay?*

She nods, letting me know—*it's not the time for sadness.* "I love your brother, Ainsley. You know I do, but I refuse to be babysat by him again."

Violet beckons Piper over. "Hey, I may know a more suitable substitute for Luke. That is, since a certain someone told me you might be interested in interning for Anderson Oil this summer. Is that true?"

Piper's eyes widen. "Are you serious?" She looks at me, then back at Violet.

"It's the least I can do. Besides, it will give Ainsley another reason to visit Texas."

"Gosh. I thought I blew that interview because I talked too much. Plus, my sorority president had to give a recommendation and that wretched mosquito probably wrote something awful."

"We host an annual summer fundraiser, and they always take on a dozen or so interns. Actually, Ainsley, if you're interested too, you can meet—"

I shake my head. "No parties, balls, or cotillions. No soirees, or any entertainment-based drama that isn't on Netflix. It's all banned until I'm healed and don't look like I lost in the first round of *Fight Club* in a dress. Or maybe, I don't know . . . forever."

Turns out, Gramma Gertrude wasn't telling the truth. Sometimes, you can fix death, given the fact that most of us had miraculously survived—except Jamie, of course—against all odds. But I have no plans to tempt fate again.

Six of us started this journey. Five got out alive. Not counting Laney or Riley. But even with two people behind bars, we still don't have all the answers. We don't know who messed with Willa Kennedy's food or if it was an *actual* accident, and no one has admitted to tampering with Gus's brakes, though I'm certain that was Sara. We also never found out who the guy was leaving Jane's party in his boxers. And of course, the biggest one—*who poisoned Alexandra?*

The Madisons and Sara all denied responsibility, and honestly, poison doesn't seem like Cooper's style. While I once suspected Violet may have played a part, I know in my heart—*she wouldn't hurt a fruit fly.*

Hopefully, one day the truth will come out. But just as important, if not more, I'm praying the next batch of debutantes learn a lesson from our tainted season.

Either way, my ass is staying at home, or in a stadium seat with Violet and friends nearby. There isn't anywhere I'd rather be than sitting here, coaching these goofy idiots through their lame attempt at baseball.

I'm happy to be away from the spotlight and out from under my own magnifying glass with no finish lines to reach or comparisons to match. Though I still plan to apply for that internship, this time, I'm hoping I can land it on my own merit.

Violet leans over. "What are you thinking about?"

"You," I say.

She smiles.

Those vapid twits think they've won.

If only it were that simple. I may be behind bars of steel, but it's no different from where I've been the last few years. Imprisoned in self-constructed walls of guilt. Locked behind incessant thoughts, chattering daily: You let Ophelia die. This is your fault.

It is my fault. I let her take the fall. I paved the way for Ophelia to steal Cooper from Ashley. Then coaxed her into playing a game with Cooper she never wanted to play. He was a means to an end. A ticket to get us on the debutante circuit. And it worked. For both of us. Until it didn't.

What's ironic is most think Cooper's either the villain or hero of this tale, depending on how they spin it. Some say his grief propelled him to seek revenge for love. But he's neither villain nor hero. Ophelia never loved him. She loved me. Cooper was simply my pawn. An accomplice now. An accomplice then. Ophelia used him to get us in. I used him to take them out.

Now, it's done. Or is it?
Can we ever really break the cycle or stop the copycats?

After all, there's that matter of Alexandra . . . and hey, it really wasn't me. I wish it had been, but afraid I can't take the credit. Guess we'll have to wait for next season.
Until then—

ACKNOWLEDGMENTS

After a decade of writing and working so hard to bring this vision to life, I'm gratefully aware how far out at sea I'd be without the people in my life that have kept me afloat. This is my thank-you to them. I hope this book will prove I'm worthy of their precious time.

Thank you, Mom. Your dazzling stories and ingenious mind inspire me to write. And thank you, Dad: you support us both by being the sanest person in the house.

Thank you to my family, whom I love dearly—including my second mom, Rosa—and to those who, I hope, are still looking out for us from above.

To loved ones and friends, thanks for listening to me rant and rave about chapter details and obsessive word counts. I promise I won't kill you off in any of my books—yet.

Thank you to those who helped make this book the best it can be, including my editors—Betsy Thorpe, for her wonderful insight and help during the publishing process, and Katherine Bartis, who honed my grammar. Thanks to Kamil Rekosz for a beautiful cover and Robert Harrison for his formatting wizardry.

And special thanks to my dog, Lore, who didn't do anything but wag his tail, but that's more than enough because he owns my heart and happiness.

To everyone who has something to say to the world, please know, there are people who want to listen. When the world tries to knock you down, remember, the next round is yours to take.

ABOUT THE AUTHOR

Payton Frischhertz, poet, novelist, and native-born New Orleanian, is the author of *Under the Gown*, a YA mystery/thriller novel set in her hometown. When she's not crafting new plots or writing, she practices mixed martial arts and spends time with her German shepherd, Lore.

To learn about her upcoming novels, visit Payton Frischhertz.com or Wolffish Press.com to sign up for email updates.

AUTHOR'S NOTE

If you enjoyed *Under the Gown*, please consider leaving a review at your favorite review site. Reviews are the best way to spread the word about a book and introduce other readers to it. I would appreciate it so much! Thank you!

    – Payton Frischhertz